Creación y realización
Equipo editorial **CLASA**

Redacción y autoría
Adriana Ballesteros

Ilustraciones
Gloria Saavedra

CATALOGACIÓN EN LA FUENTE

291   Ballesteros, Adriana
BAL   El mágico mundo de las hadas / Adriana Ballesteros. --
      Montevideo, Rep. Oriental del Uruguay : © Latinbooks International S.A.,
      2006.
      56 p. : il. ; 24 x 34 cm.

      ISBN 9974-7930-5-X

      1. MITOLOGÍA FANTÁSTICA. 2. MUNDO MÁGICO.
      3. LITERATURA INFANTIL. 4. PERSONAJES DE LA FANTASÍA.
      5. SERES FANTÁSTICOS. 6. MITOS DEL MUNDO. 7. HADAS. I. Título.

Impreso en Pressur Corporation, S. A.
R. O. del Uruguay

Derechos de edición internacional
© **LATINBOOKS INTERNATIONAL S.A.**
ISBN 9974-7930-5-X

Edición 2005-2006

El mágico mundo de Las Hadas

A Modo de Presentación

Este libro fue encontrado en el árbol
sesenta y tres del Bosque de los cedros azules.
Según los especialistas, la autora es el "Hadabuela"
Cirella Titanus, descendiente directa de Titania,
reina de las hadas, y sobrina nieta de la
célebre dama del lago. ¡Qué bueno que así sea!,
pues nadie mejor que ella podría
conocer el maravilloso mundo
de las hadas.

¿Cuál es el origen de las hadas? ¿Dónde viven?
¿Son siempre buenas? Estas y otras preguntas son
formuladas constantemente tanto por las hadas
jóvenes como por las niñas.
Por ello, decidí redactar este libro en el que intento
responder algunos interrogantes y despejar las dudas.
Lo dedico a todas las curiosas haditas, a las niñas
que creen en nosotras, y muy especialmente a mi
nieta Mailen, una pequeña hada cuyos hechizos no
están saliendo del todo bien últimamente.

¡Que lo disfruten!

Cirella Titanus

REINAS del BOSQUE

Presten atención ¡Shh…! Silencio…
¿oyen la música?¿Escuchan los acordes suaves de
una melodía? Ahora miren con cautela hacia la luz
y distinguirán pequeñas figuras del color del aire…
Son bellas damitas que bailan en ronda. Algunas
tienen largos cabellos azules y trajes verdes, otras
parecen sirenas, pero no lo son. Todas son hadas.

¿Quiénes son las hadas?

Supongo que hoy en día, las hadas necesitan que se las describa de
algún modo, ya que se volvieron bastante raras y tímidas con la gente.
Hubo buenas y poderosas razones para que esto ocurra, pero eso lo
aclararé más adelante. Las hadas son seres femeninos hechos de una
materia similar a la de la luz, el sonido y el aire. Habitan, junto a otros
seres mágicos, el vasto y luminoso reino de lo maravilloso, repleto de música,
de asombrosos avatares, de disparatados aprietos y aventuras prodigiosas.
Bosques, valles y lagos son el paisaje ideal para albergarlas. Allí danzan y
cantan en rondas, siempre descalzas. No entienden ni gustan de las máquinas
ni de los aparatos de la nueva tecnología, a decir verdad, no los necesitan
ya que con frecuencia acuden a la magia, desde la común, que las ayuda a
desaparecer en silencio y rápidamente cuando la gente se acerca, hasta la
que requiere de varitas, hechizos y palabras especiales.

Etéreas como el viento

Las hadas visten ropas tejidas con hebras de flores o hilos de agua. Algunas sólo admiten ponerse vestidos del color del cielo, otras, de gustos más amplios, llevan tenues ropas color oro, verde y amarillo. No usan zapatos, porque prefieren trasladarse por el aire o el agua. Poseen bellísimos rostros, frágiles cuerpos, risas cantarinas y melodiosas. A decir verdad, no todas: Cudilia, una de mis tías, tiene una risa que suena como la sirena del carro de bomberos, pero algo más desafinada. Por lo general intentamos contarle cosas aburridas o tristes, para evitar que la pobre estalle en ruidosas carcajadas.

¿Qué idioma hablan las hadas?

Las hadas comprendemos todas las lenguas de los seres terrestres, tanto la que usan los humanos como los animales. Pero entre nosotras utilizamos un idioma tan antiguo como la sal, tan duradero como la arena y tan melodioso como la música del arpa. Nuestra lengua es poderosa ya que con ella expresamos nuestros pensamientos y emociones y también pronunciamos las fórmulas mágicas. Lamentablemente no puedo revelar nuestro idioma porque es un secreto tan celosamente guardado, que el hada que se atreviese a romperlo sería de inmediato tildada de traidora y llevada ante el tribunal mágico para ser juzgada. Sin embargo, se me ha permitido obsequiarles algunas palabras: "afg∂b∂i\Z", es una fórmula mágica para desaparecer en el aire, y "FDOJW" es la palabra que se usa para distraer dragones.

¿De dónde proviene el nombre?

—*Jalea acta est*— ¿Cómo que no se entiende lo que digo? Perdón, hace tanto que vuelo por el mundo que los idiomas se me confunden y a veces olvido que algunos cayeron en el olvido; resulta que la denominación "hada" nace en el idioma que acabo de hablar: el latín. Es la lengua que utilizaban para conversar y escribir los antiguos habitantes del Imperio Romano. La palabra hada deriva del término *fata* o *fatum* que significa tanto destino como predicción.

¿Cuál es el origen de las hadas?

Para esta pregunta no existe una sola respuesta sino muchas teorías. El origen de las hadas viene de muy atrás, de los Días Antiguos, ya perdidos y olvidados. Hay quienes afirman que son ángeles caídos, imposibilitados de retornar al Paraíso, sin embargo hay evidencias que revelan que las hadas andaban por el mundo mucho antes de que los libros registraran esta versión. Los antiguos griegos las consideraban diosas capaces de influir sobre el destino de los mortales. Muchos afirman que las hadas son en verdad las almas de los árboles y las plantas.

El nacimiento de las hadas
-Relato-

Hace mucho tiempo atrás, cuando el mundo era joven, un enorme y cruel gigante aterrorizaba a los tranquilos habitantes de la Aldea. Incontables eran los daños que Iryn, tal era el nombre del malvado, había ocasionado. Solía soltar su furia en tempestuosos huracanes, tormentas de nieve o sequías interminables. No os relataré todas las maldades de las que era capaz el gigante, pero creedme, eran muchas y a veces terribles. Los aldeanos sufrían a más no poder. Mientras el gigante dormía, su furia dormía con él, pero apenas despertaba soltaba toda su maldad sobre la pobre gente. La rabia del gigante se desataba porque sí y porque no, ninguna razón la motivaba y tampoco había manera de prevenirla.

Y una vez se enojó de tal modo que incendió todo el bosque.

Robles, arrayanes y maitenes fueron convertidos en cenizas.
Donde antes había verde vida sólo quedaba muerte gris. Cuando
los aldeanos vieron el desastre sollozaron con pena y desesperación.
Sin bosque no habría leña, ni frutos ni animales silvestres para comer.
—Debemos derrotar al gigante —dijo el más anciano.
Todos estuvieron de acuerdo y juntos marcharon a desafiarlo. Se desató
una lucha desigual. Una batalla terrible que duró todo un día y una
larga noche que conviene olvidar. Hacia la madrugada el cruel
gigante fue derrotado y herido de muerte, con tan mala suerte
que su cuerpo cayó sobre el pueblo y lo destruyó. El horror
había sido vencido, pero la Aldea estaba devastada.
—Moriremos todos —sollozaron los aldeanos.
De pronto, de la herida del gigante comenzaron a brotar
gusanos, cientos de ellos, miles… A medida que
aparecían se convertían en luces. Algunos tomaron la
forma de pequeñas damas bellas como el Sol, pero otros
absorbieron la maldad del gigante y eran
oscuros y siniestros. Ante el mudo asombro
de los aldeanos, luces blancas y luces
negras se enfrentaron. Por fin, los seres
oscuros huyeron al fondo de la tierra
convertidos en elfos.
Las damas triunfantes pronunciaron
palabras nuevas y el cuerpo del gigante
desapareció en el aire. En su lugar se
alzaban las casas recompuestas y un nuevo
y bello bosque. Las damas se refugiaron
allí donde moran desde aquel día.

¿Cómo son las Hadas?

Con frecuencia he escuchado preguntas como estas: ¿las hadas son altas o diminutas? ¿Son todas damas o hay también hados? ¿Son buenas o son malas?. Ahora intentaré responderlas. Veamos…

Seres mágicos

Por empezar sepan que todas las hadas son seres femeninos, existen otras especies de criaturas como los duendes, elfos y demás espíritus mágicos que no son hadas; en cuanto al tamaño, éste varía, las hay muy altas y robustas –como yo– y diminutas. Es importante entender que cada hada posee una personalidad única que la diferencia del resto, pero en general son muy curiosas y sensibles, les encanta bailar y cantar y fundamentalmente son grandes defensoras de la naturaleza. Adoran las plantas y son absolutamente felices en los valles donde abundan las flores silvestres.

¿Hay hadas malvadas?

Escuché decir a muchos humanos que no es verdad que las hadas sean espíritus bondadosos, algunos han llegado al extremo de afirmar que son criaturas terribles, capaces de ocasionar grandes daños sólo porque sí. Puede ser que en algunas oportunidades la conducta de las hadas aparezca como caprichosa ante los ojos de las gentes. Sin embargo, debo preguntar: ¿cómo reaccionarían ustedes si de pronto un grupo de extraños destruyese vuestras casas, o si absolutos desconocidos irrumpiesen y, sin hacer el menor caso de vuestra presencia, construyesen sus pueblos encima de vuestros hogares? ¿No sentirían enfado? Muchas hadas habitan en el corazón de los árboles añosos, en las raíces de las hierbas más antiguas y no son pocos los humanos que destrozan lo que encuentran a su paso sólo por diversión. Cuando esto ocurra, estén seguros de que las hadas se enfadarán…

Advertencia:

¡Niñas! Si por ventura llegan a toparse con un grupo de hadas bailando o cantando ¡no se les ocurra interrumpirlas! Muéstrense amables y quizás sean invitadas a danzar con ellas (aunque esta posibilidad puede ser cansadora para alguien poco entrenado: me contó mi bisabuela Titania, que durante una fiesta bailaron ¡siete años seguidos!). Si tal cosa os ocurre, pídanle a un compañero que les tome la mano y jale con fuerza por fuera de la ronda.

11

¿Dónde está el REINO de las HADAS?

Es difícil saberlo con precisión. Los libros antiguos cuentan que en un pasado muy lejano, las hadas habitaban las colinas huecas situadas al oeste del mundo, entre los Altos Valles y el Bosque Grande, pero un día salieron a conquistar el mundo.

La conquista de nuevas tierras

En aquellos lejanos tiempos, por las noches, las colinas aparecían encendidas con miles de luces doradas; este efecto se debía a que las hadas, además de emplearlas como vivienda, las utilizaban como escondite para guardar el oro allí. Pero un buen día, no se sabe con certeza por qué, las hadas abandonaron las colinas y emprendieron un largo viaje hacia distintos territorios. Algunas se dirigieron hacia los lagos, otras al mar, muchas elfinas se quedaron en los campos y las demás treparon hacia el aire. Desde entonces se las distingue por los sitios que eligieron para morar. Sin embargo, hay quienes aseguran que aún antes de abandonar las colinas, además de las solitarias, las hadas ya se habían dividido en tres ramas: del agua, de la tierra y del fuego. (Hay quienes aseguran que éstas últimas son las más antiguas ya que aparecen referencias sobre ellas en los escritos primitivos, antes aún de la entrada en la historia). Hoy en día, según el último censo –hecho en el mes áureo se el calendario de las hadas– se registran cuatro tipos de hadas: del agua, del aire, del fuego y de la tie

HADAS de la TIERRA

Las hadas de la tierra se esparcieron por el mundo, algunas de espíritu inquieto vagabundearon por mil caminos hasta llegar a la cima de los vientos. Otras permanecieron en las tierras ásperas y muchas, de temple reposado y sereno, adoptaron los árboles como morada.

Las damas verdes

Cuentan los libros primeros que muchas hadas subieron hasta la cima del viento, desde entonces, entre los bosques de las más altas cumbres, moran las damas verdes. Como la mayoría de las hadas, viven en comunidades regidas por una reina (Titania, mi bisabuela es la reina de todas las comunidades de hadas); pero en ocasiones algunas de ellas prefieren vivir solas. Tal es el caso de la dama verde de Caerphilly, que recorre los castillos más antiguos y toma forma de hiedra cuando alguien se acerca. Pero la verdad es que es una equivocación suponer que ella deambula en soledad, y con su permiso contaré la verdad…

La dama verde y el fantasma Wimbledon
-Relato-

Hace largo tiempo atrás, la dama verde de Caerphilly vagaba por el castillo de la Antigua Escocia una mañana otoñal, neblinosa y sombría. Cuando de pronto, desde su escondite de hiedra, vio el bello rostro dorado de Eduardo Wimbledon, escudero del rey. Esa mañana, el hada pensó que ése era el joven más bello y encantador que había visto nunca jamás. Esa tarde supo que se había enamorado de él. Entonces aguardó la llegada cómplice de la noche y emitió un grito especial para lograr que Wimbledon abandonara el lecho y saliera al jardín. Apenas el joven se acercó a la hiedra, se presentó ante él, tan bella y tan verde como la enredadera que cubría el muro. Wimbledon la miró maravillado y mudo. Aterrado, fascinado y confundido, contempló los ojos inmensos que lo miraban de frente, tan verdes como la larga cabellera que la cubría por completo. Cuando pudo formular un pensamiento pensó que ese hada era el ser más bello que había visto nunca jamás. Y esa noche, Wimbledon supo que se había enamorado de ella. Poco después decidieron casarse. Fue una mala idea, ya que por aquel entonces no estaban bien vistas las uniones entre humanos y hadas y se desataron feroces persecuciones. Fueron tantas y tan terribles, que la dama verde para salvarlo de las furias sueltas le propuso un trato a su amado: se encontrarían nuevamente en ese muro, al lado de la hiedra, cien años después. El hada viajó por los cielos y los mundos, siempre pensando en su amado. Y así, un día de otoño, un siglo más tarde, regresó en busca de Wimbledon que la aguardaba feliz y sonriente junto a la hiedra, convertido en fantasma. Desde entonces, recorren juntos castillos y parques umbrosos. Si alguna vez se topan con ellos no se asusten. Sonrían y dejen junto a la fuente semillas de hiedra, de roble o de castaño, que el hada y el fantasma se los van a agradecer.

15

Las alseides

Son el grupo más representativo y numeroso de las hadas terrestres ya que habitan en los campos floridos. Temen poco o nada a las gentes y es habitual ver sus retratos en cuadros, grabados y libros. Son tan populares entre los humanos que algunos creen erróneamente que son éstas las únicas hadas que existen. Les gusta hacer amistad con los artistas, sobre todo con los pintores, pero al igual que todas las hadas, detestan ser fotografiadas. Sus motivos son muy simples: el avance tecnológico y los aparatos que ha generado –instrumentos de la falsa magia– las enojan y a muchas, incluso, las asustan. Aclaración para las jóvenes hadas: avance tecnológico es el modo en que los humanos llaman a la falsa magia.

Las dríades

Son las más sabias de entre todas las hadas, pues
poseen pensamientos profundos como raíces, y sueños
altos como las copas de los árboles que eligen para morar.
Poseen larga cabellera verde y ojos color castaño.
Hoy en día habitan en los árboles más ocultos de los bosques
umbrosos porque han decidido rehuir el contacto con las gentes.
En los días pasados, las dríades tenían estrechos vínculos con los humanos,
éstos les pedían consejo y ayuda para sortear las dificultades, los problemas
difíciles y los cotidianos. Hay un tipo de hada para cada árbol y hace tiempo atrás,
el hada del roble, el hada del castaño, el hada del fresno –con cuyas ramas se hacen
las mejores varitas mágicas– solían conversar emitiendo voces iguales al arrullo
de las hojas, con los seres humanos que conocían el lenguaje de los árboles.
Pero el tiempo fue pasando y los pueblos celtas fueron cambiando de costumbres y
mudando de idiomas, sus culturas se volvieron distintas y sus tradiciones se han ido
perdiendo. Sin embargo, hoy en día son muchas las personas que piden
la protección de las hadas antes de entrar a los bosques a fin de que las cuiden.
Claro que conviene no internarse en los bosques durante las noches, porque la
oscuridad no es buena consejera de las hadas y suele asustar a las gentes,
y el susto rara vez conduce a buenos resultados.

Las anjaras

Sin lugar a dudas, ellas son de todas las hadas las más bondadosas
y solidarias. Suelen llevar consigo varitas mágicas hechas de espino
y una botella con un brebaje capaz de curar. Pequeñas, de unos pocos
centímetros de altura, de brillantes ojos negros y larga cabellera dorada
adornada con trenzas, flores y lazos de colores, suelen socorrer a los
animales heridos o enfermos y aliviarlos con su brebaje. Habitan en
los bosques, donde cuidan y ayudan a todos sus habitantes, protegen
los rebaños y limpian los arroyos. Como además de bonitas son muy
pulcras, suelen llevar vaporosos vestidos impecables y claros.
En cuanto a los humanos, pueden premiar a los que sean generosos
y respeten la Naturaleza y sus seres, pero son capaces de castigar
duramente a quienes lastimen, rompan o dañen a los animalitos
silvestres, las plantas o las flores, como sucedió cierta vez...

El cazador y el hada
-*Relato*-

Un cazador cruzaba el bosque muy enfadado porque ese día no había logrado atrapar ninguna presa. Tras varios disparos fallidos, una liebre se cruzó en su camino. "Quizás no esté perdido el día", pensó y de inmediato comenzó a disparar, pero por más que apuntó no logró acertar ni una sola vez. Su rabia crecía más y más. De pronto, sorprendido, vio cómo la liebre se transformaba en una bella joven que lo miraba sonriendo. El cazador la contempló con miedo y se le acercó con cautela, pero ella no se movió. "Cómo te llamas", le preguntó, pero ella no contestó. El cazador le tocó una mano, pero ella no reaccionó. Entonces, decidido, la abrazó; pero apenas lo hizo, la joven se transformó en un enorme leño encendido. El cazador corrió a toda velocidad hacia un arroyo y desesperado, se arrojó al agua para aliviar la quemazón. Entonces escuchó una voz musical que le decía: "Cazador corazón de hielo, tu maldad hizo arder el leño". El hombre, aterrado y confundido, dejó de ser cazador y desde aquel día procuró divertirse con otra actividad.

Las villes

Sobre las laderas rocosas, cerca de las montañas nubladas, viven las villes. Estas doncellas se destacan por sus largos cabellos castaños que las cubren por completo. Si bien todas las hadas son muy hermosas, según mi opinión, ellas son las más bellas, gracias a su espesa cabellera castaña, sus ojos brillantes, sus brazos esbeltos y sus fuertes piernas de cabra que les otorgan gran agilidad para trepar los montes más escarpados. (El resto de nosotras no tiene otro remedio que subir volando). Conocidas como las señoras de los bosques, protegen a los seres que viven en ellos: cuidan los rebaños, los ríos, y los animales que pueblan sus territorios. Si un humano se atreve a dañar a uno solo de sus amigos, ellas son capaces de enojarse mucho. Sin embargo, como no son amantes de las guerras, sino todo lo contrario, procuran, en general, alejar de su reino a aquellas gentes que les inspiran poca o ninguna confianza.

El oro de las hadas
-Relato-

Cierta vez mi bisabuela Titania me entregó un anillo hecho de un precioso metal amarillo.
—Puedes lucirlo cuantas veces quieras —me dijo—, pero debes ocultarlo siempre de las miradas de las gentes.
Tal recomendación me intrigó. ¿Por qué debía esconderlo? La explicación me sorprendió aún más:
—No sabemos los motivos —comentó—, ¿pero ves el metal con que está hecho? Pues tiene la particularidad de enloquecer a las personas. Te contaré una historia para que lo comprendas: Hace mucho tiempo atrás, la zona de los valles floridos estaba habitada por campesinos tranquilos y trabajadores. Entre los pobladores no habían existido nunca peleas muy graves ni nadie albergaba rencores por más de dos soles. Un buen día paseaba yo con las hadas de mi corte por el bosque que rodea la aldea, cuando de pronto vimos un extraño cofre de madera. Tú sabes lo curiosas que son mis cortesanas, así que de inmediato abrimos la caja para ver qué guardaba en su interior y nos sorprendimos al ver que estaba repleta de collares, pulseras, anillos, coronas y hasta capas hechas con ese bonito metal dorado. Todas nos adornamos, y por pura diversión hicimos una ronda.
Estábamos tan entretenidas que no notamos que no estábamos solas. Escondido entre las moreras del lado norte se hallaba Glub, el campesino, y oculto entre las hiedras del sur estaba Glob, el labriego. Ambos lo habían visto todo.
Hacia el crepúsculo, decidimos guardar las joyas y continuamos con la ronda, seguimos danzando hasta que llegó la noche. Entonces, fuimos testigos de un episodio que no olvidaremos jamás: Glob, el labriego, abandonó su escondite y comenzó a avanzar hacia el cofre.

Su mirada, antes serena, lucía un brillo oscuro de sombra. Parecía haber mudado de alma. Nunca sabremos si nos vio o no, pero no hizo ningún caso de nuestra presencia, caminaba directo hacia el oro como si fuera un autómata. Desde el lado opuesto, pero en igual dirección, se aproximaba Glub, también su rostro, siempre plácido, se había transformado en una máscara siniestra. Ambos tomaron a la vez el cofre, y ante nuestra sorpresa, Glub golpeó a Glob con tanta fuerza que éste cayó desmayado al suelo. El campesino tomó la caja dispuesto a partir con ella, pero nosotras se lo impedimos lanzando sobre sus piernas y brazos nuestras cuerdas de telas de araña. Una vez que lo inmovilizamos, lo tendimos al lado de su vecino a fin de que reflexionara sobre lo que acababa de hacer. Pero en ese momento despertó Glob que, ya repuesto del golpe, se incorporó y tomó la caja. Y ya hubiera partido con ella si no fuera porque nosotras sin pérdida de tiempo, lanzamos sobre él nuestras cuerdas de telas de arañas y lo tendimos junto a su vecino. Al día siguiente, Glub y Glob despertaron en medio del bosque, se vieron sucios, cubiertos de babas de araña y pensaron que habían sufrido un mal sueño. Se incorporaron y juntos regresaron al pueblo. Poco tardaron en olvidar este feo y extraño episodio y ambos vivieron felices y tranquilos por siempre. En cuanto a nosotras, las hadas, aprendimos la lección. Comprendimos que ese metal amarillo, que por cierto se llama oro, era en extremo peligroso para las gentes, y decidimos guardarlo por siempre en las colinas huecas a fin de evitar la locura de los hombres.

HADAS del AGUA

En tiempos remotos, muchas hadas, amantes de las olas y los vuelos húmedos, abandonaron las colinas huecas y se dirigieron al agua. Por aquellos tempranos días, mares, ríos, manantiales, estanques, pozos y hasta algunas fuentes fueron escenario de la llegada de mágicas doncellas, que construyeron sus casas, aldeas y comarcas.

En el río, el manantial y el mar...

Es posible que las comunidades de hadas acuáticas sean las más numerosas de todas. Toda buena aprendiz sabe que numerosos reinos se alzan detrás de cascadas, en lo profundo del mar, en lo más hondo de algunos lagos y ríos. Las señoras del agua suelen reflejar el medio en el que se mueven, así las damas del río varían su humor con una facilidad admirable; las mujeres del mar, de temple a veces manso a veces furibundo, son capaces de desatar feroces tempestades, mientras que las doncellas de los lagos son pacíficas, y serenas. Pero todas ellas conforman, sin lugar a dudas, el grupo más enamoradizo de hadas y son innumerables las historias de amor que se cuentan entre ellas y los mortales.

Moradoras de las aguas

El arte de la edificación subacuática bien pudo provenir de las sirenas, pero las hadas del agua lo practicaban a su manera. No construían edificios ni castillos de más de tres pisos, esto último quizás se deba a la dificultad que representa para la mayoría de las hadas contar más allá del número tres.

Las casas de paredes redondas estaban hechas de perlas, oro y corales. Este tipo de construcción fue mejorando y cambiando con el tiempo, ya que las damas fueron incorporando nuevas técnicas y procedimientos (por supuesto ajenos por completo a la falsa magia o como la llaman los humanos: la tecnología).

HADAS de los LAGOS

Las habitantes de los lagos, son las más amigables y tranquilas de las damas acuáticas, muy hermosas, tienen la piel suave y delicada, los ojos serenos y los cabellos azules.

Gwragedd annwn

Son hadas de larga cabellera azul y ojos color del tiempo. Por las noches de luna llena suelen bailar en las playas hasta el amanecer. En noches como esas, es habitual distinguir las siluetas moviéndose al compás del viento. Como la mayoría de las hadas del agua, las gwragedd annwn son muy enamoradizas.

Pociones y Hechizos Mágicos

Hechizo de luna y amor

Para lograr que el dueño de los suspiros nos mire, se pide al hada del avellano que nos otorgue una vara mágica. Cuando la rama caiga a nuestros pies, se escribe en la tierra el nombre del ser amado; luego, se colocan en un frasco 2 cucharadas de miel, 3 pétalos de rosa, y 5 hojas caídas del laurel, y se lo entierra bajo un espino una noche de luna llena o al pie del árbol que haya en el jardín.

Si al cabo de tres meses el joven no da ninguna señal, es porque no es él quien nos conviene, pero seguramente el acertado pronto aparecerá.

Poción de amor

Otra maravillosa poción para enamorar a un joven se hace hirviendo 3 barras de canela, 1 cucharada de anís, 3 cucharadas de aceite de almendras dulces, 3 cucharadas de miel, pétalos de 5 rosas y un cabello de la persona deseada... Una vez tibio, dar a beber tres gotitas al joven elegido. Si al cabo de tres semanas nada sucede, lo mejor es olvidarlo.

Hechizo del olvido

Se toman pétalos de jazmín marchitos, marchitos también han de estar los tres tréboles de tres hojas y una flor de pensamiento seca.
Se hace la mezcla en una bolsita de tela y se la entierra junto al nombre del ser a olvidar. Se dicen los versos del poeta: "Ya no lo quiero, es cierto, pero quizás lo quiero, es tan corto el amor y tan largo el olvido".
Se aguarda. Poco a poco el hechizo hará efecto y un día cualquiera sucederá: el dolor que había ya no estará.

Hechizo para detener la envidia

Si los hechizos no nos salen bien y nos da una cosita en la panza ver que a otras les salen, el Hadabuela tiene una receta fantástica:
Juntar tres hojas caídas del laurel y dos flores secas de pensamientos. Dejar macerar en agua de rocío. Sobre la hierba regar diciendo:
"Si no me sale, ya me saldrá".
Repetir.

Las asrai

Son pequeñas, tímidas y delicadas. Estas frágiles hadas viven en los lagos fríos, muy próximos a las grandes montañas de hielo. Suelen tener el cabello verde y la piel muy blanca. Aunque son muy inquietas, jamás abandonan el lago porque el contacto con el sol les resulta en extremo peligroso: un solo rayo tibio basta para que se desvanezcan y diluyan en el agua. Por este motivo nunca andan cerca de las costas. De noche, sin embargo, salen a la superficie y bailan sobre el lago a la luz de la luna. En esos momentos de fiesta disfrutan enormemente jugando con la espuma y el suave oleaje que producen sus movimientos. Su origen es un misterio, pero algunas versiones afirman que antes de emigrar a los lagos, vivían en las altas cumbres de hielo, muy próximas a la región de las nieves.

La dama del lago (mi tía abuela)

Muchas hadas viven en los lagos, pero el lago en el que habita mi tía abuela tiene la peculiaridad de ser imaginario. Cuando ella encuentra un lugar en el bosque que le agrada, construye su hogar del color del aire. Con un solo pase mágico logra que la hierba parezca un lago y así tanto ella como su reino quedan ocultos de las miradas indiscretas. La dama del lago es muy sabia y poderosa y actualmente cuida, junto a tres poderosas hadas, la espada Excalibur.

Un secreto oculto bajo las aguas

No sé si ella estará de acuerdo con lo que les voy a contar porque detesta hablar de su vida privada, pero lo cierto es que, cuando el mago Merlín la vio, se enamoró de ella al instante. Durante un tiempo fueron inseparables y él le enseñó todo lo que sabía sobre magia y hechicería, pero ella es muy inteligente y al poco tiempo su poder superó al del mago. Como se imaginarán, a Merlín esto no le causó ninguna gracia y entonces comenzaron las peleas. Ella decidió alejarse. Hasta que un buen día Merlín fue a buscarla y le pidió que fuese ella la guardiana de la gran espada Excalibur. Cuentan que cuando el rey Arturo fue mortalmente herido, arrojó la espada al lago y desde entonces, ella la mantiene oculta. La dama del lago junto con sus hadas, llevó al rey a Avalón, la isla mágica donde Arturo fue curado y de donde no puede salir.

HADAS de las FUENTES

Nadie crea que las fuentes son pequeños remansos donde nada sucede. Si las miramos con detenimiento, quizás podamos descubrir los anillos que se forman alrededor de los revoloteos de las delicadas y etéreas hadas que las pueblan.

Damas de la noche

Son hermosas damas que viven en las fuentes y salen a la superficie recién cuando anochece, pero lo hacen sólo si están seguras de que nadie las observa. Quizás se trate de las hadas más laboriosas del reino. Lavan sus ropas, hechas de tul, y las ponen a secar bajo la luz de la luna. Estas delgadas hadas de larga y brillante cabellera pasan horas y horas, hilando, cocinando y realizando las labores del hogar.

Las xanas

El nombre xana proviene del latín, y hay quienes aseguran que antiguamente tenían algún tipo de parentesco con Diana, la diosa de la caza. Aunque la veracidad de esta versión es poco probable, las xanas, al igual que la deidad griega, son muy valientes, audaces y generosas. En la mañana de San Juan es posible verlas a la orilla de una fuente, peinando sus cabellos. Son tan coquetas que entre sus objetos personales suelen llevar un peine de nácar y oro y un espejo. Son unas hadas dulces y pacíficas, pero no te atrevas a robarles su peine porque entonces sacarán toda su rabia y te perseguirán y amenazarán hasta que se lo devuelvas.

El juramento
de las xanas

Me contó mi bisabuela que custodian enormes
tesoros y que son guardianas de la fuente
de la Eterna Juventud, por eso han tenido grandes
problemas con algunos seres mágicos y muchos humanos
muy ambiciosos. Es una pena porque son naturalmente solidarias, y están siempre
dispuestas a ayudar. Sin embargo la gran cantidad de inconvenientes que les causaron
las gentes indiscretas las llevaron a tomar una drástica decisión: se reunieron un verano
en el fondo de las fuentes y realizaron un juramento inquebrantable: "No volverían a
socorrer nunca jamás a ningún mortal". La promesa que realizaron es indestructible,
sin embargo no fue esa la última vez que brindaron su auxilio a las personas. Ya verán...

La xana y el rey Mauregato
-Relato-

Hace mucho tiempo, cerca de las mesetas áridas, se alzaba el reino de Mauregato, un monarca poderoso y guerrero. Tantas tierras había conquistado, tantos eran sus enemigos y tantas batallas libraba que en una oportunidad le tocó perder. Los soldados del ejército vencedor que también habían participado en numerosas cruzadas, eran hombres crueles, sanguinarios y vengativos. De modo que, cuando entraron en el reino vencido destrozaron todo a su paso. Tan terribles y feroces fueron que Mauregato decidió pactar con ellos.

—¡Queremos las tierras! —exigieron los vencedores.

—¡Imposible! —contestó Mauregato—. Sin las tierras y los cultivos mi pueblo y yo moriremos de hambre.

—Entonces, danos los ríos —propusieron los vencedores.

—No, señor —volvió a negarse el rey—, sin los ríos para navegar tampoco tendremos agua y moriremos de sed.

—Pues entonces deberás entregarnos cien doncellas cada año para hacerlas nuestras esposas. Y esta es nuestra oferta final.

Al rey no le pareció un buen trato, pero debió aceptar. Y desde ese día, cada primavera, los soldados del reino vencedor, elegían a las jóvenes más lindas y se casaban con ellas a la fuerza. Mientras tanto, en el pueblo vecino de Illés vivía Galinda, una jovencita muy hermosa que andaba a caballo mejor que el más hábil de los jinetes del rey, manejaba la ballesta y sabía disparar con precisión.

—Si vienen por mí, me defenderé —solía decir.

—Son muchos soldados y muy poderosos, hija, te matarán antes de que puedas contar hasta tres —le decía afligida su madre.

Pero Galinda era joven y se creía indestructible, creía que nada malo le podía ocurrir.

Ese invierno pasó por la aldea el general del ejército vencedor y vio a la muchacha cabalgando.

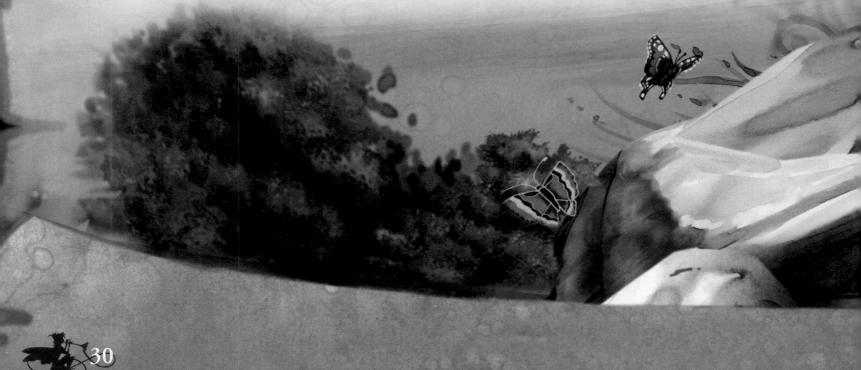

Le pareció tan bella que tomó una decisión: "Esta primavera vendremos a Illés a buscar esposas, y ésta será la mía". La madre de la joven estaba buscando agua en la fuente cuando oyó al general y rompió a llorar con gran desconsuelo:

—¡Ella se va a negar y entonces ese hombre malvado la matará!

Una de las xanas de la fuente escuchó su lamento y sintió una pena infinita por la mujer y quiso ayudarla. Sin embargo, la reina de las xanas se negó con firmeza:

—Ya tuvimos muchos problemas, ¿recuerdas? Tú hiciste el juramento, y no lo puedes romper. Ya sabes: ¡nada de ayudar a las personas!

La xana se quedó pensativa. Una de las últimas noches del invierno, antes de la llegada de la primavera, el general llegó a Illés con su ejército. Al oír los cascos de los caballos, Galinda montó su alazán, preparó su ballesta y huyó. Pero no pudo ir lejos: la aldea estaba rodeada y no había modo de escapar. Galinda se detuvo cerca de la fuente a pensar.

—Allí está —se escuchó de la voz del general— ¡Atrápenla!

Galinda oyó el galope de los caballos acercándose a gran velocidad.
Iba a gritar de furia cuando oyó una voz que le decía:

—Bebe el agua.

—¿Qué?, ¿quién habla? —preguntó Galinda.

—¡Que bebas el agua! ¡Ya!

La joven lo hizo y de pronto vio con asombro que los soldados
pasaban a su lado como si ella no existiese.

—¿Dónde está? —oyó que preguntaba el general.

—Me he vuelto invisible —comprobó con alegría—.
Pero, ¿cómo fue?

—Fuiste tú —dijo la xana de la fuente—.
Te convertiste en un hada, no sé si te agrada la idea,
pero era la única forma de ayudarte.

—¡Muchas gracias! —dijo Galinda emocionada.

Pero en ese momento vio que perseguían a otra joven.

—¡Xana! —gritó— ¡No hay tiempo!
¡Salvemos a todas las demás!

El hada se ensombreció y le contestó:

—Lo siento mucho —dijo—. Juré, al
igual que todas las xanas, que no ayudaríamos
a ningún humano más, por eso para salvarte
no tuve más remedio que convertirte en hada.

—¡Ah…! Un juramento… —dijo Galinda—,
pero… Yo nunca juré y ahora soy un hada, ¿verdad?

—Sí —admitió la xana—, es verdad, pero ¿qué tramas?

—Ya lo verás— sonrió la flamante hada.

Cuando los soldados regresaron en busca de Galinda, la vieron
sentada al borde de la fuente, bella como siempre, pero ahora sus
cabellos negros eran azules y le sentaban muy bien.

Los soldados se lanzaron sobre ella, dieron un paso, uno solo y al instante, comenzaron a balar. Mientras tanto, el general esperaba impaciente a sus soldados que tardaban en regresar y al ver que no llegaban fue a buscar al rey.

—Mauregato —lo instó—, los guerreros no han vuelto: algo les ha sucedido.

El general y el rey fueron con sus guardias a la fuente donde los soldados habían sido vistos por última vez y se encontraron con Galinda rodeada de corderos.

—¿Dónde están mis soldados? —le gritó el general.

—¿Qué soldados? ¿Te refieres a esos corderos? —dijo Galinda señalando a los soldados.

El rey y el general se volvieron, y con estupor, comprobaron que los guardias que los acompañaban también eran corderos.

Atemorizados por el poder de la xana, le suplicaron que dejara libres a sus soldados:

—Yo libero a los soldados, pero tú, Mauregato, romperás tu trato con el enemigo y nunca más entregarás a una joven. También quiero que regresen todas las damas que se fueron contra su voluntad.

—Así será— prometió el rey.

—Más te vale. Pero si no lo haces, cada vez que un soldado toque a una muchacha se convertirá en cordero. El rey y el general comprobaron con asombro cómo los corderos se transformaban en soldados.

Así fue que la alegría volvió al lugar. Y los días que siguieron fueron puro festejo porque regresaron las jóvenes raptadas. Desde entonces, la xana Galinda mora en la fuente y libre del juramento, protege siempre a las niñas y a las mujeres de la ciudad.

33

Hadas de los Mares

Alguien nos hizo creer que los mares son el reino de las sirenas y que un hada jamás podría llegar a las profundidades marinas. Sin embargo, el silencio del mar profundo está poblado de hadas muy particulares…

Las nereidas

Las nereidas, son unas hermosas y jóvenes ninfas, de piel blanca y hermosa voz, que habitan en el fondo de los mares. A estas bellísimas hadas de larga cabellera verde mar y ojos amarillos, no les causa gracia ser observadas por los humanos sin su permiso. Les encanta en cambio, jugar con los delfines y se comenta que siempre aparecen en compañía de estos simpáticos animales. Hay quienes las confunden con sirenas, porque algunas (no todas) tienen torso de mujer y piernas de pescado, sin embargo son fáciles de reconocer porque muchas de ellas van vestidas de blanco y dorado y siempre llevan un chal en sus manos. Aunque introvertidas, son muy generosas y ayudan a los hombres en alta mar, sobre todo cuando hay tormentas, pues tienen el poder de controlar las aguas. Pero es importante no confundirse: son muy celosas de su intimidad, no les gusta la presencia de los mortales y mucho menos la de los curiosos. Y si alguno se atreve a mirarlas mientras se bañan, le robarán la voz.

Las hijas de Océano

Cuando el dios Nereo se casó con Doris, hija del titán Océano, tuvieron cincuenta hermosas hijas: las nereidas, consideradas diosas menores. Desde siempre se destacaron por su gran belleza y cuentan que a Jasón y a los Argonautas los salvaron en una tempestad, cuando iban en la nave Argos en busca del vellocino de oro.

Las selkies o hadas focas

En los mares fríos, más allá de las tierras heladas, nadan las tímidas selkies, también llamadas hadas focas. Su aspecto, a simple vista, no resulta el más agradable. Sin embargo cada primavera las selkies se desprenden de su piel y llegan a las costas terrestres transformadas en bellas doncellas. Son muy bondadosas con todos los seres, animales y humanos, exceptuando, claro está, a los cazadores de focas. Con ellos abandonan sus modales dulces y tranquilos y pueden llegar a ser despiadadas.

A diferencia del resto de las hadas acuáticas, los humanos no les resultan atractivos y no se enamoran nunca de ellos, pero si un hombre logra apoderarse de su piel, la selkie no puede volver al mar y se ve obligada a convertirse en una obediente, aunque muy melancólica esposa. Sin embargo, cuando por un descuido del raptor, la selkie logra encontrar su abrigo, retorna de inmediato a su hogar.

HADAS de los RÍOS

Las aguas cristalinas de los ríos correntosos y de algunos lagos esconden un mundo de náyades y ondinas, hadas bastante más sociables que las de mar, pero también de increíble belleza.

Las náyades

El escritor griego Homero decía que eran hijas de Zeus, pero otras versiones aseguran que, en realidad, son hijas de muchos dioses. Protegen las fuentes, los ríos y los lagos. Su color preferido es el azul por eso están vestidas con telas de ese tono. Les encanta contemplar a los seres humanos y son curiosas y algo traviesas. Poseen el don de curar. Son grandes nadadoras y saben sumergirse y nadar perfectamente bajo el agua.

Las ondinas

Estas bellas hadas de los ríos, poseen larga y húmeda cabellera verde. Su origen es un tema de controversia entre los especialistas, porque mientras algunos libros antiguos afirman que son hijas del dios Odín, otra versión las emparenta con las náyades. Según esta teoría, por motivos que se desconocen, algunas náyades se habrían visto obligadas a emigrar hacia los ríos del norte. Y en un territorio más propicio habrían establecido las primeras comunidades de lo que luego se conocería como ondinas. Al igual que a las sirenas (con quienes no hay que confundirlas) se las acusa de seducir a los marinos con su dulce voz. Lo cierto es que textos muy antiguos narran historias de amor entre ellas y apuestos marineros que las cautivaron obsequiándoles sus joyas favoritas: collares de perlas.

Por culpa de la reina de corazón de hielo
-Relato-

Según una antigua costumbre de las épocas ya idas, cuando nacía alguna jovencita (sobre todo si se trataba de una princesa) a las hadas nos asignaban la misión de brindarle nuestra protección. En el año dorado de la edad áurea, yo debí ser el hada madrina de una princesa asombrosamente bella. La más hermosa niña que habíamos visto nunca jamás, sin embargo aunque su rostro eclipsaba al mismísimo Sol, su carácter era un tanto... cómo decirlo... ¡espantoso! Ya desde muy temprana edad demostró cierta mezquindad. Solía ser egoísta con sus amigas y cruel con los niños que suspiraban por sus ojos brillantes y su piel de seda nueva. Pero, aunque no parecía ser una niña del todo buena, ¿quién iba a imaginar entonces, lo que luego habría de suceder?

Cuando cumplió quince años se convirtió en una joven bellísima, de ojos enormes y cabellera luminosa. Alta y altiva, era sin dudas la más bella princesa de toda la región, qué diré, ¡de todo el mundo! Como su xana madrina le obsequié tres presentes invaluables.

¡Ay, no debí haberlo hecho jamás!

—Toma: un peine de oro para que ese metal nunca falte en tu hogar, un frasco del agua con el cual conservarás tu belleza por siempre jamás y, éste es el regalo más importante, un espejo mágico que te dirá siempre la verdad. Espero que seas prudente con estos obsequios.

La joven, educada como buena princesa, agradeció los presentes.

Sin embargo, nuestras buenas intenciones no bastaban y lo cierto es que a medida que el tiempo pasaba, estos obsequios le hicieron cada vez peor. El peine de oro la convirtió en la reina más rica, poderosa y déspota del lugar; su belleza increíble se eternizó merced al agua mágica y así logró ocultar la maldad de su corazón. Todos los días bebía unas gotas del frasco y le preguntaba al espejo:

—Espejito, espejito que dices siempre la verdad, dime, ¿quién es la más bella del reino?

—Tú, mi señora —respondía el espejo sin dudar.

Y la reina se tranquilizaba, pero sólo hasta el día siguiente cuando volvía a preguntar:

—Espejito, espejito que dices siempre la verdad: ¿quién es la más bella del reino?

—Mi Señora, ¿es que no deseas conocer otras respuestas? —preguntó cierta vez el espejo—, puedo darte mucha sabiduría sobre todo lo que existe...

Pero entonces la mujer enfureció:

—¿Acaso me tratas de tonta? ¡¡¡Te arrepentirás!!!

—No, claro que no —se resignó el espejo. Desde aquella vez no volvió a cuestionar a la reina. Pero una mañana de primavera, la reina lo interrogó como siempre y el espejo, obligado a decir la verdad, respondió:

—Eres muy hermosa señora, pero hay una niña que lo es aún más.

La reina enloqueció de ira he hizo cosas terribles para deshacerse de su rival.

Por suerte, la pobre muchachita se salvó de la crueldad de mi malvada ahijada y se casó con un príncipe azul. Pero las xanas, preocupadas por el daño que, sin querer habíamos provocado, nos reunimos en más de una oportunidad. Finalmente nuestra reina tomó una decisión:

—A partir de ahora, ninguna xana se entrometerá nunca más en los asuntos humanos —dijo, y todas tuvimos que hacer aquel juramento.

HADAS del AIRE

En tiempos muy antiguos, cuando las hadas moraban en las colinas huecas, había entre ellas un grupo que se distinguía del resto por su carácter alegre. Inquietas, sobrevolaban con las mariposas y las aves los jardines más perfumados.

Alegres e inquietas viajeras

Por aquellos tiempos estas hadas deambulaban por bosques, cerros y prados y se sabe que fueron ellas las que llevaron al resto de las hadas, las noticias sobre la existencia del mar. Al abandonar las colinas huecas, estas hadas decidieron no quedarse en un solo sitio y treparon al viento para viajar con él.

Amantes de las flores

Son muy bellas, tienen cabelleras tenues y piel muy suave, cuyo color varía de acuerdo al lugar donde se encuentren. Pero como pueden huir con asombrosa facilidad, no les preocupan los peligros ni temen a los humanos. Aman las flores cuyo perfume adoran, son en extremo sensibles a los aromas, y es por eso que suelen pasar largo tiempo entre las rosas, los jazmines y las madreselvas y rara vez resisten la tentación de posarse sobre un jardín florido.

Los silfos

Estas bellas hadas azules vuelan en bandadas como los pájaros, por eso, muchas veces, las confunden con gaviotas. Como se mueven a gran velocidad y cambian de forma y color en el aire, les resulta muy sencillo escapar de los peligros. Con frecuencia ayudan a las hadas de la tierra, ya que colorean las flores y dan sabor a los frutos, y no se equivocan jamás.

Las figyar

Son un grupo de hadas muy simpáticas y es raro verlas de mal humor. Adoran bailar en los jardines floridos al compás del viento pero rara vez permanecen más de dos días en un mismo jardín. Sin embargo, cuando un sitio les agrada suelen regresar a él. A diferencia de las hadas acuáticas, nunca se enamoran de los hombres, pero tienen predilección por las familias, a las que, pese a su espíritu inquieto, les encantaría pertenecer. Por eso, muchas veces eligen una familia y la visitan cada tanto, generalmente sin que ésta llegue a saberlo ni a conocerlas jamás. Esto claro está, no era lo que sucedía antes, pero algo cambió la historia…

Blancamar y "su" familia
-Relato-

En un país muy lejano, en una casa situada al este del arco iris vivía la familia Alcalá, conformada por Amanda, la mamá, Adán, el papá, Alan, el niño mayor y Aldana, la niña menor. Era primavera y unas haditas del aire revoloteaban entre las rosas del jardín, cuando de pronto una sombra peluda oscureció la tarde: "Miau", dijo la sombra y entonces, al levantar la vista, lo vieron: era Don Botas, el gato de la familia, que acechaba cerca del nogal.

En un santiamén huyeron todas las hadas, todas menos una:
Blancamar, el hada más blanca,
enredó su vestido en el rosal y no pudo escapar.

—Ahh —gritó el hada aterrada.

—¿Don Botas, qué haces? —se escuchó la voz de Aldana, la niña menor. —¡Un hada! —gritó al ver a Blancamar enredada en su rosal.

Con cuidado, la niña la desenredó y la colocó sobre el capullo de una rosa.

—Ahora ya puedes volar —le dijo.

El hada sonrió agradecida, y movió las alas con suavidad, luego más fuerte, y finalmente las agitó a toda velocidad, sin poder elevarse.

—¿Qué ocurre? —le preguntó la niña.

—Las alas fallan —explicó el hada.

—Te llevaré a mi cuarto —dijo la niña—. Allí veremos si te puedo curar.

El hada afligida se dejó llevar.

—¿Sanará mañana? —preguntó.

—Seguramente —dijo la niña y la acomodó en una cama de muñecas.

—Aguarda, iré por ayuda —dijo y fue corriendo a buscar a su hermano mayor.

—¡Alan! —llamó—, ven pronto.

—¿Qué ocurre?

—¡Es que tengo un hada en mi cuarto!

—Ah... era eso... —dijo Alan y siguió leyendo.

—¡Es verdad!

—Sí, claro y yo tengo un dragón en la sala.

—Ven... —dijo la niña jalándolo del brazo.

—Bien, pero no empujes —protestó el muchacho.

Alan abrió los ojos como platos grandes y redondos cuando la vio.

—¡Qué es eso! —tartamudeó.

—Blancamar jamás fallaba —dijo el hada a modo de presentación.

—Llamemos a mamá —dijo Alan cuando reaccionó.

Esa tarde la familia Alcalá en pleno se reunió en el cuarto de Aldana para ayudar.

—Tiene un ala herida —dijo finalmente la mamá al revisarla con cuidado.

—Papá —pidió Alan— , tú eres médico, cúrala por favor.

—No puedo —dijo el padre—, no sé sanar alas de hada.

—Quizás ella sepa qué hacer —dijo la mamá y mirando a Blancamar le preguntó—, ¿recuerdas algún remedio con el que te podamos curar?

El hada se puso muy seria y comenzó a pensar en voz alta: "Papas para las patas malas, ramas anaranjadas para las nalgas aplastadas, para las alas… para las alas…"

De pronto recordó con ilusión:

— ¡Para las alas, calas!

Al día siguiente la familia consiguió una planta de calas y la plantó en el jardín. El hada se puso muy feliz: "Las hadas alabarán a Blancamar, cantarán para aclamarla", cantaba.

Y cuando la flor se abrió colocaron al hadita en su interior.

Ella aspiró el perfume tres veces, movió las alas y se elevó.

—Muchas gracias —dijo a todos.

—¡Puedes volar! —festejó la niña.

—¡Y hablas con todas las letras! —dijo Alan.

—Ven a visitarnos —pidieron todos.

Cada primavera el hada visita a la familia, que la recibe feliz de verla.

Pero esta historia sigue…

Blancamar contó su experiencia a todas las demás: "Ahora tengo una familia más".

—Nosotras también deseamos el amor de una familia —dijeron las hadas. Desde aquel día, las hadas del aire visitan a una familia que les guste y cuando escuchan algún deseo, lo hacen realidad.

Por eso, niñas: ¡estén atentas!

43

HADAS del FUEGO

Estas son damas muy, pero muy antiguas y también poderosas. En los libros aparecen referencias sobre ellas que datan de los tiempos anteriores a la historia, cuando los hombres se reunían en torno a las fogatas. Además son muy sabias, atesoran secretos que el resto de las hadas ignora.

Lejos de los mares...

Las hadas del fuego moran en las "colinas de corazón ardiente", llamadas volcanes por las gentes. Suelen vivir lejos de los ríos y los lagos, y hasta donde se sabe, ninguna de ellas ha navegado nunca. Muchas incluso, jamás vieron el mar. Se dice que la mayoría de las hadas del fuego miran con gran desconfianza todos los cauces de agua y a tal punto llega su aversión, que términos como mar, lluvia o cascada se han transformado en palabras horrorosas que conviene no pronunciar en su presencia.

Limníades

Estas chispeantes y diminutas damas adoran las fiestas y los bailes. A diferencia de otras hadas, les gusta dejarse ver por las gentes a quienes frecuentemente invitan a bailar. No es del todo aconsejable aceptar sus convites porque son incansables y capaces de danzar indefinidamente. Aunque sienten gran desilusión cuando son rechazadas, no son vengativas porque su espíritu festivo hace que rápidamente olviden cualquier ofensa.

Las salamandras o señoras del fuego

Son hadas muy sabias y poderosas.
Nunca es aconsejable ofender a un hada, pero si se trata
de una salamandra, este consejo debe acatarse a perpetuidad.
Si se ofenden o se sienten heridas, las salamandras
son capaces de soltar su furia y ¡ay de quien las enfrente!
Sin embargo, a pesar de su carácter irascible,
son muy generosas y no dudan en brindar su ayuda
a las demás hadas y a las gentes todas las veces que
pueden y sin pedir nada a cambio jamás.

Con estas sí, con estas no

Al igual que la mayoría de las hadas,
viven en comunidades regidas por una reina
(ya les dije que Titania, mi bisabuela es la
reina de todas las comunidades). Cada siete
años todas las hadas se reúnen para
deliberar asuntos o para festejar un
acontecimiento especial. Durante
estas convenciones suele reinar la
armonía, pero hay que admitir
que entre algunos grupos
existen ciertas desavenencias,
que si bien no hay por qué
exagerar, tampoco conviene
ignorar. Las hadas del agua se
llevan muy bien con las
damas de la tierra, y las
señoras del fuego suelen
congeniar de maravillas con
las damitas del aire, pero
entre las damas del mar y
las salamandras suele
haber roces frecuentes e
indirectas varias.

Un mar de pesadillas
-Relato-

Todo comenzó hace mucho tiempo atrás, en las épocas lejanas en que las hadas moraban en las colinas huecas.

Las hadas del aire, inquietas y aventureras, en uno de sus paseos, descubrieron el mar.

—¡Qué maravilla! ¡Qué gran y asombrosa inmensidad! —dijeron a coro y, felices, no dudaron en volar veloces y narrar lo que habían visto a las demás hadas.

Estaban tan entusiasmadas que les costaba contar lo que habían descubierto.

—¡La gran sabana salada nada de acá para allá! ¡A la mañana es más brava y se calma al alba!

Cuando por fin se tranquilizaron, lograron explicar con más claridad la maravilla que habían contemplado, pero no todas las hadas reaccionaron del mismo modo: las damas de la tierra sonrieron plácidas e indiferentes a las buenas nuevas.

—Nos alegramos de que tal belleza exista —dijeron simplemente antes de olvidar el asunto.

A las hadas del agua, en cambio, les fascinó tanto lo que oyeron que decidieron viajar sin demora a conocer ese extraño y mágico lugar.

Cuando vieron el mar, se quedaron quietas, mudas de maravilla y de asombro.

La impresionante y brava inmensidad, a veces azul, a veces verde, las fascinó de tal modo que en ese instante muchas de ellas decidieron permanecer por siempre allí.

Pero a las hadas de fuego, lo que escucharon no les gustó nada. La entusiasta descripción de la extraña inmensidad húmeda les causó terror y no quisieron saber nada más.

A aquellas hadas del agua que habían elegido el mar para vivir, esta actitud, las molestó.

—¡Caramba! Vosotras, tan sabias, deben conocer el sitio más maravilloso que hay! —insistían una y otra vez.

Las limníades se limitaron a esconderse al calor de una fogata y no hicieron más caso, pero las salamandras contestaron con fervor:

—¡No queremos volver a oír hablar de esa cuestión! No nos digan más.

Pero a las hadas del mar no les gusta que las callen y son algo insistentes.

—Nos oirán contar todo lo que queramos, ustedes no nos van a callar —dijeron.

Entonces las señoras del fuego que no se destacan justamente por su gran paciencia, la perdieron del todo.

—¡Basta ya! —advirtieron.

—¡Tan poderosas y con tanto miedo! —se burlaron las damas del mar.

¡Ay!, las salamandras, de temperamento irascible no podían soportar las burlas con facilidad, y furiosas dijeron cosas feas de esas que no conviene repetir ni recordar.

Las hadas del mar, dolidas y muy ofendidas, juraron no volverles a hablar.

Desde aquellos días remotos perduran la rabia y el rencor entre las comunidades de hadas.

Las demás hadas piensan que es infantil conservar el encono a través de los siglos, pero las damas marítimas y las señoras del fuego aún no las quieren escuchar.

Quizás lo hagan en un par de siglos más…

¿Cómo contactar a las HADAS

Esto no es algo muy sencillo. No basta sólo con desearlo, ellas también deben estar dispuestas. Que accedan, por cierto es muy difícil, porque, aunque pueden estar entre nosotros, no siempre quieren manifestarse corpóreamente a nuestros ojos.

Para convocar a las hadas

Para llamar a las hadas:
Preparen un ramillete de prímulas con un número exacto y luego toquen con él una roca de hadas. Entonces se les abrirá la entrada a su país.

Para la segunda receta deben conseguir serpol, procurando arrancarlo cerca de una colina que visiten las hadas, y mezclarlo con algunas hierbas que crezcan junto a un "tronco de hadas". Preparen una infusión, que al beberla, les permitirá verlas.

Si las están buscando…
nunca lleven "hierro", lo desprecian.
No silben en los bosques: esto rompe el aura natural del lugar.
Tengan en cuenta que el mejor momento es a
la luz de la luna llena.

¿Cómo atraerlas al jardín?

Para que visiten sus casas habitualmente, no olviden…
poner casas de pájaros y comederos en sus jardines.
Sembrar flores y plantas atractivas a las abejas y las mariposas.
Las hadas se sienten atraídas por los lugares donde merodean las mariposas.
Instalar en el jardín una pequeña fuente de agua. A las hadas y a los duendes del agua les gusta el sonido de las cascadas y ver las fuentes.
Estas son algunas de las plantas que atraen mariposas y hadas al jardín:
crisantemo, tomillo, lavanda, rosas, petunia, verbena, zinnia.

¿Cómo mantenerlas cerca?

A las hadas les encanta el jengibre y la cebada. Por eso, si ponen un pequeño cesto con estas plantas en el jardín, se quedarán siempre cerca, especialmente si las reemplazan periódicamente. También les gusta ver siempre en el jardín tomillo y trébol, este último sólo de tres hojas.

El invierno

Durante el invierno las hadas duermen, tal y como hacen sus plantas y sus árboles. Si quieren, las hadas pueden pasar el invierno en sus casas, sólo deberán tener paciencia.

Hechizo para convocar a las hadas

Sentarse donde el gato se sienta.
Cruzar los dedos de los pies.
Cerrar los ojos y oler una rosa,
mientras decimos:
"Yo creo en las hadas,
efectivamente ellas están.
¡Gadflykins! ¡Gladtrypins!
¡Gutterpuss y Cass!
Venga a mí el fairily.
¡Vengan haditas a mí!"

HADAS SOLITARIAS

Como ya les conté, la mayoría de las hadas "reside" en comunidades regidas por una reina, pero no todas viven así. Algunas deambulan solas por los cielos, los mares o los bosques…

Habetot

A diferencia de la mayoría de las hadas, Habetot es una viejecita, de pelo canoso y desaliñado. No es linda, porque la belleza no le interesa, pero sí es tierna y bondadosa. Le encanta hilar y coser y antiguamente enseñaba sus artes a las jovencitas. Luego con el advenimiento de la vida moderna y la llegada de la falsa magia, todo cambió y ahora Habetot no sabe cómo ayudar.

Mab

Esta diminuta y traviesa hada del aire, montada en un carro de una
sola perla, guiado por insectos, lleva consigo miles de sueños.
Concede deseos, siempre que puede, pero si no están a su alcance otorga
alegría y esperanzas al deseante dormido. Mab cuenta con muchos
amigos entre las gentes, sobre todo poetas y pintores.
Bondadosa y desobediente, tiene una debilidad: le encanta ser famosa,
punto tal que llegó a decir que era ella la reina de todas las hadas y
así aparece retratada en miles de obras. Titania, al principio,
se enojó, pero luego se echó a reír y dejó que el
viento corriera con el rumor.

Morgana

Este hada del mar, que reside en la isla mágica de Avalón, junto a la
dama del lago, Nínive y la maga Eliane, cuida del rey Arturo.
La leyenda de "Morgana, el hada malvada" proviene del tiempo en
que ella habitó la corte de aquel rey. Morgana, aprendió los secretos
que encierran los números, lo que la convirtió en una maga
poderosa y despertó algunas envidias. Su belleza deslumbrante
llamaba la atención de los caballeros, y, como nunca fue muy
simpática, contestaba las atenciones con cierta indiferencia y
frialdad. Cuando la agredían se limitaba a responder con risas de
superioridad. ¡Ay! ¡Nada más efectivo para despertar
las furias de los humanos! Y los rumores comenzaron a rodar,
pero deben saber que son sólo eso, rumores y nada más.

Un mágico secreto
-Relato-

Voy a contarles un secreto pero si prometen no difundirlo jamás. Sucedió un día entre los días, hace tiempo.

Yo volaba plácidamente por los aires cuando de pronto apareció Mab, montada en su carro de perla. Se la veía más inquieta de lo habitual, lo que es decir mucho…

—Hadabuela —me llamó, y sin esperar siquiera mi respuesta, blandió un papel y exclamó—: ¡Mi amigo el poeta cayó prisionero! ¡Está en el castillo de Morgana, en Avalón!

—Caramba —me entristecí, pero de inmediato me asombré—. ¿En la isla de Avalón? ¿Y cómo llegó hasta allí?

El rubor repentino de Mab me dio la respuesta:

—¡Tú lo llevaste, Mab! ¿Qué has hecho?

—Sí —admitió ella con un pedacito de voz—, fue uno de sus deseos y era su cumpleaños y yo… Pero —continuó de pronto con su voz completa—, ¡Morgana lo descubrió y lo apresó! Y tú sabes lo estricta que suele ser.

—Sí, lo sé. Y también conozco las reglas ¡que tú ignoraste! ¡Ningún humano puede jamás entrar allí!

—Por favor, Hadabuela —rogó Mab—, ¡debes ayudarme a liberarlo!..., es inofensivo, no contará nada y si lo hace…, ¡qué más da! ¡Es poeta! ¿Quién va a creer que lo que cuenta es verdad?

Tuve que admitir que estaba en lo cierto. Muchos poetas se cansaron de describir a Mab (y contra su voluntad también a Titania) sin que nadie sospechase ni remotamente que lo que contaban era realidad.

—Bien, te ayudaré —Mab saltó de alegría—, pero que ésta sea la última vez —advertí.

Llegar a Avalón sin invitación no era una tarea fácil, había que prepararse bien, por eso fui en busca de mi mejor vara mágica, elegí la más poderosa que estaba hecha con una rama de fresno y me había sido otorgada especialmente por la reina Titania.

—Vamos antes de que lo piense bien —le dije a Mab.

Los caminos hacia Avalón son complicados, sobre todo si uno acude sin llevar tarjeta de invitación. Tuvimos que convencer al gigante que cuida la isla y luego confundir a los siete vientos que casi nos hacen caer.

Cuando por fin llegamos, volamos directo hacia la torre del gran castillo donde mora Morgana.

Desde la pequeña ventana vimos al poeta, se lo notaba triste y su rostro reflejaba una expresión de hondo dolor.

La puerta se abrió
y apareció el hada,
hermosa
y altiva como siempre…
—¿Quién anda por allí?
—preguntó
— Soy yo, el Hadabuela
—me anuncié.
En el rostro de la dama se notaba
una mueca de sorpresa.
—¡Hadabuela! ¿Qué haces aquí?
Era inútil mentir:
—Vine a pedir por el poeta —le dije—.
Bella reina, por favor, déjalo partir.
El hada hizo un gesto de fastidio, mezclado
con una pizca de furia.
—Pero sucede que… —comenzó a decir, pero no siguió.
De pronto quedó inmóvil y muda.
—¿Que pasó? —pregunté.
—Fui yo —dijo Mab que se había escondido en mi bolsillo—,
le lancé un hechizo… Y mirando al poeta ordenó:
—Vamos, que Morgana no va a tardar en deshacerse de mi magia.
El poeta la contemplaba lánguido y melancólico, pero no se movía.
—¿Acaso estás sordo? —lo increpó Mab—, ¡apresúrate, te vinimos a liberar!
—¡Ay! —suspiró el joven—, ¡hada bondadosa, la prisión que me apresa es
mucho más poderosa de la que tú o cualquier maga me pueda soltar!
—¿De qué habla? —le pregunté a Mab— ¿Tu amigo ha enloquecido?
Él me miró y dijo:
—No, no más que antes.
—¡En la nota me decías que estabas prisionero! —chilló ya cansada Mab e impaciente
porque veía que la poderosa hada ya se liberaba del hechizo y comenzaba a moverse.
—Sí —continuó el poeta—, y sigo prisionero, pero de amor.

—Me enamoré de Morgana ni bien la vi.
Por eso es que sufro…
—Les quería explicar —dijo Morgana molesta—, pero ella
me lanzó ese estúpido hechizo.
—Caramba, te pedimos mil disculpas,
por favor —rogué a Morgana—. No sabíamos la verdad.
—Bueno —volvió a hablar Mab—, entonces Hadabuela,
lánzale un hechizo para que se libere de su pasión.
—¡Nunca!—clamó el poeta.
—No, por favor —pidió Morgana casi con desesperación…
—Reina, ¿por qué no? Tú tienes muchos caballeros que
suspiran por ti, ¿por qué no consientes en dejarlo ir? —pregunté.
—Pues… —el rostro pálido de la altiva
hada enrojeció—, pues… ¡Porque no!
—Ah…, ya veo… —comprendí—,
vinimos a solucionar un problema
que ya no existe —exclamé furiosa mirando
a Mab—, aunque… quizás no hayamos viajado en
vano y aún podemos hacer algo útil y bueno, ¿verdad?
—suspiré y volví a mirar al hada diminuta.
Ella pareció entenderme
porque se acercó al poeta y le dijo:
—Deja de sufrir, Morgana te quiere.
Pero ella no te lo dirá tan fácilmente.
El rostro del muchacho se iluminó de dicha:
—Reina, ¿es eso, verdad? —preguntó.
Morgana no contestó, pero sus ojos dijeron sí.
—Es hora de irnos, Mab —me apresuré a decir.
Saludamos a los novios y sin más
ceremonia partimos de una buena vez.
—¡Es la última… —estaba por regañar al hada más
traviesa del mundo cuando uno de los siete vientos
que habíamos burlado nos vio, y vengativo,
comenzó a soplar.
Sopló tan fuerte que nos hizo tropezar.
Yo me distraje y solté mi vara mágica.
¡La mejor! ¡La más poderosa que tenía y que
jamás tendré!
Grité desesperada, pero ya era demasiado tarde…
Vi caer mi varita y estrellarse contra la montaña
del hielo azul, la vi estallar y romperse en mil
y un pedazos. En ese momento,
el viento bandido sopló tan fuerte que los trozos
mágicos se esparcieron por todo el mundo.
Nada que hacer, tan sólo podía
resignarme y volver.

Y aquí va mi secreto…

La magia de la varita se esparció por todo el mundo y todavía
hoy los trocitos pueden tocar lo que sea y a quien sea.
Si eso ocurre, la persona rozada será al instante y por un rato, un hada.
A todas las niñas en cualquier momento les puede pasar.
Tal vez ya les haya ocurrido.
Piénsenlo bien…
Si aún no sucedió, quizás suceda pronto.
¿Cómo se darán cuenta?
Pues no lo sé. Simplemente,
estén atentas…

ÍNDICE

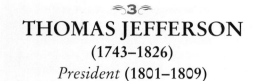

❧3❧
THOMAS JEFFERSON
(1743–1826)
President (1801–1809)

The American Renaissance Man of his age, Jefferson was curious about everything: "There was not a sprig of grass... uninteresting to me, nor anything that moves."

> *I know well that no man will ever bring out of that office the reputation which carries him into it. The honeymoon would be as short in that case as in any other, and its moments of ecstasy would be ransomed by years of torment and hatred."*
> **THOMAS JEFFERSON, 1796**

BIOGRAPHY
Date of Birth: 13 April 1743
Place of Birth: Goochland (Albemarle) County, Virginia
Father: Peter Jefferson (1708–57)
Mother: Jane Randolph Jefferson (1720–76)
Wife: Martha Wayles Skelton (1748–82)
Children: 4
Date of Death: 4 July 1826
Place of Death: Charlottesville, Virginia
Burial: Monticello, Charlottesville, Virginia
Number of terms: 2
Dates of inaugurations: (1) 4 March 1801, (2) 4 March 1805
Age at first inauguration: 57

Vice-President: Aaron Burr, George Clinton
Sec. of State: James Madison
Sec. of Treasury: Samuel Dexter, Albert Gallatin, Albert Gallatin

HIGHLIGHTS
1762 Graduated from College of William and Mary, Williamsburg, Virginia
1767 Admitted to the Virginia bar
1769 Elected to the Virginia legislature. Began construction of Monticello
1772, 1 January Married wealthy widow, Martha Wayles Skelton
1774 Authored Summary View of the Rights of British America
1776 Drafted The Declaration of Independence
1776–79 Served in the Virginia House of Delegates
1779–81 Governor of Virginia
1782 Death of Martha Jefferson
1782 Elected a delegate of the Continental Congress
1785–89 US Minister to France
1789 Secretary of State in Washington's first administration
1793 Resigned as Secretary of State
1796 Lost presidential election to John Adams. Became vice-president
1801, 4 March Sworn in as third president in Washington, D.C.
1803 Purchased Louisiana from France for $15 million – three cents an acre
1804 Won second term
1804 Sent Lewis and Clark on their expedition to the West
1809 Returned to Monticello
1810 Primary founder of University of Virginia
1826, 4 July Died at Monticello

> *I have the consolation...of having added nothing to my private fortune during my public service, and of retiring with hands as clean as they are empty."*
> **JEFFERSON, 29 MARCH 1807**

Jefferson's heavily edited draft of the Declaration of Independence.

❧4❧
JAMES MADISON
(1751–1836)
President (1809–1817)

Although physically unimpressive, James Madison was an intellectual power-house among the founding fathers. John F. Kennedy called him "our most underrated President."

BIOGRAPHY
Date of birth: 16 March 1751
Place of birth: Port Conway, Virginia
Father: James Madison (1723–1801)
Mother: Eleanor Conway Madison (1731–1829)
Wife: Dolley Payne Todd (1768–1849)
Children: none
Date of death: 28 June 1836
Place of death: Montpelier, Virginia
Burial: Montpelier, Virginia
Number of terms: 2
Dates of inaugurations: (1) 4 March 1809, (2) 4 March 1813
Age at first inauguration: 57
Vice-President: George Clinton, Elbridge Gerry
Sec. of State: Robert Smith, James Monroe
Sec. of Treasury: Albert Gallatin, George W. Campbell, Alexander J. Dallas

HIGHLIGHTS
1771 Graduated from College of New Jersey at Princeton
1776 Contributed to Virginia state constitution
1776–77 Member of Virginia legislature
1780–83 Delegate to Congress
1787–88 Wrote many of The Federalist papers
1801–9 Secretary of State under Jefferson
1809–17 Fourth President
1826 Rector of University of Virginia

> *Justice is the end of government. It ever has been, and ever will be pursued, until it is obtained, or until liberty be lost in the pursuit."*
> **JAMES MADISON**

> *Not withstanding a thousand faults and blunders, his administration has acquired more glory and established more union, than all three predecessors put together."*
> JOHN ADAMS ON JAMES MADISON'S PRESIDENCY.

1802 ✦ GAS STOVE INVENTED BY GERMAN-BORN FREDERICK WINSOR IN ENGLAND.

1803 ✦ OHIO ADMITTED TO STATEHOOD. LOUISIANA PURCHASED FROM FRANCE FOR $15 MILLION.

1804 ✦ AARON BURR (VICE-PRESIDENT IN JEFFERSON'S FIRST CABINET) KILLED ALEXANDER HAMILTON (SECRETARY OF THE TREASURY IN WASHINGTON'S CABINETS) IN A DUEL.

1804–1806 ✦ LEWIS AND CLARK EXPEDITION. MERIWETHER LEWIS AND WILLIAM CLARK EXPLORE THE COUNTRY FROM THE MISSISSIPPI TO THE PACIFIC

1805 ✦ US WARSHIPS DEFEAT THE BARBARY PIRATES OF NORTH AFRICA IN THE TRIPOLITANIAN WAR.

1807 ✦ USS *CHESAPEAKE* FIRED ON BY BRITISH HMS *LEOPARD* CAUSING BRITISH WARSHIPS TO BE BANNED FROM AMERICAN WATERS.

1811 ✦ LONDON WAS THE FIRST CITY TO EXCEED 1 MILLION POPULATION.

United States declares war on Great Britain

1812 ✦ AMERICA DECLARES WAR ON BRITAIN (18 JUNE).

1814 ✦ BRITISH CAPTURE AND BURN WASHINGTON DC.

1815 ✦ BRITISH DEFEATED BY ANDREW JACKSON AT THE BATTLE OF NEW ORLEANS.

1816 ✦ FRENCHMAN RENÉ LAËNNEC INVENTED THE STETHOSCOPE IN PARIS.

1817 ✦ MISSISSIPPI ADMITTED TO STATEHOOD.

1953 Worked as bookkeeper for Carter's peanut business in Plains, Georgia
1971-75 Lived in Atlanta during Carter's term as governor of Georgia
1975-76 Campaigned full-time for Carter across the country, by car and plane
1976, December Attended inauguration of Mexico's new president; presided over a mental health conference in Philadelphia
1977 Took a controversial trip to seven Central and South American countries and gave foreign policy speeches
1978 Attended the Camp David summit meeting with Middle Eastern leaders and wives
1979 Testified in Congress for increased funds for the Mental Health Systems Act
1981 to present Returned to Plains, Georgia; continues mental health advocacy and humanitarian work throughout the world through the Carter Center in Atlanta
1984 Wrote her autobiography, *First Lady from Plains*, a bestseller

> **“** *I have found that the more that she and I can share responsibilities, with her being in an unofficial position and me in an official position, then that tends to strengthen the personal kind of relationship between husband and wife.”*
> JIMMY CARTER, IN *THE NEW YORK TIMES*

Nancy Davis
REAGAN
(1921–   )
First Lady (1981–1989)

Nancy Reagan's lifework was Ronald Reagan. Willful, driven, devoted, she powerfully influenced his presidency and his staff, expanding "the role of first lady into a sort of Associate Presidency." [New York Times] She is credited with steering Reagan from cold warrior to peacemaker.
  Her first year in the White House, 1981, was rocky. Criticized for over-spending and seeking private donations, she also endured the attempted assassination of her husband. Her popularity rose when in the mid-80's she led the national campaign against drug abuse among the young. Nancy Reagan devoted ten years to caring for her husband, stricken with Alzheimer's.

> **“** *Abigail Adams helped invent America. Dolley Madison helped protect it. Eleanor Roosevelt was FDR's eyes and ears. Nancy is my everything....I say to myself, but also on behalf of the nation, 'Thank you, partner. Thanks for everything.'”*
> RONALD REAGAN, 1985

BIOGRAPHY
Date of birth: 6 July 1921
Place of birth: New York City
Father: Kenneth Robbins
Mother: Edith Luckett
Education: Smith College, Northampton, Massachusetts
Husband: Ronald Reagan
Marriage: 4 March 1952
Children: Patricia Ann "Patti"; Ronald Prescott

HIGHLIGHTS
1929 Legally adopted by Dr. Loyal Davis, her mother's second husband
1946 Appeared in the Broadway play *Lute Song*
1949–56 Film career; acted in 11 movies; and met Ronald Reagan in 1951
1981 Refurbished the White House, largely with private donations
1981, March Attempted assassination of President Reagan
1982 Wrote *To Love A Child*, about the Foster Grandparent Program
1982-88 Promoted national campaign against drug abuse; spokeswoman for "Just Say No" Foundation
1985, July President Reagan's cancer surgery; Nancy reportedly "in charge in the White House"
1987 Underwent surgery for breast cancer
1988 Secretary of Treasury Donald Regan's *For the Record* published, claiming Nancy consulted her astrologer to schedule president's activities
1988 Criticized for "borrowing" designer clothing and jewelry and not returning most
1989 Awarded the Council of Fashion Designers of America's Lifetime Achievement Award for her contribution to fashion
1989 *My Turn* published, her memoirs
1990 to present Serves on the board of the Ronald Reagan Presidential Foundation; works with the national Alzheimer's Association and its affiliate, the Ronald & Nancy Reagan Research Institute in Chicago, Illinois.

> **“** *Everything began with you, my whole life—so you'd better be careful and take care of yourself because there'd be nothing and I'd be no one without you.”*
> NANCY REAGAN, IN LETTER TO HUSBAND, 1967

Barbara Pierce
BUSH
(1925–   )
First Lady (1989–1993)

Unpretentious, candid, and spirited, Barbara Bush immediately endeared herself to the American people with her comment (below) at the inauguration. As first lady she promoted adult literacy and launched the Barbara Bush Foundation for Family Literacy.
  Today she lives with her husband in Houston, Texas, and in a summer home in Kennebunkport, Maine. She serves on the Boards of AmeriCares and the Mayo Clinic, and continues her work for literacy.

BIOGRAPHY
Date of birth: 8 June 1925
Place of birth: Rye, New York
Father: Marvin Pierce
Mother: Pauline Robinson Pierce
Education: Attended Smith College, Northampton, Massachusetts
Husband: George H. W. Bush
Marriage: 6 January 1945
Children: George W., John E. "Jeb", Neil M., Marvin P., Dorothy W. "Doro"

HIGHLIGHTS
1942 Met George Bush at a Christmas dance in Greenwich, Connecticut; married in 1945 at First Presbyterian Church, Rye, New York
1949 Mother died in automobile accident
1953 Daughter Robin died of leukemia at age three
1970–74 Lived in New York City while Bush was US Representative to the United Nations; later in Washington D.C, and Beijing, China
1980 Began efforts to promote national literacy
1983 Named trustee of the Morehouse School of Medicine, Atlanta, Georgia
1984 Wrote *C. Fred's Story* (family dog) to promote her literacy project
1989 Organized and named honorary chairperson of the Barbara Bush Foundation for Family Literacy
1990 Commencement speaker with Raisa Gorbachev at Wellesley College
1990 Wrote *Millie's Book*, "autobiography" of the White House dog
1992 Opposed the anti-abortion plank in Republican platform

> **“** *I want you all to take a look at me. Please notice – hairdo, makeup, designer dress. Look at me good this week, because it's the only week.”*
> BARBARA BUSH, TO REPORTERS DURING THE INAUGURAL FESTIVITIES, 1989

Hillary Rodham CLINTON
(1947–)
First Lady (1993–2001)

Hillary Rodham Clinton arrived at the White House after serving as first lady of Arkansas for twelve years. A lawyer and activist, she focused early on a career in public service, especially the welfare of children. In 1974, she served as counsel on the staff of the House Judiciary Committee which was considering impeachment of then-President Richard Nixon.

As first lady, after an unsuccessful reform of health care, public humiliation in her private life and legal allegations in her professional life, she became an effective global advocate for women and children.

> *If I want to knock a story off the front page, I just change my hairstyle.*
>
> HILLARY RODHAM CLINTON

In 2000, she was elected United States Senator from New York. She is the first first lady to run for public office and the first woman elected statewide in New York. As senator, she has made homeland security, economic security, and national security her top priorities.

There is much speculation about her running for president in 2008.

> *I'm having a great time being the Pres, I mean Senator from New York.*
>
> HILLARY RODHAM CLINTON

BIOGRAPHY
Date of birth: 26 October 1947
Place of birth: Park Ridge, Illinois
Father: Hugh E. Rodham
Mother: Dorothy Howell Rodham
Education: Wellesley College, Wellesley, Massachusetts; Yale Law School
Husband: Bill Clinton
Marriage: 11 October 1975
Children: Chelsea Victoria

> *Our lives are a mixture of different roles. Most of us are doing the best we can to find whatever the right balance is . . . For me, that balance is family, work, and service.*
>
> HILLARY RODHAM CLINTON, 1992

HIGHLIGHTS
1969 Graduated from Wellesley with high honors; was class speaker at ceremony
1969-73 Attended Yale Law School, where she met Bill Clinton
1972 Campaigned for Senator George McGovern for president
1973 Worked at Children's Defense Fund in Cambridge, Massachusetts
1974 Staff lawyer of House Judiciary Committee considering impeachment charges against President Richard Nixon
1974-77 Taught at University of Arkansas (Fayetteville) Law School
1977 Named partner in Rose Law Firm, Little Rock, Arkansas
1979-81; 1983-92 First lady of Arkansas
1988 and **1991** Named one of nation's most influential lawyers by *National Law Journal*
1992 *"60 Minutes"* TV interview about the Gennifer Flowers affair
1993 Appointed by Clinton as chair of Task Force on Health Care Reform
1995 Wrote a weekly newspaper column, "Talking It Over" – her observations of women, children, and families she met around the world.
1995 Spoke at UN Conference on Women in Beijing, China
1996 Testified before grand jury on Whitewater charges
1996 Wrote *It Takes A Village* about the role of community in raising children
2000, February Announced her candidacy for Senator from New York state; won the election in November
2003 Published her autobiography *Living History*, a huge bestseller
2003 Traveled at Thanksgiving to Afghanistan and Iraq to visit the troops
2004 Senator Clinton serves on the Senate Committees for Environment and Public Works; Health, Education, Labor and Pensions; and is the first New York Senator to serve on the Senate Armed Services Committee.

Laura Welch BUSH
(1946–)
First Lady (2001–2009)

Poised, cheerful, and non-controversial, Laura Bush has largely remained above the political fray. But in the 2004 campaign she moved into a new role, emerging as a formidable fund-raiser and a vigorous defender of the president and his policies. In August 2004 she gave a prime-time speech at the Republican National Convention.

Laura Bush's interest in education and reading began early and led her to a career as teacher and librarian. As first lady in 2001, she launched the first National Book Festival. In November 2001, she became the first first lady to record a full presidential radio address, on the plight of Afghan women and children under the Taliban.

> *My husband didn't want to go to war, but he knew the safety and security of America and the world depended on it.*
>
> LAURA BUSH, IN HER SPEECH TO THE REPUBLICAN NATIONAL CONVENTION, 2004

BIOGRAPHY
Date of birth: 4 November 1946
Place of birth: Midland, Texas
Father: Harold Welch
Mother: Jenna Hawkins Welch
Education: Southern Methodist University, Dallas, Texas; University of Texas (Austin)
Husband: George W. Bush
Marriage: 5 November 1977
Children: Barbara, Jenna

HIGHLIGHTS
1968-72 Taught in Texas public schools
1973 Earned a Master of Library Science degree in library science and worked as librarian
1977 Met George Bush; married four months later
1994-2000 First Lady of Texas; started the Texas Book Festival
2001, 8 September Organized first National Book Festival
2001, February Launched Ready to Read, Ready to Learn education program
2002, May Addressed people of Afghanistan through Radio Liberty in Prague
2003 Accompanied the president on a tour of Africa
2004 Campaigned in key states across the U.S.

≈1≈ GEORGE WASHINGTON
(1732–1799)
President (1789–1797)

"The son of a prosperous planter, and grandson of an English settler, George Washington trained as a surveyor before taking up a military career. Although the owner of thousands of acres, he had to borrow money to attend his own inaugural.

BIOGRAPHY

Date of Birth: 22 February 1732
Place of Birth: Pope's Creek, Westmoreland County, Virginia
Father: Augustine Washington (1694-1743)
Mother: Mary Ball Washington (1708-89)
Wife: Martha Dandridge Custis (1731-1802)
Children: 2
Date of death: 14 December 1799
Place of death: Mount Vernon, Virginia
Burial: Mount Vernon, Virginia
Number of terms: 2
Age at first inauguration: 57
Date of inaugurations: (1) 30 April 1789; (2) 4 March 1793
Vice-President: John Adams (1 & 2)
Sec. of State: Thomas Jefferson, Edmund Randolph, Timothy Pickering
Sec. of Treasury: Alexander Hamilton, Oliver Wolcott, Jr.

HIGHLIGHTS

1747 Became land surveyor after leaving school at 14
1753 Appointed major in Virginia militia
1754 Surrendered Fort Necessity to the French
1759 With Braddock at his defeat at Monongahela River
1759 Married Martha Dandridge Custis
1774 Delegate to First Continental Congress, Philadelphia
1775, 15 June Elected Commander-in-Chief of the Continental Army
1775, 17 June Battle of Bunker Hill
1776, 1 July Defeated at Battle of Brooklyn
1776, 4 July Declaration of Independence, Independence Hall, Philadelphia
1776, 26 December Defeated British, battles of Trenton and Princeton (27 December)
1777, 11 September Defeated at Brandywine

> *I walk, as it were, on untrodden ground, so many untoward circumstances may intervene in such a new and critical situation, that I shall feel an insuperable diffidence in my own abilities.*
> **GEORGE WASHINGTON AT HIS FIRST INAUGURATION, 30 APRIL 1789**

1777, 17 October British defeated at Saratoga
1777–78 Winter at Valley Forge
1778, June Chased British out of Philadelphia
1781, 19 October British surrender at Yorktown
1787 President of Constitutional Convention
1789–93 First term as president
1792 Established first presidential veto
1793–97 Second term

> *To make and sell a little flour annually, to repair houses (going fast to ruin), to build one for the security of my papers of a public nature, and to amuse myself in agricultural and rural pursuits, will constitute employment for the few years I have to remain on this terrestrial globe. If...I could now and then meet the friends I esteem, it would fill the measure and add zest to my enjoyments; but, if this ever happens, it must be under my own vine and fig tree.*
> **GEORGE WASHINGTON ON HIS RETIREMENT, MAY 1797**

Washington arriving in New York City for his inauguration, 30 April 1789.

≈2≈ JOHN ADAMS
(1735–1826)
President (1797–1801)

A deep thinker, a man of unshakable integrity and independence of mind, Adams was often a difficult man to get on with.

> *He is vain, irritable and a bad calculator of the force and probable effect of the motives which govern men...He is profound in views...accurate in his judgment.*
> **THOMAS JEFFERSON ON JOHN ADAMS**

BIOGRAPHY

Date of birth: 30 Oct 1735
Place of birth: Braintree (Now Quincy), Mass.
Father: John Adams (1691–1761)
Mother: Susanna Boylston Adams (1709-97)
Wife: Abigail Smith (1744–1818)
Children: 5
Date of death: 4 July 1826
Place of death: Quincy, Mass.
Burial: First Unitarian Church, Quincy, Mass.
Age at inauguration: 61
Number of terms: 1
Date of inauguration: 4 March 1797
Age at inauguration: 61
Vice President: Thomas Jefferson
Sec of State: Timothy Pickering, John Marshall (from 6 Jun 1800)
Sec of Treasury: Oliver Wolcott Jr, Samuel Dexter (from 1 Jan 1801)

> *No man who ever held the office of President would congratulate a friend on obtaining it.*
> **JOHN ADAMS**

1789 ✦ FIRST CONGRESS MET AT NEW YORK (4 MARCH).

1790 ✦ FIRST PATENT FOR A MECHANICAL SEWING MACHINE ISSUED TO ENGLISHMAN THOMAS SAINT.

1791 ✦ THOMAS PAINE PUBLISHED HIS INFLUENTIAL THE *RIGHTS OF MAN*.

1790 ✦ SAMUEL SLATER OPENS THE FIRST TEXTILE FACTORY IN THE U.S.

1792 ✦ THE FIRST STONE OF THE WHITE HOUSE (KNOWN AS THE EXECUTIVE MANSION UNTIL THE 20TH CENTURY) WAS LAID.

1793 ✦ REVOLUTIONARIES IN FRANCE EXECUTE THE KING, LOUIS XVI.

1794 ✦ THE WHISKEY REBELLION IN WESTERN PENNSYLVANIA SUPPRESSED BY THE MILITARY.

1796 ✦ PRESIDENT WASHINGTON'S FAREWELL ADDRESS (18 SEPTEMBER).

1797 ✦ FIRST PARACHUTE DESCENT (BY ANDRÉ-JACQUES GARNERIN IN PARIS)

President Washington

1798 ✦ NAPOLEON INVADED EGYPT AND DEFEATED THE MAMELUKE ARMY AT THE BATTLE OF THE PYRAMIDS.

1799 ✦ FIRST WORKABLE ELECTRIC BATTERY PRODUCED BY ITALIAN ALESSANDRO VOLTA.

Napoleon

1799 ✦ AMERICAN ROBERT FULTON BUILT THE FIRST PROPELLER-DRIVEN SUBMARINE.

1800 ✦ ON 1 NOVEMBER JOHN ADAMS BECAME THE FIRST PRESIDENT TO SLEEP IN THE NEWLY ERECTED WHITE HOUSE.

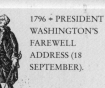

⁖5⁖
JAMES MONROE
(1758–1831)
President (1817–1825)

The fourth President to have come from Virginia, and the last to have fought in the War of Independence.

BIOGRAPHY
Date of birth: 28 April 1758
Place of birth: Westmoreland County, Virginia
Father: Spence Monroe (d.1744)
Mother: Elizabeth Jones Monroe (dates unknown)
Wife: Elizabeth Kortright (1768-1830)
Children: 3
Date of death: 4 July 1831
Place of death: New York City
Burial: Hollywood Cemetery, Richmond, Virginia
Number of terms: 2
Dates of inauguration: 4 March 1817, 5 March 1821
Age at first inauguration: 58
Vice-Presidents: Daniel D. Tompkins
Sec. of State: Richard Rush, John Quincy Adams
Sec. of Treasury: William H. Crawford

> *The American continents, by the free and independent condition which they have assumed and maintain, are henceforth not to be considered as subjects for future colonization by any European powers."*
> **JAMES MONROE TO CONGRESS, 2 DECEMBER 1823**

HIGHLIGHTS
1776–80 Fought in War of Independence
1782 Member of Virginia legislature
1786, 16 February Married Elizabeth Kortright
1790–94 US Senator for Virginia
1794–96 Minister to France
1799–1802 Governor of Virginia
1803–07 Minister to Britain
1811–17 Secretary of State under Madison
1814–15 Secretary of War under Madison
1817–25 Fifth President

⁖6⁖
JOHN QUINCY ADAMS
(1767–1848)
President (1825–1829)

The first son of a President to become President himself, John Quincy Adams had an unhappy four years in the White House.

BIOGRAPHY
Date of birth: 11 July 1767
Place of birth: Quincy, Massachusetts
Father: John Adams (1735-1826)
Mother: Abigail Smith Adams (1744-1818)
Wife: Louisa Catherine Johnson (1775-1852)
Children: 4
Date of death: 23 February 1848
Place of death: Washington D.C.
Burial: First Unitarian Church, Quincy, Massachusetts
Number of terms: 1
Date of inauguration: 4 March 1825
Age at inauguration: 57
Vice-President: John C. Calhoun
Sec. of State: Henry Clay
Sec. of Treasury: Richard Rush

> *I am not formed to shine in company, nor be delighted with it..."*
> **JOHN QUINCY ADAMS**

⁖7⁖
ANDREW JACKSON
(1767–1845)
President (1829–1837)

The first president to come from poverty, "Old Hickory" made his reputation as a tough Indian fighter and fearless duelist.

BIOGRAPHY
Date of birth: 15 March 1767
Place of birth: The Waxhaws, South Carolina
Father: Andrew Jackson (d.1767)
Mother: Elizabeth Hutchinson Jackson (d.1781)
Wife: Rachel Donelson Robards (1767–1828)
Children: 1
Date of death: 8 June 1845
Place of death: Nashville, Tennessee
Burial: The Hermitage, Nashville, Tennessee
Number of terms: 2
Date of inaugurations: (1) 4 March 1829, (2) 4 March 1833
Age at first inauguration: 61
Vice-President: John C. Calhoun, Martin Van Buren
Sec. of State: Martin Van Buren, Edward Livingston, Louis McLane, John Forsyth
Sec. of Treasury: (1) Samuel D. Ingham, Louis McLane, (2) Louis McLane, William J. Duane, Roger B. Taney, Levi Woodbury

> *As the meeting of Congress approaches, my labors increase. I am engaged preparing for them, and this with my other labors, employs me day and night. I can with truth say mine is a situation of dignified slavery."*
> **ANDREW JACKSON, 30 NOVEMBER 1829**

⁖8⁖
MARTIN VAN BUREN
(1782–1862)
President (1837–1841)

The first president to have been born an American citizen, Martin Van Buren was also the first to use 'modern' political methods based on the party machine.

BIOGRAPHY
Date of birth: 5 December 1782
Place of birth: Kinderhook, New York
Father: Abraham Van Buren (1737–1817)
Mother: Maria Hoes Van Alen Van Buren (1747–1818)
Wife: Hannah Hoes (1783–1819)
Children: 4
Date of death: 24 July 1862
Place of death: Kinderhook, New York
Burial: Kinderhook, New York
Number of terms: 1

> *...one of the most frank men I ever knew, with talents combined with common sense."*
> **ANDREW JACKSON ON MARTIN VAN BUREN**

1817–18 → ANDREW JACKSON INVADED FLORIDA DURING THE SEMINOLE WARS.

1818 → BRITAIN AND AMERICA AGREE THE 49TH PARALLEL AS THE FRONTIER BETWEEN CANADA AND THE UNITED STATES.

1819 → ALABAMA ADMITTED TO STATEHOOD.

1821 → FIRST NATURAL GAS STREET LIGHTING IN THE USA – AT FREDONIA, NEW YORK.

1823 → THE MONROE DOCTRINE DECLARED (2 DEC). NO EUROPEAN POWER TO BE ABLE TO COLONIZE ANY PART OF THE AMERICAN CONTINENT.

1825 → ERIE CANAL COMPLETED (BEGUN 1817) AND OPENS UP SETTLEMENT OF THE WEST.

1826 → FRENCH PHYSICIST, JOSEPH NIEPCE MADE THE FIRST PHOTOGRAPH.

1828 → FIRST PUBLIC RAILROAD IN THE US – BALTIMORE & OHIO – BEGAN CONSTRUCTION.

1830 → MORMON CHURCH FOUNDED IN FAYETTE, NEW YORK, BY JOSEPH SMITH.

Joseph Smith

1829 → PRESBYTERIAN MINISTER SYLVESTER GRAHAM PRODUCES THE GRAHAM CRACKER.

1832 → NEW ENGLAND ANTI-SLAVERY SOCIETY ESTABLISHED, FOLLOWED IN 1833 BY AMERICAN ANTI-SLAVERY SOCIETY.

1837 → AMERICAN SAMUEL MORSE PATENTED THE TELEGRAPH SYSTEM. FIRST MESSAGE WAS SENT BETWEEN BALTIMORE AND WASHINGTON DC, 1844.

1839 → ENGLISHMAN WILLIAM TALBOT INVENTED THE NEGATIVE-POSITIVE PROCESS WHICH LAID THE BASIS FOR MODERN PHOTOGRAPHY.

HIGHLIGHTS

1932–34 Worked in New York City as X-ray technician to save money for college

1935 Worked as movie extra; appeared in movie The Great Ziegfeld (1936)

1937–38 After graduation from college, taught at Whittier (California) High School, and acted at Whittier Little Theater where she met Richard Nixon

1942–46 Worked in a San Francisco bank and then as economist for the Office of Price Administration while Nixon served in the navy

> " I do or I die. I never cancel out."
>
> PAT NIXON

1958 Traveled with Vice President Nixon to Caracas, Venezuela

1968 Daughter Julie married Dwight David Eisenhower II in New York City

1969 Trip to South Vietnam, the first first lady to visit a combat zone

1971 Daughter Tricia married Edward Cox in the White House Rose Garden

1974 Retired with president to San Clemente, California, and later to New York City and New Jersey

Elizabeth "Betty" Bloomer Warren FORD
(1918-)
First Lady (1974–1977)

Honest and outspoken on controversial issues, and a strong advocate of women's rights, Betty Ford won the attention and respect of many

Americans. But she won the gratitude of people everywhere when she openly discussed her breast cancer and, later, her chemical dependency. In 1982, she established the Betty Ford Center for treatment of alcohol and drug addiction. To date, the Center has helped over 90,000 alumni throughout the world.

> " Lying in the hospital, thinking of all those women going for cancer checkups because of me, I'd come to recognize more clearly the power of the woman in the White House. Not my power, but the power of the position, a power which could be used to help."
>
> BETTY FORD,
> AFTER HER BREAST CANCER SURGERY

BIOGRAPHY

Date of birth: 8 April 1918
Place of birth: Chicago, Illinois
Father: William S. Bloomer
Mother: Hortense Neahr Bloomer
Husband: (1) William C. Warren; (2) Gerald R. Ford
Marriage: (1) 1942 (2) 15 October 1948
Children: (2) Michael Gerald, John Gardner, Steven Meigs, Susan Elizabeth

HIGHLIGHTS

1935–39 Studied dance at Calla Travis Dance Studio and at Bennington (Vermont) College; joined the Martha Graham New York Concert Group

1942 Married William C. Warren; divorced in 1947

1947 Met Gerald Ford; they married in 1948

1949–74 Lived in Washington during Ford's years as congressman and vice-president

1974 Held first press conference announcing she would campaign for ratification of the Equal Rights Amendment and abortion rights

1974, September Underwent surgery for breast cancer

1975 Received the Anti-Defamation League's Human Relations Award for championing women's rights

1975 Named a Fellow of the National Academy of Design

1982 Established the Betty Ford Center, a chemical dependency recovery center in Rancho Mirage, California

1982 Received the American Cancer Society's Hubert Humphrey Award

1987 Wrote Betty: A Glad Awakening, about her parents' and her own alcoholism

> " I do not believe that being first lady should prevent me from expressing my views."
>
> BETTY FORD

Rosalynn Smith CARTER
(1927–)
First Lady (1977-1981)

Rosalynn and Jimmy Carter are, and have always been, the closest of life partners, from navy days, the peanut business, the Georgia governorship to the presidency and their humanitarian work today.

At the White House Rosalynn lobbied for the Equal Rights Amendment, and was the first first lady since Eleanor Roosevelt to testify before Congress – for more funds for mental health.

She is currently vice chair of The Carter Center in Atlanta, founded in 1982 to promote peace and human rights worldwide. She continues her advocacy for greater access to mental health care. She also is a partner with the ex-president in projects to promote human rights, improve global health, and build democracy in some 65 countries.

> " ....there is a general presumption that the projects of a first lady will be substantive, highly publicized, and closely scrutinized. I am thankful for the change."
>
> ROSALYNN CARTER

BIOGRAPHY

Date of birth: 18 August 1927
Place of birth: Plains, Georgia
Father: Edgar Smith
Mother: Allie Murray Smith
Education: Georgia Southwestern College
Husband: Jimmy Carter
Marriage: 7 July 1946
Children: John William, James Earl III, Jeffrey, Amy Lynn

HIGHLIGHTS

1945 First date with Ensign Jimmy Carter, home on leave from Annapolis; married in 1946

1946-53 Lived at various navy posts on the mainland and Hawaii

York ; George Washington University
Husband: (1) John F. Kennedy; (2) Aristotle Onassis
Marriage: (1) 12 September 1953; (2) 20 October 1968
Children: Caroline, John F., Jr.
Date of death: 19 May 1994
Place of death: New York City
Burial: Arlington National Cemetery, Virginia

HIGHLIGHTS
1951 Worked for the Washington Times-Herald as "Inquiring Camera Girl"
1951 Met JFK at a dinner party ; they attended Eisenhower's inaugural ball in 1953
1953, 12 September Married John F. Kennedy at St. Mary's Church, Newport, Rhode Island; settled in McLean, Virginia
1961 Initiated plans to restore original furnishings to the White House; set up White House fine arts commission
1961 Visited Paris ("I am the man who accompanied Jacqueline Kennedy to Paris.") and Vienna
1961 Voted "Woman of the Year" by editors of over 100 periodicals
1962 Spearheaded drive to preserve Lafayette Square in Washington, D.C.
1962 Conducted a nationwide televised tour of the restored White House
1963, 9 August Baby Patrick died, two days old
1963, 22 November Kennedy assassinated
1964 Moved to New York City
1968, 20 October Married Aristotle Onassis; he died in 1975
1975–94 Worked as consulting editor at Viking Press and senior editor at Doubleday & Company, book publishers; lived in New York City, Bernardsville, New Jersey, and Martha's Vineyard
1994 Died from non-Hodgkin's lymphoma

> ❝ *Lyndon lives in a cloud of troubles, with few rays of light.... I am counting the months until March 1968 when, like Truman, it will be possible to say, 'I don't want this office, this responsibility, any longer, even if you want me. Find the strongest and most able and God bless you. Good-bye.'*
>
> LADY BIRD JOHNSON, IN HER DIARY

Claudia Alta
"Lady Bird" Taylor
⚜ JOHNSON ⚜
(1912–   )
First Lady (1963–1969)

She was called "pretty as a ladybird" by a nursemaid; family and friends call her "Bird." Seven weeks after she met Lyndon Johnson, they were married. When Congressman Johnson served in World War II, Lady Bird took over his duties without pay, gaining confidence and independence. In 1961-62 as vice president's wife, she filled in for Jackie Kennedy at numerous political events. Lady Bird's over 25 years in Washington prepared her well for her abrupt ascent to first lady in November 1963. Married to one of the most dominant men of the 20th century, she played a pivotal role in his administration. Her signature project was the environment – a national beautification of neighborhoods with trees and wildflowers and highways without billboards – the first major legislation launched by a first lady. A grandmother of seven, today Lady Bird still supports causes dear to her, the National Wildflower Research Center and the LBJ Library. She also serves on the Board of the National Geographic Society as a trustee emeritus.

BIOGRAPHY
Date of birth: 22 December 1912
Place of birth: Karnack, Texas
Father: Thomas Jefferson Taylor
Mother: Minnie Pattillo Taylor
Education: University of Texas
Husband: Lyndon B. Johnson
Marriage: 17 November 1934
Children: Lynda Bird, Luci Baines

HIGHLIGHTS
1934 Met Lyndon Johnson at the home of a mutual friend in Austin, Texas; married on 17 November
1942 Invested an inheritance in a radio station, KTBC, in Austin; it became the successful Texas Broadcasting Corporation
1964 Launched beautification project, a campaign to improve the landscape of America; traveled 200,000 miles
1965 Highway Beautification Act signed, the first important legislation by a first lady
1968 Retired with the president to the LBJ Ranch in Texas
1970 Published *A White House Diary*, a record of her years as first lady
1983 Founded the National Wildflower Research Center

Thelma Catherine
"Pat" Ryan
⚜ NIXON ⚜
(1912–1993)
First Lady (1969–1974)

Pat Ryan grew up in poverty, was orphaned at 18, and worked to pay her way through college. She graduated cum laude and became an enthusiastic, popular teacher. When Nixon ran for Congress in 1945 she helped finance his campaign. She kept a low profile during her White House years, both because of her desire for privacy and the fact that neither her husband nor the staff took her projects seriously. She entertained more visitors and gave more tours than most predecessors, and answered every letter individually. Pat Nixon was the most widely traveled first lady, visiting 83 nations and crisscrossing the US several times.

BIOGRAPHY
Date of birth: 16 March 1912
Place of birth: Ely, Nevada
Father: William Ryan
Mother: Kate Halberstadt Ryan
Education: University of Southern California
Husband: Richard M. Nixon
Marriage: 21 June 1940
Children: Patricia "Tricia", Julie
Date of death: 22 June 1993
Place of death: Park Ridge, New Jersey
Burial: grounds of Nixon Library, Yorba Linda, California

> ❝ *I knew that the road had been hardest of all for Pat. For almost twenty years of public life she had been wife, mother and fulltime campaigner....She had done it all, not because she loved the attention or reveled in the publicity – she didn't. She had done it because she believed in me. And she had done it magnificently. Now she was loved by millions and no woman ever deserved it more. My deepest hope was that she felt that it had all been worth it.*
>
> RICHARD NIXON IN HIS MEMOIRS

Age at inauguration: 54
Date of inauguration: 4 March 1837
Vice-President: Richard M. Johnson
Sec. of State: John Forsyth
Sec. of Treasury: Levi Woodbury

≈9≈
WILLIAM HENRY HARRISON
(1773–1841)
President (1841)

The first president to die in office, one month after his inauguration, Harrison was a candidate of the new Whig party and won the election against the incumbent Van Buren.

BIOGRAPHY
Date of birth: 9 February 1773
Place of birth: Berkeley, Virginia
Father: Benjamin Harrison (1726-91)
Mother: Elizabeth Bassett Harrison (1730-92)
Wife: Anna Symmes (1775-1864)
Children: 10
Date of death: 4 April 1841
Place of death: Washington, D.C.
Burial: North Bend, Ohio
Length of term: 1 month
Age at inauguration: 68
Date of inauguration: 4 March 1841
Vice-President: John Tyler
Sec. of State: Daniel Webster
Sec. of Treasury: Thomas Ewing

≈10≈
JOHN TYLER
(1790–1862)
President (1841–1845)

At Harrison's death, John Tyler became the nation's first vice president to become president by "act of God".

BIOGRAPHY
Date of birth: 29 March 1790
Place of birth: Greenway, Virginia
Father: John Tyler (1747–1813)
Mother: Mary Armistead (1761–97)
Education: College of William and Mary
Wife: (1) Letitia Christian (1790–1842); (2)

Julia Gardiner (1820–89)
Children: (1) 7; (2) 7
Date of death: 18 January 1862
Place of death: Richmond, Virginia
Burial: Richmond, Virginia
Number of terms: 1
Age at inauguration: 51
Date of inauguration: 6 April 1841
Vice-President: none
Sec. of State: Daniel Webster, Abel P. Upshur, John C. Calhoun
Sec. of Treasury: Thomas Ewing, Walter Forward

≈11≈
JAMES KNOX POLK
(1795–1849)
President (1845–1849)

A supporter of "manifest destiny", a belief that the nation should rule across the whole North American continent, Polk increased the size of the country more than any president since Jefferson. In one term he accomplished all four goals he had set in his campaign.

BIOGRAPHY
Date of birth: 2 November 1795
Place of birth: Pineville, North Carolina
Father: Samuel Polk (1772–1827)
Mother: Jane Knox Polk (1776–1852)
Wife: Sarah Childress (1803–91)
Children: none
Date of death: 15 June 1849
Place of death: Nashville, Tennessee
Burial: Nashville, Tennessee
Number of terms: 1
Age at inauguration: 49
Date of inauguration: 4 March 1845
Vice-President: George M. Dallas
Sec. of State: James Buchanan
Sec. of Treasury: Robert J. Walker

HIGHLIGHTS
1818 Graduated from the University of North Carolina
1820 Admitted to the bar to practice law in Tennessee
1823–25 Elected to state legislature of Tennessee
1824, 1 January Married Sarah Childress
1825–39 U.S representative from Tennessee
1835–39 Speaker of the House of Representatives

1839–41 Governor of Tennessee
1845–49 President of the United States
1846 Walker Tariff, reducing tax on imports
1846 Independent Treasury Act
1846 Oregon Treaty, settling boundary dispute
1846–48 Mexican War; Mexico ceded to U.S. all or part of California, Nevada, Utah, Wyoming, Colorado, Texas, New Mexico, and Arizona

≈12≈
ZACHARY TAYLOR
(1784–1850)
President (1849–1850)

A national hero after victory in the Mexican War (1847), Taylor won election with no previous political experience. Although a slaveholder, he opposed the right of secession.

BIOGRAPHY
Date of birth: 24 November 1784
Place of birth: Orange County, Virginia
Father: Richard Taylor (1774–1829)
Mother: Sarah Strother Taylor (1760–1822)
Wife: Margaret Mackall Smith (1788–1852)
Children: 6
Date of death: 9 July 1850
Place of death: Washington, D. C.
Burial: Louisville, Kentucky
Length of term: 16 months
Age at inauguration: 64
Date of inauguration: 5 March 1849
Vice-President: Millard Fillmore
Sec. of State: John M. Clayton
Sec. of Treasury: W.M. Meredith

≈13≈
MILLARD FILLMORE
(1800–1874)
President (1850–1853)

Becoming president on the death of Zachary Taylor, Fillmore supported the Compromise of 1850 as a "final settlement" of the differences between North and South.

BIOGRAPHY
Date of birth: 7 January 1800
Place of birth: Locke, New York

1841 ✦ FIRST EMIGRANT WAGON TRAIN REACHES OREGON TERRITORY.

1841 ✦ EDGAR ALLAN POE PUBLISHES THE MURDERS IN THE RUE MORGUE, THE FIRST AMERICAN DETECTIVE STORY.

1842 ✦ FIRST USE OF ETHER AS AN ANESTHETIC, BY GEORGIA PHYSICIAN.

1844 ✦ FIRST MESSAGE OVER FIRST TELEGRAPH LINE SENT BY INVENTOR SAMUEL F.B. MORSE.

1845 ✦ TEXAS ADMITTED TO THE UNION.

1846 ✦ ELIAS HOWE INVENTED SEWING MACHINE.

1847 ✦ FIRST ADHESIVE U.S. POSTAGE STAMPS ON SALE.

1846–48 ✦ U.S.-MEXICAN WAR. MEXICO CEDED TEXAS, CALIFORNIA, AND OTHER TERRITORY.

1848 ✦ GOLD DISCOVERED IN CALIFORNIA.

1852 ✦ UNCLE TOM'S CABIN BY HARRIET BEECHER STOWE PUBLISHED.

1852 ✦ ELISHA OTIS BUILT FIRST SAFETY ELEVATOR.

Prospectors

1850 ✦ LEVI STRAUSS SAILS TO SAN FRANCISCO; MAKES DURABLE PANTS CALLED JEANS FOR GOLD MINERS.

1855 ✦ WALT WHITMAN PUBLISHED LEAVES OF GRASS.

1861 ✦ WESTERN UNION COMPLETED FIRST TRANSCONTINENTAL TELEGRAPH LINE.

1861 ✦ SEVEN SOUTHERN STATES FORMED CONFEDERATE STATES OF AMERICA.

1862 ✦ BATTLE OF ANTIETAM, THE BLOODIEST ONE-DAY BATTLE OF THE CIVIL WAR.

1863 ✦ LINCOLN DECLARED THANKSGIVING DAY AN OFFICIAL NATIONAL HOLIDAY.

Father: Nathaniel Fillmore (1771–1863)
Mother: Phoebe Millard Fillmore (1780–1831)
Wife: (1) Abigail Powers (1798–1853); (2)
Caroline McIntosh (1813–81)
Children: (1) 2
Date of death: 8 March 1874
Place of death: Buffalo, New York
Burial: Buffalo, New York
Number of terms: 1 (incomplete)
Age at inauguration: 50
Date of inauguration: 10 July 1850
Vice-President: none
Sec. of State: Daniel Webster, Edward Everett
Sec. of Treasury: Thomas Corwin

⇜14⇝
FRANKLIN PIERCE
(1804–1869)
President (1853–1857)

Handsome and congenial, Pierce is the only president who served a complete term without making a single change in his Cabinet. Although against slavery, Pierce was influenced by pro-slavery Southerners and lost the renomination in 1856.

BIOGRAPHY
Date of birth: 23 November 1804
Place of birth: Hillsboro, New Hampshire
Father: Benjamin Pierce (1757–1839)
Mother: Anna Kendrick Pierce (1768–1838)
Education: Bowdoin College, Brunswick, Maine
Wife: Jane Means Appleton (1806–63)
Children: 3
Date of death: 8 October 1869
Place of death: Concord, New Hampshire
Burial: Concord, New Hampshire
Number of terms: 1
Age at inauguration: 48
Date of inauguration: 4 March 1853
Vice-President: William R.D. King
Sec. of State: William L. Marcy
Sec. of Treasury: James Guthrie

> *...it would ruin a noble character (though one of limited scope) for him to admit any idea that were not entertained by the fathers of the Constitution and the Republic....*"
> NATHANIEL HAWTHORNE

⇜15⇝
JAMES BUCHANAN
(1791–1868)
President (1857–1861)

The only president who never married, Buchanan presided over a nation rapidly dividing over the issue of slavery. Seven states withdrew from the Union during his administration.

BIOGRAPHY
Date of birth: 23 April 1791
Place of birth: near Mercersburg, Pennsylvania
Father: James Buchanan, Sr. (1761–1821)
Mother: Elizabeth Speer Buchanan (1767–1833)
Education: Dickinson College, Carlisle, Pennsylvania
Wife: none
Children: none
Date of death: 1 June 1868
Place of death: Wheatland, near Lancaster, Pennsylvania
Burial: Lancaster, Pennsylvania
Number of terms: 1
Age at inauguration: 65
Date of inauguration: 4 March 1857
Vice-President: John C. Breckinridge
Sec. of State: Lewis Cass, Jeremiah S. Black
Sec. of Treasury: Howell Cobb, Philip F. Thomas, John A. Dix

⇜16⇝
ABRAHAM LINCOLN
(1809–1865)
President (1861–1865)

Unpretentious, plain-spoken, with a ready wit, Lincoln had a dark side and wrestled with severe bouts of depression. He estimated he had about one year of formal education and a childhood that "can be condensed into a single sentence: 'The short and simple annals of the poor.'"

BIOGRAPHY
Date of birth: 12 February 1809
Place of birth: Hardin (now Larue) County, Kentucky
Father: Thomas Lincoln (1778–1851)
Mother: Nancy Hanks Lincoln (1784–1818)

> *A house divided against itself cannot stand. I believe this government cannot endure permanently half slave and half free.*"
> ABRAHAM LINCOLN, 16 JUNE, 1858

Wife: Mary Todd (1818–81)
Children: 4
Date of death: 15 April 1865
Place of death: Washington, D.C.
Burial: Springfield, Illinois
Number of terms: 1 (2nd incomplete)
Age at first inauguration: 52
Date of inaugurations: 4 March 1861; 4 March 1865
Vice-President: Hannibal Hamlin, Andrew Johnson
Sec. of State: William H. Seward
Sec. of Treasury: Salmon P. Chase, William P. Fessenden, Hugh McCulloch

HIGHLIGHTS
1832 Served as captain in Black Hawk War
1833–36 Appointed postmaster of New Salem, Illinois
1834–42 Elected to Illinois legislature
1836 Licensed to practice law
1842, 4 November Married Mary Todd
1847 Elected to Congress as representative from Illinois
1858 Campaigned unsuccessfully for U.S. Senate; debated slavery issue with Stephen Douglas
1859 Nominated and elected president
1861, 12 April Confederates take Fort Sumter; Civil War begins
1862, September Issued the Emancipation Proclamation
1853, November Delivered Gettysburg Address
1864 Won reelection to a second term
1865, 9 April Lee's surrender to Grant at Appomattox, Virginia
1864, 14 April Wounded by assassin John Wilkes Booth
1865, 15 April Died in Washington, D.C.

> *If any personal description of me is thought desirable,...I am, in height, six feet, four inches, nearly; lean in flesh, weighing, on an average one hundred and eighty pounds; dark complexion, with coarse black hair and grey eyes....*"
> ABRAHAM LINCOLN, 1859

1865 ✦ PHILADELPHIA HATMAKER JOHN B. STETSON CREATED THE FIRST STETSON HAT.

1867 ✦ ALASKA SOLD TO U.S. BY RUSSIA FOR $7,200,000.

1868 ✦ FIRST PRACTICAL TYPEWRITER PATENTED BY CHRISTOPHER SHOLES.

1868 ✦ LOUISA MAY ALCOTT PUBLISHED *LITTLE WOMEN*.

1869 ✦ FIRST COLLEGE FOOTBALL GAME – RUTGERS V. PRINCETON.

1869 ✦ FIRST TRANSCONTINENTAL RAILROAD LINE COMPLETED AT PROMONTORY, UTAH.

1871 ✦ THE GREAT CHICAGO FIRE.

1872 ✦ FIRST NATIONAL PARK ESTABLISHED BY CONGRESS – YELLOWSTONE.

1876 ✦ ALEXANDER GRAHAM BELL PATENTED THE TELEPHONE.

1877 ✦ THOMAS EDISON INVENTS THE PHONOGRAPH.

1879 ✦ FRANK W. WOOLWORTH OPENED THE GREAT FIVE CENT STORE IN UTICA, NEW YORK.

1879 ✦ SALOON OWNER JAMES RITTY PATENTED THE CASH REGISTER, CALLED THE INCORRUPTIBLE CASHIER.

1881 ✦ NURSE CLARA BARTON FOUNDED THE AMERICAN RED CROSS.

Clara Barton

the first U.S. delegation to the United Nations; chairman of the UN Commission on Human Rights
1948 Universal Declaration of Human Rights signed
1958 Published *On My Own*
1961–62 Reappointed by President Kennedy to the UN; head of the Commission on the Status of Women
1961 Published *The Autobiography of Eleanor Roosevelt*

Elizabeth 'Bess' Virginia Wallace TRUMAN
(1885–1982)
First Lady (1945–1953)

Raised in a prominent Independence, Missouri, family, Bess Wallace met Harry Truman when they were children in Sunday School – and subsequently had the longest courtship of any presidential couple – 15 years. It was a union of two very different temperaments, and a first family that White House staff agreed was the closest they ever knew. With a deep desire for privacy, Bess canceled the press conferences started by Eleanor Roosevelt. When questioned by reporters, her usual response was "No comment."

BIOGRAPHY
Date of birth: 13 February 1885
Place of birth: Independence, Missouri
Father: David W. Wallace
Mother: Madge Gates Wallace
Husband: Harry S Truman
Marriage: 28 June 1919
Children: Margaret
Date of death: 18 October 1982
Place of death: Independence, Missouri
Burial: Harry S Truman Library, Independence, Missouri

HIGHLIGHTS
1890 Met Harry Truman; she was five, he was six
1919, 28 June Married Harry Truman at Trinity Episcopal Church, Independence, Missouri
1935–45 Worked as secretary to her husband when he was in the Senate
1949 Made a rare public statement that **Cong**ress should repair the White House rather than construct a new one
1949–52 Lived at Blair House while White House was under repair
1953 Retired with the president to her childhood home in Independence

Mamie Geneva Doud EISENHOWER
(1896–1979)
First Lady (1953-1961)

Married for 36 years when she became First Lady, moving almost yearly from one army post to the next, Mamie was ever the proud, supportive wife to Eisenhower. Unaffected, friendly, with a penchant for youthful gowns, Mamie seemed as familiar as the woman next door. In the post-war White House, she and "Ike" entertained an unprecedented number of heads of state and leaders of foreign governments.

BIOGRAPHY
Date of birth: 14 November 1896
Place of birth: Boone, Iowa
Father: John Sheldon Doud
Mother: Elvira Carlson Doud
Husband: Dwight D. Eisenhower
Marriage: 1 July 1916
Children: John Sheldon Doud
Date of death: 11 November 1979
Place of death: Gettysburg, Pennsylvania
Burial: Abilene, Kansas

HIGHLIGHTS
1916, 1 July Married Lieutenant Dwight D. Eisenhower at her parents' home in Denver, Colorado; lived at Fort Sam Houston in San Antonio, Texas
1921 First-born son died at age three
1922-39 Lived in Panama and the Philippines, and numerous army bases
1943-45 Remained in Washington while Eisenhower served as Supreme Allied Commander in Europe
1951-52 Lived in Paris, France when Eisenhower was Commander of NATO
1961 Retired with the president to Gettysburg, Pennsylvania, their first permanent home
1973 Responded to rumors of alcoholism that she had carotid sinus, a condition that causes

imbalance
1979 Suffered a stroke and died
1980 Birthplace in Boone, Iowa, dedicated a historic site

Jacqueline Lee Bouvier KENNEDY
(1929–1994)
First Lady (1961–1963)

More words have been written about Jacqueline Kennedy than any other first lady except Eleanor Roosevelt. She has been described as glamorous, sophisticated, intelligent, an aesthete, a devoted mother, shy, aloof, an ethereal charmer. Her first official project, begun just a week after JFK's inauguration, was to restore the original White House furnishings, to make it "a showcase of American art history." An unprecedented array of major artists, performers, and Nobel laureates appeared at the Kennedy state dinners. Generally, however, Jackie kept herself and, above all, her children, out of the public eye. Jackie's last official event was directing the mourning and funeral for her husband in November, 1963. During those four unforgettable days, she showed the impeccable taste and flair, the self-control, and the focus on history, that everyone admired.

BIOGRAPHY
Date of birth: 28 July 1929
Place of birth: Southampton, New York
Father: John V. Bouvier III
Mother: Janet Lee Bouvier
Education: Vassar College, Poughkeepsie, New

HIGHLIGHTS

1902 Graduated from the University of Vermont

1902 Reading instructor at Clarke Institute for the Deaf, Northampton, Massachusetts

1903 Met Calvin Coolidge, shaving at an open window in Northampton; married 4 October 1905

1921 Moved to Washington when Coolidge elected Vice President

1923 Lighted first national Christmas tree on White House lawn

1924 Death of son Calvin, Jr., at 16 from blood poisoning

1927 Hosted party for Charles Lindbergh following his transatlantic flight

1927 Moved to house on Dupont Circle in Washington during renovation of White House

1929 Published her poetry

1941–57 During World War II, supported the Red Cross, civil defense, and scrap drives, and continued to work for the deaf until her death in 1957

Lou Henry
⚞ HOOVER ⚟
(1874–1944)
First Lady (1929–1933)

Described as tall and graceful, with beautiful silver hair, Lou Hoover went to the White House with wide experience for the position of first lady. With a geology degree from Stanford University, she had lived in all parts of the world. She spoke five languages, including Mandarin Chinese, and together the Hoovers translated an important book on metallurgy from Latin to English. During the 1930's depression, she paid for many White House expenses with her own money and spoke by radio to the nation to encourage donations and volunteer work.

BIOGRAPHY

Date of birth: 29 March 1874
Place of birth: Waterloo, Iowa
Father: Charles D. Henry
Mother: Florence Weed Henry
Education: Stanford University, Stanford, California
Husband: Herbert Hoover
Marriage: 10 February 1899
Children: Herbert, Jr., Allan
Date of death: 7 January 1944

> ❝ *She does not keep the rules, but mixes the great and the near-great with the obscure and the near obscure.* ❞
> WOMAN'S HOME COMPANION

Place of death: New York City
Burial: Palo Alto, California; later West Branch, Iowa

HIGHLIGHTS

1898 Graduated with a major in geology from Stanford University, Stanford, California

1899, 10 February Married Herbert Hoover; the next day sailed to Tientsin, China where Hoover worked as mining engineer

1899–1900 Witnessed the Boxer Rebellion in China

1903–10 Lived and traveled throughout Europe and Asia during Hoover's career as engineer

1907 Translated Agricola's *De Re Metallica*, from Latin to English; published in 1912

1919 Decorated by King Albert of Belgium for her aid to Belgian refugees in World War I

1921–28 Served as national president of the Girl Scouts of America

1931–33 Gave radio talks to the nation from 2nd floor of White House, encouraging voluntarism

1932 Encouraged Hoover to amend Civil Service to open nominations to women

Anna Eleanor Roosevelt
⚞ ROOSEVELT ⚟
(1884-1962)
First Lady (1933-1945)

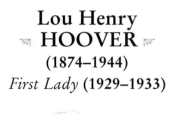

She grew up shy and insecure, an orphan before adolescence, and matured from political helpmate to a confident, independent champion of human rights First Lady for 12 years, Eleanor Roosevelt was the humane side of the presidency, its conscience and voice of the underdog. She was the first to hold formal press conferences. She traveled to all parts of the country, gave lectures and radio broadcasts, and expressed her opinions in a daily syndicated newspaper column, "My Day." After FDR's death, she continued an active public life as "First Lady of the Western World."

> ❝ *What other single human being has touched and transformed the existence of so many? She walked in the slums and ghettos of the world, not on a tour of inspection, but as one who could not feel contentment when others were hungry.* ❞
> ADLAI STEVENSON

BIOGRAPHY

Date of birth: 11 October 1884
Place of birth: New York City
Father: Elliott Roosevelt
Mother: Anna Hall Roosevelt
Education: Allenswood, London, England
Husband: Franklin D. Roosevelt
Marriage: 17 March 1905
Children: Anna Eleanor, James, Elliott, Franklin D., Jr., John Aspinwall
Date of death: 7 November 1962
Place of death: New York City
Burial: Hyde Park, New York

> ❝ *If I ... worried about mudslinging, I would have been dead long ago.* ❞
> ELEANOR ROOSEVELT

HIGHLIGHTS

1902 Social worker in New York City slums

1905, 17 March Married Franklin D. Roosevelt, her fifth cousin; her uncle, President Theodore Roosevelt, gave her away

1910–13 Commuted from Albany to New York City to teach school

1921 FDR stricken with polio; Eleanor nursed him and made public appearances on his behalf

1933 Traveled 40,000 miles during her first year in White House

1937 Published *This Is My Story*

1939 Resigned from Daughters of the American Revolution in protest over their barring black singer Marian Anderson from performing at Constitution Hall

1939 Welcomed King George VI and Queen Elizabeth to White House, the first British monarchs to visit America

1945 At FDR's death, moved to an apartment in New York City and to Val-Kill, Hyde Park, New York

1946–52 Appointed by President Truman to

> ❝ *The bottom dropped out of my own particular world. I faced myself, my surroundings, my world, honestly for the first time.* ❞
> ELEANOR ROOSEVELT, ON LEARNING OF FDR'S LOVE LETTERS FROM LUCY MERCER

～17～
ANDREW JOHNSON
(1808–1875)
President (1865–1869)

A defender of the rights of the working man and loyal to the Union, Johnson presided over the bitterly divisive "reconstruction" of the former Confederate states, and in 1867, the purchase of Alaska. Johnson was impeached, but acquitted, over his dismissal of the Secretary of War.

BIOGRAPHY
Date of birth: 29 December 1808
Place of birth: Raleigh, North Carolina
Father: Jacob Johnson (1778–1812)
Mother: Mary McDonough Johnson (1783–1856)
Wife: Eliza McCardle (1810–76)
Children: 5
Date of death: 31 July 1875
Place of death: Carter Station, Tennessee
Burial: Greenville, Tennessee
Number of terms: 1
Age at inauguration: 56
Date of inauguration: 15 April 1865
Vice-President: none
Sec. of State: William H. Seward
Sec. of Treasury: Hugh McCulloch

> " No man has a right to judge Andrew Johnson in any respect who has not suffered and done as much as he for the Nation's sake."
>
> PRESIDENT ABRAHAM LINCOLN, 1864

～18～
ULYSSES S. GRANT
(1822–1885)
President (1869–1877)

A graduate of West Point and a professional soldier, Grant served in the Mexican War and the Civil War, rising to general of the army, the first commander since Washington to hold that rank. Grant was the first president whose administration was marked by major scandals.

BIOGRAPHY
Date of birth: 27 April 1822
Place of birth: Point Pleasant, Ohio
Father: Jesse Root Grant (1794–1873)
Mother: Hannah Simpson Grant (1798–1883)
Wife: Julia Dent (1826–1902)
Children: 4
Date of death: 23 July 1885
Place of death: Mount McGregor, New York
Burial: New York City
Number of terms: 2
Age at first inauguration: 46
Date of inaugurations: 4 March 1869; 4 March 1873
Vice-President: Schuyler Colfax, Henry Wilson
Sec. of State: Elihu B. Washbourne, Hamilton Fish
Sec. of Treasury: Alexander T. Stewart, George S. Boutwell, William A. Richardson

HIGHLIGHTS
1843 Graduated from West Point
1846–48 Served in the Mexican War
1848, 22 August Married Julia Dent
1861 Joined the Union army, rising to rank of lieutenant general
1865, 9 April Accepted Lee's surrender at Appomattox, Virginia
1868, November Elected president under campaign slogan, "*Let us have peace.*"
1869–77 Administrations marked by major scandals
1870 Fifteenth Amendment ratified, outlawing discrimination in voting rights due to race, color, or previous servitude
1873, September Panic of 1873 leading to five-year depression

～19～
RUTHERFORD B. HAYES
(1822–1893)
President (1877–1881)

A Civil War major and governor of Ohio, Hayes ran for president against the Democrat Samuel J. Tilden. Tilden won the popular vote, the voting was disputed and Hayes won by a margin of one electoral vote.

BIOGRAPHY
Date of birth: 4 October 1822
Place of birth: Delaware, Ohio
Father: Rutherford Hayes (1787–1822)
Mother: Sophia Birchard Hayes (1792–1866)
Education: Kenyon College, Gambier, Ohio
Wife: Lucy Ware Webb (1831–89)
Children: 8
Date of death: 17 January 1893
Place of death: Fremont, Ohio
Burial: Fremont, Ohio
Number of terms: 1
Age at inauguration: 54
Date of inauguration: 5 March 1877
Vice-President: William A. Wheeler
Sec. of State: William M. Evarts
Sec. of Treasury: John Sherman

～20～
JAMES A. GARFIELD
(1831–1881)
President (1881)

The last president born in a log cabin, he became a major-general in the Union army. He was assassinated on his way to his college reunion.

BIOGRAPHY
Date of birth: 19 November 1831
Place of birth: Orange, Ohio
Father: Abram Garfield (1799–1833)
Mother: Eliza Ballou Garfield (1801–88)
Education: Williams College, Williamstown, Massachusetts
Wife: Lucretia Rudolph (1832–1918)
Children: 7
Date of death: 19 September 1881
Place of death: Washington, D.C.
Burial: Cleveland, Ohio
Length of term: 200 days
Age at first inauguration: 49
Date of inauguration: 4 March 1881
Vice-President: Chester A. Arthur
Sec. of State: James G. Blaine
Sec. of Treasury: William Windom

～21～
CHESTER A. ARTHUR
(1829–1886)
President (1881–1885)

Arthur, a lawyer by training, and known as the "Gentleman Boss" of the Republican party in New York City, was an organizational rather than inspirational politician.

BIOGRAPHY
Date of birth: 5 October 1829
Place of birth: Fairfield, Vermont

1882 ✦ CHINESE EXCLUSION ACT. ALL CHINESE IMMIGRANT LABORERS DENIED ACCESS TO U.S.

1883 ✦ BROOKLYN BRIDGE COMPLETED. DESIGNED BY JOHN ROEBLING.

1883 ✦ BUFFALO BILL CODY'S WILD WEST SHOW OPENED IN OMAHA, NEBRASKA. BEGINNING A 30-YEAR RUN.

Buffalo Bill

1883 ✦ SCOTTISH NOVELIST ROBERT LOUIS STEVENSON PUBLISHED *TREASURE ISLAND*.

1883 ✦ U.S. RAILROAD COMPANIES ADOPT THE FOUR TRANSCONTINENTAL TIME ZONES THAT WE USE TODAY.

1884 ✦ FIRST ROLLER COASTER IN THE U.S. OPENED AT CONEY ISLAND IN NEW YORK CITY.

1884 ✦ MARK TWAIN'S *THE ADVENTURES OF HUCKLEBERRY FINN* PUBLISHED.

1885 ✦ BRITISH GENERAL GORDON AND HIS FORCE MASSACRED AT KHARTOUM, SUDAN BY TROOPS OF THE MAHDI.

1885 ✦ FIRST PETROL-POWERED AUTOMOBILE (A THREE-WHEELER) BUILT IN GERMANY BY KARL BENZ.

Father: Reverend William Arthur (1796–1875)
Mother: Malvina Stone Arthur (1802–69)
Education: Union College, Schenectady, New York
Wife: Ellen Lewis Herndon (1837–80)
Children: 3
Date of death: 18 November 1886
Place of death: New York City
Burial: Albany, New York
Number of terms: 1
Age at inauguration: 51
Date of inauguration: 20 September 1881
Vice-President: none
Sec. of State: James G. Blaine
Sec. of Treasury: William Windom, Charles J. Folger, Walter Q. Gresham, Hugh McCulloch

~22 & 24~
GROVER CLEVELAND
(1837–1908)
President (1885–1889; 1893–1897)

Cleveland is the only president to serve two non-consecutive terms, and to be married in the White House. After four prosperous years of his first term, his second term began with a severe economic depression – the Panic of 1893.

BIOGRAPHY
Date of birth: 18 March 1837
Place of birth: Caldwell, New Jersey
Father: Reverend Richard Cleveland (1804-53)
Mother: Ann Neal Cleveland (1806-82)
Wife: Frances Folsom (1864-1947)
Children: 5
Date of death: 14 June 1908
Place of death: Princeton, New Jersey
Burial: Princeton, New Jersey
Number of terms: 2
Age at first inauguration: 47
Date of inaugurations: 4 March 1885; 4 March 1893
Vice-President: Thomas A. Hendricks, Adlai E. Stevenson
Sec. of State: Thomas F. Bayard, Walter Q. Gresham, Richard Olney
Sec. of Treasury: Daniel Manning, Charles S. Fairchild, John G. Carlisle

HIGHLIGHTS
1859 Admitted to the bar to practice law
1871–73 Served as sheriff of Erie County, New York
1883 Elected Governor of New York
1884 Elected twenty-second president
1886, 2 June Married Frances Folsom at the

White House
1889–93 Practiced law in New York City
1893 Elected twenty-fourth president
1901 Trustee of Princeton University

~23~
BENJAMIN HARRISON
(1833–1901)
President (1889–1893)

A grandson of President William Henry Harrison, a soldier, lawyer, and senator from Indiana, Harrison saw the continuing growth of the nation with six new states admitted during his term. By 1890 the country was settled from coast to coast.

BIOGRAPHY
Date of birth: 20 August 1833
Place of birth: North Bend, Ohio
Father: John Scott Harrison (1804-78)
Mother: Elizabeth Irwin Harrison(1810-1948)
Education: Miami University, Oxford, Ohio
Wife: (1) Caroline Lavinia Scott (1832-92); (2) Mary Scott Dimmick (1858-1948)
Children: (1) 2; (2) 1
Date of death: 13 March 1901
Place of death: Indianapolis, Indiana
Burial: Indianapolis, Indiana
Number of terms: 1
Age at inauguration: 55
Date of inauguration: 4 March 1889
Vice-President: Levi P. Morton
Sec. of State: James G. Blaine, John W. Foster
Sec. of Treasury: William Windom, Charles Foster

~25~
WILLIAM McKINLEY
(1843–1901)
President (1897–1901)

Although a conciliator by nature McKinley was drawn into war with Spain over Cuba. He was assassinated shortly after the start of his second term.

BIOGRAPHY
Date of birth: 29 January 1843
Place of birth: Niles, Ohio
Father: William McKinley, Sr. (1807-92)
Mother: Nancy Allison McKinley (1809-97)

Wife: Ida Saxton (1847-1907)
Children: 2
Date of death: 14 September 1901
Place of death: Buffalo, New York
Burial: Canton, Ohio
Number of terms: 1 (incomplete 2nd term)
Age at first inauguration: 54
Date of inaugurations: 4 March 1897; 4 March 1901
Vice-President: Garret A. Hobart, Theodore Roosevelt
Sec. of State: Lyman J. Gage

~26~
THEODORE ROOSEVELT
(1858–1919)
President (1901–1909)

The youngest man to become president, "TR" brought zest and vitality to the nation at the start of a new century. Though a sickly boy, he was a believer in the strenuous life and enjoyed boxing, judo, horseback riding, hiking, mountain climbing, and big game hunting. The teddy bear was named for him after a cartoon showed him sparing the life of a cub while hunting.

BIOGRAPHY
Date of birth: 27 October 1858
Place of birth: New York City
Father: Theodore Roosevelt, Sr. (1831–78)
Mother: Martha Bulloch Roosevelt (1834–84)
Wife: (1) Alice Hathaway Lee (1861–84); (2) Edith Kermit Carow (1861–1948)
Children: (1) 1; (2) 5
Date of death: 6 January 1919
Place of death: Oyster Bay, New York
Burial: Oyster Bay, New York
Number of terms: 2 (partial 1st term)
Age at first inauguration: 42
Date of inaugurations: 14 September 1901; 4 March 1905
Vice-President: Charles W. Fairbanks
Sec. of State: John Hay, Elihu Root, Robert Bacon
Sec. of Treasury: Lyman J. Gage, Leslie M. Shaw, George B.Cortelyou

HIGHLIGHTS
1880 Graduated from Harvard College
1880, 27 October Married Alice Hathaway Lee
1882–84 New York State assemblyman
1886 Candidate for mayor of New York City
1886, 2 December Married Edith Kermit Carow

1886 → WORLD'S FIRST SKYSCRAPER COMPLETED, THE AUDITORIUM BUILDING, IN CHICAGO.

1886 → COCA-COLA FIRST SOLD, AT JACOB'S PHARMACY IN ATLANTA.

1886 → STATUE OF LIBERTY, A GIFT FROM FRANCE, INAUGURATED.

1892 → ELLIS ISLAND OPENED TO IMMIGRANTS.

Statue of Liberty

1893 → THE DURYEA BROTHERS TESTED THEIR "GASOLINE BUGGY," THE FIRST US-BUILT GASOLINE-POWERED AUTOMOBILE.

1894 → MILTON HERSHEY STARTED HERSHEY CHOCOLATE COMPANY.

1895 → KING C. GILLETTE INVENTED THE FIRST SAFETY RAZOR WITH A DISPOSABLE BLADE.

1897 → FIRST U.S. SUBWAY OPENED IN BOSTON.

1900 → L. FRANK BAUM PUBLISHED *THE WONDERFUL WIZARD OF OZ.*

1900 → EASTMAN KODAK INTRODUCED THE BROWNIE BOX CAMERA.

1903 → WRIGHT BROTHERS MADE THE WORLD'S FIRST FLIGHT IN A HEAVIER-THAN-AIR MACHINE AT KITTY HAWK, NC.

1905 → ALBERT EINSTEIN PRESENTED HIS THEORY OF RELATIVITY.

1908 → FORD MOTOR COMPANY INTRODUCED THE MODEL T, PRICED AT $850.

Edith Bolling Galt
WILSON
(1872–1961)
First Lady (1915–1921)

Edith Galt, who proudly traced her ancestry to Pocahontas, was a widow when introduced at the White House to President Wilson. It was an ardent love affair. As first lady during World War I, she rationed food and fuel and replaced manpower with sheep to mow the lawn. After Wilson's stroke in 1919, Edith took over routine details for her husband during what she called "my stewardship" and others called "Mrs. Wilson's Regency" as "Acting First Man." In later life she directed the Woodrow Wilson Foundation, published her memoirs (1938), and attended the inauguration of John F. Kennedy in 1961.

> **"** *We have petticoat government! Mrs. Wilson is President!"*
> SENATOR ALBERT FALL OF NEW MEXICO

BIOGRAPHY
Date of birth: 15 October 1872
Place of birth: Wytheville, Virginia
Father: William Bolling
Mother: Sallie White Bolling
Education: Martha Washington College, Abingdon, Virginia
Husband: (1) Norman Galt; (2) Woodrow Wilson
Marriage: (1) 1896; (2) 18 December 1915
Children: none
Date of death: 28 December 1961
Place of death: Washington, D.C.
Burial: Washington Cathedral, Washington, D.C.

> **"** *I am absolutely dependent on intimate love for the right and free and most effective use of my powers and I know by experience…what it costs my work to do without it."*
> WOODROW WILSON TO EDITH GALT, 1915

Florence Kling de Wolfe
HARDING
(1860-1924)
First Lady (1921-1923)

A divorcee with a young son, Florence DeWolfe met Warren Harding when he moved to Marion, Ohio as reporter and, later, owner of the Marion Star. After their marriage, she herself worked at the newspaper for 14 years (keeping watch over her husband's roving eye) and learning the value of good publicity. Strong-willed but gullible, Florence consulted mediums and fortune-tellers; one predicted, accurately, that her husband would die in office and herself soon afterward.

> **"** *Watch me!"*
> FLORENCE'S RESPONSE TO A SENATOR'S REMARK THAT DOLLEY MADISON OR FRANCES CLEVELAND WAS THE MOST SUCCESSFUL FIRST LADY IN HISTORY.

BIOGRAPHY
Date of birth: 15 August 1860
Place of birth: Marion, Ohio
Father: Amos Kling
Mother: Louisa Bouton Kling
Husband: (1) Henry DeWolfe; (2) Warren G. Harding
Marriage: (1) 1880; (2) 8 July 1891
Children: (1) 1
Date of death: 21 November 1924
Place of death: Marion, Ohio
Burial: Marion, Ohio

HIGHLIGHTS
1870s Studied at the Cincinnati Conservatory of Music
1880 Married Henry DeWolfe; 6 months later gave birth to a son; divorced in 1886
1882 Moved back to Marion, Ohio, to teach piano

> **"** *Not a bit of it. I am going to have that bill defeated. Do you think that I am going to have those Coolidges living in a house like that? A hotel apartment is plenty good enough for them."*
> FLORENCE HARDING'S RESPONSE TO THE IDEA OF A PERMANENT RESIDENCE FOR THE VICE PRESIDENT.

1891 Married Warren G. Harding, new owner of the Marion (Ohio) Star
1891-1905 Worked as circulation manager of the Star; called "the real driving power in its success."
1915 Moved to Washington when Harding elected to Senate
1921 Moved to the White House; an expert in public relations, she opened it to thousands of visitors
1922 Suffered an attack of nephritis
1923, 2 August Harding died in California; Florence accompanied his body on cross-country train trip back to Washington
1923 Returned to Marion, Ohio, until her death in 1924

Grace Anna Goodhue
COOLIDGE
(1879-1957)
First Lady (1923-1929)

Charming and vivacious Grace Goodhue married frugal and taciturn Calvin Coolidge and it mystified everyone. But they shared a dry sense of humor. Though she limited herself to a traditional role as first lady, she injected a refreshing informality and wit in whatever she did. The White House staff had a code name for her: "Sunshine."

> **"** *I burst out laughing; I couldn't help myself. He heard me and turned to look at me. When he learned who I was, he managed to arrange a formal introduction – and that is how I became Mrs. Calvin Coolidge."*
> GRACE COOLIDGE'S ACCOUNT OF FIRST MEETING HER HUSBAND, SHAVING IN FRONT OF AN OPEN WINDOW, WEARING LONG UNDERWEAR AND A HAT

BIOGRAPHY
Date of birth: 3 January 1879
Place of birth: Burlington, Vermont
Father: Andrew I. Goodhue
Mother: Lemira Barrett Goodhue
Husband: Calvin Coolidge
Marriage: 4 October 1905
Children: John, Calvin, Jr.
Date of death: 8 July 1957
Place of death: Northampton, Massachusetts
Burial: Plymouth, Vermont

Edith Kermit Carow
ROOSEVELT
(1861–1948)
First Lady (1901–1909)

Growing up in New York City, Edith Carow was "the girl next door" to Theodore Roosevelt and her best friend, his sister Corinne. After Theodore's wife Alice died, Edith and "Teedie" met again and married in London. In the White House, Edith managed a large rambunctious family and renovated the mansion to separate the personal quarters (upstairs) from the official quarters (downstairs). Confident and efficient, Edith was the first first lady to hire a social secretary.

BIOGRAPHY
Date of birth: 6 August 1861
Place of birth: Norwich, Connecticut
Father: Charles Carow
Mother: Gertrude Tyler Carow
Husband: Theodore Roosevelt
Marriage: 2 December 1886
Children: Theodore, Jr., Kermit, Ethel Carow, Archibald Bulloch, Quentin
Date of death: 30 September 1948
Place of death: Oyster Bay, New York
Burial: Oyster Bay, New York

HIGHLIGHTS:
1870s Attended Comstock School, New York City
1886, 2 December Married Theodore Roosevelt at St. George's Church, London. The groom wore bright orange gloves.
1887 Settled in a house at Sagamore Hill, Oyster Bay, New York
1902–09 Enlarged and remodeled the White House at a cost of $475,000, constructing a separate office wing. Established weekly meetings with wives of cabinet members. Began collection of portraits of first ladies.
1906 Hosted wedding of stepdaughter Alice Roosevelt to Nicholas Longworth at the White House

---

1919 Traveled extensively after husband's death.
Contributed to *American Backlogs,* a travel book written by her children.

Helen Herron
TAFT
(1861–1943)
First Lady (1909–1913)

Ambitious and politically astute, "Nellie" Taft said that at 17, when she visited the Hayes at the White House, she first dreamed of becoming first lady. A valued confidante to her husband, she was the first wife to ride down Pennsylvania Avenue with the president after inauguration. In the White House she arranged for 3,000 Japanese cherry trees to be planted along the Washington Tidal Basin – a top tourist attraction to this day.

> **❝** *Of course there was objection, but I had my way and in spite of protests took my place at my husband's side."*
> **HELEN TAFT, AFTER INAUGURATION, 1909**

BIOGRAPHY
Date of birth: 2 June 1861
Place of birth: Cincinnati, Ohio
Father: Judge John W. Herron
Mother: Harriet Collins Herron
Education: Cincinnati College of Music
Husband: William Howard Taft
Marriage: 19 June 1886
Children: Robert Alphonso, Helen Herron, Charles Phelps
Date of death: 22 May 1943
Place of death: Washington, D.C.
Burial: Arlington National Cemetery, Virginia

> **❝** *Had it not been for his wife, Mr. Taft would never have entered the Presidential race."*
> *LADIES HOME JOURNAL,* **MARCH 1909**

HIGHLIGHTS:
1879 Met "Will" Taft at a bobsledding party in Cincinnati, Ohio; married 19 June 1886
1886 Toured Europe on 3–month honeymoon
1900–04 Lived in the Philippines when Taft was governor there
1909 Potomac Drive in Washington opened, a project she sponsored
1909 Suffered a stroke two months after Taft took office
1911 Celebrated silver wedding anniversary with 5,000 guests at White House
1912 Planted first of 3,000 cherry trees with wife of Japanese ambassador
1912 Moved to New Haven, Connecticut where Taft taught at Yale Law School
1921 Returned to Washington when Taft appointed chief justice

Ellen Louise Axson
WILSON
(1860–1914)
First Lady (1913–1914)

First lady for only 15 months, Ellen Wilson was an accomplished artist who donated the proceeds to charity. In the White House she championed housing reform, and hosted the weddings of two of her daughters. At her death of Bright's disease, President Wilson was so devastated that he said he hoped he would be assassinated.

BIOGRAPHY
Date of birth: 15 May 1860
Place of birth: Rome, Georgia
Father: Reverend Samuel E. Axson
Mother: Margaret Hoyt Axson
Education: Rome Female College, Rome, Georgia; Art Students' League, New York City
Husband: Woodrow Wilson
Marriage: 24 June 1885
Children: Margaret Woodrow, Jessie Woodrow, Eleanor Randolph
Date of death: 6 August 1914
Place of death: Washington, D.C.
Burial: Rome, Georgia

> *While President I have been President, emphatically; I have used every ounce of power there was in the office and I have not cared a rap for the criticisms of those who spoke of my 'usurpation of power'….*"
>
> THEODORE ROOSEVELT

1889–95 Commissioner of U. S. Civil Service
1895–97 President of New York City Police Board
1897–98 Assistant Secretary of the Navy
1898 Colonel of the "Rough Riders" in Spanish-American War, leading charge on San Juan Hill
1899–1900 Governor of New York
1901 Vice President of the United States
1901–09 President of the United States
1903 Negotiated the purchase of a canal zone from Panama
1903 Established first national wildlife refuge at Pelican Island, Florida
1904–05 Russo-Japanese War
1906 Awarded Nobel Peace Prize, the first American to win the award
1912 Defeated in presidential election

> *To waste, to destroy, our natural resources, to skin and exhaust the land instead of using it so as to increase its usefulness, will result in undermining in the days of our children the very prosperity which we ought by right to hand down to them amplified and developed.*"
>
> THEODORE ROOSEVELT, MESSAGE TO CONGRESS, 1907

Puck cartoon, 1906. 'King Teddy' Roosevelt with his chosen successor, 'Prince' William Taft on his shoulder.

◈27◈
WILLIAM HOWARD TAFT
(1857–1930)
President (1909–1913)

Taft is the only man to serve as president, and also as a chief justice of the United States – a lifelong ambition.

BIOGRAPHY
Date of birth: 15 September 1857
Place of birth: Cincinnati, Ohio
Father: Alphonse Taft (1810–91)
Mother: Louisa Maria Torrey Taft (1827–1907)
Education: Yale College, New Haven, Connecticut
Wife: Helen Herron (1861–1943)
Children: 3
Date of death: 8 March 1930
Place of death: Washington, D.C.
Burial: Arlington National Cemetery, Virginia
Number of terms: 1
Age at inauguration: 51
Date of inauguration: 4 March 1909
Vice-President: James Schoolcraft Sherman
Sec. of State: Philander C. Knox
Sec. of Treasury: Franklin MacVeagh

◈28◈
WOODROW WILSON
(1856–1924)
President (1913–1921)

Highly educated, idealistic, and an inspiring speaker, Wilson led America's effort in World War I, saying "The world must be made safe for democracy." His major defeat was the Senate's rejection of the League of Nations in 1919.

BIOGRAPHY
Date of birth: 29 December 1856
Place of birth: Staunton, Virginia
Father: Joseph Ruggles Wilson (1822–1903)

> *There will come sometime…another struggle in which, not a few hundred thousand fine men from America will have to die, but many millions…to accomplish the final freedom of the people of the world.*"
>
> WOODROW WILSON, 1919

Mother: Janet Woodrow Wilson (1830–88)
Wife: (1) Ellen Louise Axson (1860–1914); (2) Edith Bolling Galt (1872–1961)
Children: (1) 3
Date of death: 3 February 1924
Place of death: Washington D.C.
Burial: Washington, D.C.
Number of terms: 2
Age at first inauguration: 56
Date of inaugurations: 4 March 1913; 5 March l917
Vice-President: Thomas R. Marshall
Sec. of State: William Jennings Bryan, Robert Lansing, Bainbridge Colby
Sec. of Treasury: William G. McAdoo, Carter Glass, David F. Houston

HIGHLIGHTS
1879 Graduated from the College of New Jersey (now Princeton University)
1879–81 Attended University of Virginia law school
1882–83 Practiced law in Atlanta, Georgia
1885, 24 June Married Ellen Louise Axson
1885–1902 Professor at Bryn Mawr College, Wesleyan University, and Princeton University
1902–10 President of Princeton University
1911–13 Governor of New Jersey
1913–21 President of the United States
1913 17th Amendment ratified: election of senators by popular vote
1915, 18 December Married Edith Bolling Galt
1917, 6 April Declared war against Germany
1918 Issued Fourteen Points, the terms of peace; Germany signed Armistice 11 November
1918 Awarded Nobel Peace Prize
1919 18th Amendment ratified: prohibition of alcoholic beverages
1920 19th Amendment ratified: women's right to vote

> *It is not men that interest or disturb me primarily; it is ideas. Ideas live; men die.*"
>
> WOODROW WILSON

1909 ✦ ADMIRAL ROBERT E. PEARY CLAIMED TO BE FIRST TO REACH THE NORTH POLE.

1909 ✦ DR. SIGMUND FREUD BEGAN A LECTURE TOUR OF THE U.S.

1910 ✦ BOY SCOUTS FOUNDED.

1910–20 ✦ MEXICAN REVOLUTION.

Joseph Pulitzer

1911 ✦ JOSEPH PULITZER CREATES PRIZES IN THE FIELDS OF FICTION, POETRY, HISTORY, AND JOURNALISM.

1912 ✦ AMERICAN GIRL GUIDES FOUNDED (NAME CHANGED IN 1913 TO GIRL SCOUTS.)

1913 ✦ STAINLESS STEEL FIRST MANUFACTURED IN ENGLAND.

1914 ✦ ASSASSINATION OF AUSTRO-HUNGARIAN ARCHDUKE FRANZ FERDINAND TRIGGERS WORLD WAR I.

1917 ✦ AMERICA DECLARES WAR ON GERMANY AND SEND TROOPS TO FRANCE.

Lenin

1917 ✦ RUSSIAN REVOLUTION.

1918 ✦ INFLUENZA EPIDEMIC KILLED AN ESTIMATED 20 MILLION WORLDWIDE.

1918 ✦ ARMISTICE ON 11 NOVEMBER ENDS WORLD WAR I.

1921 ✦ INSULIN, NECESSARY TO CONTROL DIABETES, FIRST ISOLATED BY DR FREDERICK BANTING, TORONTO, CANADA.

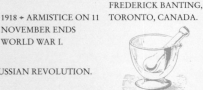

◦29◦
WARREN GAMALIEL HARDING
(1865–1923)
President **(1921–1923)**

By 1923, as America's postwar depression was giving way to prosperity, Harding had wide popular support. Behind the scenes, crime and corruption marked his administration. Harding died before the scandals were revealed.

BIOGRAPHY
Date of birth: 2 November 1865
Place of birth: Morrow County, Ohio
Father: George Tryon Harding (1843–1928)
Mother: Phoebe Elizabeth Dickerson Harding (1843–1910)
Education: Ohio Central College, Iberia, Ohio
Wife: Florence King DeWolfe (1860–1924)
Children: 2
Date of death: 2 August 1923
Place of death: San Francisco, California
Burial: Marion, Ohio
Length of term: 2 years, 5 months
Age at inauguration: 55
Date of inauguration: 4 March 1921
Vice-President: Calvin Coolidge
Sec. of State: Charles Evans Hughes
Sec. of Treasury: Andrew W. Mellon

> *My God, this is a hell of a job! I have no trouble with my enemies....But my damn friends, they're the ones that keep me walking the floor nights.*
> WARREN G. HARDING

The 'Teapot Dome' scandal enmeshed some members of Harding's administration.

◦30◦
CALVIN COOLIDGE
(1872–1929)
President **(1923–1929)**

"Silent Cal," a man of few, but witty, words, was the beneficiary of the country's growth and prosperity. By the time the Great Depression hit in October 1929, Coolidge was in retirement.

BIOGRAPHY
Date of birth: 4 July 1872
Place of birth: Plymouth Notch, Vermont
Father: John Calvin Coolidge (1845–1926)
Mother: Victoria Josephine Moor Coolidge (1846–85)
Education: Amherst College, Amherst, Massachusetts
Wife. Grace Anna Goodhue (1879-1957)
Children: 2
Date of death: 5 January 1933
Place of death: Northampton, Massachusetts
Burial: Plymouth, Vermont
Number of terms: 2 (partial 1st term)
Age at first inauguration: 51
Date of inaugurations: 3 August 1923; 4 March 1925
Vice-President: Charles G. Dawes
Sec. of State: Charles Evans Hughes, Frank B. Kellogg
Sec. of Treasury: Andrew W. Mellon

◦31◦
HERBERT C. HOOVER
(1874–1964)
President **(1929–1933)**

Hoover brought a solid record of honesty and humanitarianism to his election. The stock market crash, just seven months after he took office, spiralled the nation into the Great Depression. Hoover became a scapegoat and was badly defeated in 1932.

BIOGRAPHY
Date of birth: 10 August 1874
Place of birth: West Branch, Iowa
Father: Jesse Clark Hoover (1846–80)

Mother: Huldah Minthorn Hoover (1848–83)
Education: Stanford University, California
Wife: Lou Henry (1874–1944)
Children: 2
Date of death: 20 October 1964
Place of death: New York City
Burial: West Branch, Iowa
Number of terms: 1
Age at inauguration: 54
Date of inauguration: 4 March 1929
Vice-President: Charles Curtis
Sec. of State: Frank B. Kellogg, Henry L.Stimson
Sec. of Treasury: Andrew W. Mellon, Ogden L. Mills

◦32◦
FRANKLIN D. ROOSEVELT
(1882–1945)
President **(1933–1945)**

Charismatic and supremely confident, "FDR" was elected president a record four times. He rallied the nation through economic recovery with the New Deal and, with the Allies, led the strategy that brought victory in World War II.

BIOGRAPHY
Date of birth: 30 January 1882
Place of birth: Hyde Park, New York
Father: James Roosevelt (1828–1900)
Mother: Sara Delano Roosevelt (1854–1941)
Wife: Eleanor Roosevelt
Children: 5
Date of death: 12 April 1945
Place of death: Warm Springs, Georgia
Burial: Hyde Park, New York
Number of terms: 3 (incomplete 4th term)
Age at first inauguration: 51
Date of inaugurations: 4 March 1933; 20 January 1937; 20 January 1941; 20 January 1945
Vice-President: John Nance Garner, Henry A. Wallace, Harry S Truman
Sec. of State: Cordell Hull, Edward R. Stettinius, Jr.
Sec. of Treasury: W.H. Woodin, Henry Morgenthau, Jr.

HIGHLIGHTS
1903 Graduated from Harvard University
1904–07 Attended Columbia University Law School

1922 ✦ TOMB OF TUTANKHAMEN DISCOVERED BY BRITISH ARCHAEOLOGIST HOWARD CARTER.

1922 ✦ *READER'S DIGEST* FOUNDED.

1923 ✦ *TIME* MAGAZINE LAUNCHED.

1925 ✦ CLARENCE BIRDSEYE DEVELOPED AND MARKETED FIRST FROZEN FOOD.

1929 ✦ ST. VALENTINE'S DAY MASSACRE IN CHICAGO.

1927 ✦ CHARLES LINDBERGH COMPLETED FIRST SOLO TRANSATLANTIC FLIGHT IN SINGLE-ENGINE PLANE THE SPIRIT OF ST. LOUIS.

1929 ✦ STOCK MARKET CRASH, BEGINNING THE GREAT DEPRESSION.

1930 ✦ FIRST SUPERMARKET, KING KULLEN, OPENED IN NEW YORK CITY.

1931 ✦ EMPIRE STATE BUILDING OPENED IN NEW YORK CITY.

1936 ✦ MARGARET MITCHELL PUBLISHED *GONE WITH THE WIND.*

1937 ✦ AIRSHIP HINDENBURG BURST INTO FLAMES AND EXPLODED WHILE LANDING AT LAKEHURST, NJ.

1939 ✦ WALT DISNEY RELEASED *SNOW WHITE AND THE SEVEN DWARFS*, THE FIRST FULL-LENGTH ANIMATED MOVIE.

1939 ✦ WORLD'S FAIR OPENED IN NEW YORK.

1939 ✦ START OF WORLD WAR II.

1944 ✦ D DAY, U.S INVASION AT NORMANDY, THE GREATEST AMPHIBIOUS LANDING IN HISTORY (6 JUNE).

1945 ✦ GERMANY SURRENDERS (10 MAY). JAPAN SURRENDERS (2 SEPTEMBER).

BIOGRAPHY
Date of birth: 19 April 1832
Place of birth: Hiram, Ohio
Father: Zebulon Rudolph
Mother: Arabella Mason Rudolph
Education: Eclectic Institute, now Hiram College, Hiram, Ohio
Husband: James A. Garfield
Marriage: 11 November 1858
Children: Harry Augustus, James Rudolph, Mary, Irvin McDowell, Abram
Date of death: 14 March 1918
Place of death: South Pasadena, California
Burial: Cleveland, Ohio

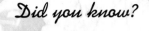

Did you know?

The Baby Ruth candy bar was named after Frances Cleveland's daughter Ruth (not Babe Ruth).

BIOGRAPHY
Date of birth: 1 October 1832
Place of birth: Oxford, Ohio
Father: Reverend John W. Scott
Mother: Mary Neal Scott
Education: Oxford Female Institute, Oxford, Ohio
Husband: Benjamin Harrison
Marriage: 20 October 1853
Children: Russell Benjamin, Mary Scott, Elizabeth
Date of death: 25 October 1892
Place of death: Washington, D.C.
Burial: Indianapolis, Indiana

Mary Arthur
McELROY
(1842–1916)
Acting First Lady (1881–1885)

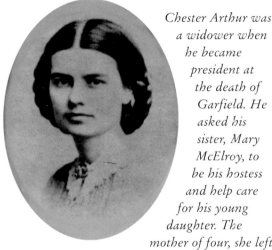

Chester Arthur was a widower when he became president at the death of Garfield. He asked his sister, Mary McElroy, to be his hostess and help care for his young daughter. The mother of four, she left her family in Albany, New York to be in Washington for the winter season. She often called on Julia Tyler and Harriet Lane as co-hostesses.

Frances Folsom
CLEVELAND
(1864–1947)
First Lady (1886–1889; 1893–1897)

A bachelor when he became president (1885) Grover Cleveland relied on his sister Rose as hostess before he married Frances Folsom in 1886. A college graduate and one of the most popular

first ladies of the century, Frances was also the youngest, the first to marry a president in the White House (in the Blue Room), and the first president's widow to remarry.

BIOGRAPHY
Date of birth: 21 July 1864
Place of birth: Buffalo, New York
Father: Oscar Folsom
Mother: Emma Harmon Folsom
Education: Wells College, Aurora, New York
Husband: (1) Grover Cleveland; (2) Thomas J. Preston
Marriage: (1) 2 June 1886; (2) 1913
Children: (1) Ruth, Esther, Marion, Richard Folsom, Francis Grover
Date of death: 29 October 1947
Place of death: Baltimore, Maryland
Burial: Princeton, New Jersey

Caroline Lavinia Scott
HARRISON
(1832–1892)
First Lady (1889–1892)

In the White House, Caroline Harrison put up the first Christmas tree and installed electricity (1891), new plumbing, and more bathrooms. She designed her own china pattern and began the collection of china from former first ladies. She supported the new Johns Hopkins Medical School on the condition it admit women on an equal basis with men. She died during Harrison's unsuccessful campaign for reelection in 1892.

Ida Saxton
McKINLEY
(1847–1907)
First Lady (1897–1901)

She was a spirited young woman, but early in what seemed an idyllic marriage, Ida McKinley lost her mother and two infant daughters. She never recovered, developed seizures and was a life-long invalid. With her devoted husband's constant care, she continued to attend White House events. After her husband's assassination, she visited his grave almost daily.

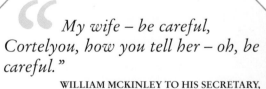

My wife – be careful, Cortelyou, how you tell her – oh, be careful.
WILLIAM MCKINLEY TO HIS SECRETARY, AFTER HE WAS SHOT BY AN ASSASSIN, 1901

BIOGRAPHY
Date of birth: 8 June 1847
Place of birth: Canton, Ohio
Father: James Saxton
Mother: Catherine DeWalt Saxton
Education: Brook Hall Seminary, Media, Pennsylvania
Husband: William McKinley
Marriage: 25 January 1871
Children: Katherine, Ida
Date of death: 26 May 1907
Place of death: Canton, Ohio
Burial: Canton, Ohio

Julia Dent
⚞ GRANT ⚟
(1826–1902)
First Lady (1869–1877)

Julia Grant was called by a journalist, "first lady of the land" – the first known use of that term. In the White House she was a favorite topic of a new crop of women reporters, and a fun-loving, extravagant hostess of the Gilded Age. After Grant's second term, she traveled with him for 28 months around the world, treated like a queen from London to the Far East. She was the first ex-president's wife to write her own autobiography. Her view of the scandals surrounding her husband was that he was naïve but not dishonest, a view held by later historians.

> ❝ *The children and I had that beautiful lawn for eight years, and I assure you we enjoyed it.*❞
> JULIA GRANT

BIOGRAPHY
Date of birth: 26 January 1826
Place of birth: near St. Louis, Missouri
Father: Colonel Frederick Dent
Mother: Ellen Wrenshall Dent
Husband: Ulysses S. Grant
Marriage: 22 August 1848
Children: Frederick Dent, Ulysses S., Jr., Ellen "Nellie" Wrenshall, Jesse Root
Date of death: 14 December 1902

> ❝ *...the light of his glorious fame still reaches out to me, falls upon me, and warms me.*❞
> JULIA GRANT

Place of death: Washington, D.C.
Burial: Grant's Tomb, New York City

HIGHLIGHTS:
1840s Met "Ulys" Grant, a classmate of her brother at West Point
1844 Began four-year engagement to Grant
1848, 22 August Married Grant at her home in St. Louis, Missouri
1874 Daughter Nellie married in lavish White House ceremony
1877 Accompanied husband on 28-month around the world trip
1885–1902 Lived in New York City
1890s Wrote autobiography, *The Personal Memoirs of Julia Dent Grant*, published in 1975

Lucy Ware Webb
⚞ HAYES ⚟
(1831–1889)
First Lady (1877–1881)

The first first lady to have graduated from college, Lucy Hayes was an early feminist and a firm Abolitionist who persuaded her husband to abandon the Whigs for the antislavery Republican party. During the Civil War she visited her husband at camp and ministered to the wounded and dying. A popular hostess, though frugal in style, she was called "Lemonade Lucy" for banning alcohol in the White House. Lucy Hayes became one of the best-loved women to preside over the White House, where the Hayeses celebrated their silver wedding anniversary in 1877.

> ❝ *[Lucy] wishes she had been in Fort Sumter with a garrison of women.*❞
> RUTHERFORD HAYES, IN LETTER TO HIS UNCLE

BIOGRAPHY
Date of birth: 28 August 1831
Place of birth: Chillicothe, Ohio
Father: James Webb
Mother: Maria Cook Webb
Education: Wesleyan Female College, Cincinnati, Ohio
Husband: Rutherford B. Hayes
Marriage: 30 December 1852
Children: Sardis Birchard, James Webb, Rutherford Platt, Frances, Scott Russell
Date of death: 25 June 1889
Place of death: Fremont, Ohio
Burial: Fremont, Ohio

HIGHLIGHTS
1847 Enrolled at Wesleyan Female College
1852, 30 December Married Rutherford B. Hayes at her mother's home
1861–65 Visited her wounded husband during Civil War when he served with a volunteer regiment
1867 Moved to Columbus, Ohio when Hayes elected governor of Ohio
1868 Raised funds to establish the state Home for Soldiers' Orphans at Xenia, Ohio
1879 Established Easter egg rolling on White House lawn as an annual children's event

> ❝ *Your ignorance of politics is not a grave offense. You could not expect to know and enjoy politics as I do.*❞
> LUCY HAYES TO A YOUNG SON

Lucretia Rudolph
⚞ GARFIELD ⚟
(1832-1918)
First Lady (1881)

Lucretia "Crete" Rudolph met James Garfield when she was 17, both students at Geauga Seminary in Chester, Ohio. Their early marriage was troubled, they were apart during the Civil War, and like so many of their contemporaries they suffered the deaths of young children, though five grew up healthy. They grew closer during the Washington years, but soon after her husband's election, Lucretia contracted malaria. And, four months after taking office, Garfield was shot by an assassin. Lucretia kept a three-month vigil at his bedside.

> ❝ *The President wishes me to say to you from him that he has been seriously hurt – how seriously he cannot yet say. He is himself and hopes you will come to him soon. He sends his love to you.*❞
> MESSAGE TO LUCRETIA GARFIELD FROM WHITE HOUSE, 2 JULY 1881

Today, in this year of war, 1945, we have learned lessons – at fearful cost – and we shall profit by them. We have learned that we cannot live alone, at peace; that our own well-being is dependent on the well-being of other nations far away. We have learned that we must live as men, not as ostriches, nor as dogs in the manger. We have learned to be citizens of the world, members of the human community. We have learned the simple truth, as Emerson said, that 'The only way to have a friend is to be one'"....

FRANKLIN D. ROOSEVELT, 4TH
INAUGURAL ADDRESS, 20 JANUARY 1945

1905, 17 March Married Eleanor Roosevelt
1907 Admitted to the bar to practice law
1911–13 New York State Senator
1913–20 Assistant Secretary of the Navy
1920 Ran unsuccessfully as Democratic nominee for vice president
1920–28 Returned to private life as lawyer and politician
1919 Crippled by an attack of polio
1929–32 Governor of New York
1932 Elected president of the United States
1933–35 Launched New Deal programs, including National Industrial Recovery Act (NRA) and Works Progress Administration (WPA)
1933 21st Amendment (prohibition) repealed
1935 Social Security legislation passed
1941, 7 December Japan attacks Pearl Harbor
1941–45 Led U.S. home front and armed forces through World War II
1941 Met with Prime Minister Winston Churchill to draft the "Atlantic Charter" with 26 countries, forming the basis of the United Nations
1945 Yalta Conference with Churchill and Stalin outlining peace terms

We look forward to a world founded upon four essential human freedoms...freedom of speech and expression...freedom of every person to worship God in his own way...freedom from want...freedom from fear."

FRANKLIN D. ROOSEVELT, 1941

⁌33⁊
HARRY S. TRUMAN
(1884–1972)
President (1945–1953)

Honest, decisive, stubborn, blunt in speech, Truman thrived on the political life and was an avid student of history. The first president to take office in wartime, in 1945 he authorized the atomic bombing of Hiroshima and Nagasaki. Guiding the nation to a peacetime economy, he launched a domestic program, the Fair Deal. In 1948 he approved a major foreign-aid program for European recovery.

(I felt) like the moon, the stars and all the planets had fallen on me."

HARRY S TRUMAN, ON TAKING OFFICE AT
ROOSEVELT'S DEATH, 1945

BIOGRAPHY
Date of birth: 8 May 1884
Place of birth: Lamar, Missouri
Father: John Anderson Truman (1851–1914)
Mother: Martha Ellen Young (1852–1947)
Wife: Elizabeth "Bess" Wallace
Children: 1
Date of death: 26 December 1972
Place of death: Kansas City, Missouri
Burial: Independence, Missouri
Number of terms: 1 (incomplete 1st term)
Age at first inauguration: 60
Date of inaugurations: 12 April 1945; 20 January 1949

If you can't stand the heat, stay out of the kitchen."

HARRY S TRUMAN

Vice-President: Alben W. Barkley
Sec. of State: Edward R. Stettinius, Jr., James F. Byrnes, George C. Marshall, Dean G. Acheson
Sec. of Treasury: Henry Morgenthau, Jr., Frederick M. Vinson, John W. Snyder

HIGHLIGHTS
1901 Graduated from Independence (Missouri) High School
1917–19 Served with an artillery battery in World War I, rising to rank of major
1919, 28 June Married Elizabeth "Bess" Wallace
1919–22 Established a haberdashery in Kansas City, Missouri
1926–34 County Judge and Presiding Judge of Jackson County, Missouri
1935–45 U.S. Senator from Missouri
1945, March-April Vice President of the United States
1945, 12 April President of the United States at

You, more than any other man, have saved Western civilization."

WINSTON CHURCHILL TO HARRY S TRUMAN

Roosevelt's death
1945, 6 and 9 August Ordered the atomic bomb dropped on Hiroshima and Nagasaki, Japan
1946, October First meeting of United Nations in London
1948 Reelected president in famous upset victory over Republican, Thomas E. Dewey
1948 Approved the Marshall Plan to rebuild Europe
1949 Helped establish the North Atlantic Treaty Organization (NATO)
1950–53 Korean War, Truman relieved General Douglas MacArthur of his command in April 1951
1951 22nd Amendment ratified, limiting future presidents to two terms in office

The Chicago Daily Tribune *jumped the gun in declaring the outcome of the 1948 presidential election.*

1945 + FIRST FLUORIDATION OF WATER, TO REDUCE TOOTH DECAY, IN GRAND RAPIDS, MICHIGAN.

1946 + DR. SPOCK'S *BABY AND CHILD CARE* PUBLISHED AS BABY BOOM BEGAN.

1947 + TEST PILOT CHUCK YEAGER BECAME THE FIRST TO BREAK THE SOUND BARRIER.

1948 + ISRAEL BECAME A STATE

1948 + TRANSISTOR DEVELOPED.

1947 + JACKIE ROBINSON JOINED THE BROOKLYN DODGERS, BREAKING THE COLOR BARRIER IN MAJOR-LEAGUE BASEBALL.

Jackie Robinson

1949 + PEOPLE'S REPUBLIC OF CHINA ESTABLISHED.

1950 + PEANUTS COMIC STRIP BY CHARLES SCHULZ APPEARED.

1950 + DINERS CLUB INTRODUCED THE FIRST CREDIT CARD.

1951 + *I LOVE LUCY* WITH LUCILLE BALL AND DESI ARNAZ PREMIERED ON TELEVISION.

1951 + J.D. SALINGER PUBLISHED *THE CATCHER IN THE RYE.*

1952 + SALK POLIO VACCINE DEVELOPED.

Lucille Ball

1953 + C.A. SWANSON & SONS INTRODUCED THE FIRST TV DINNER.

1953 + DOUBLE HELIX STRUCTURE OF DNA DISCOVERED.

⪚34⪚
DWIGHT D. EISENHOWER
(1890–1969)
President (1953–1961)

The famous Eisenhower smile reflected the friendly, gregarious man who inspired America's confidence and respect. A career soldier, hero-worshiped after World War II, he was elected twice with huge majorities, and led the nation at the onset of the Space Age and the escalation of the Cold War between communist countries and western democracies.

BIOGRAPHY

Date of birth: 14 October 1890
Place of birth: Denison, Texas
Father: David Jacob Eisenhower (1863–1942)
Mother: Ida Elizabeth Stover Eisenhower (1862–1946)
Wife: Mamie Geneva Doud (1896–1979)
Children: 2
Date of death: 28 March 1969
Place of death: Washington, D.C.
Burial: Abilene, Kansas
Number of terms: 2
Age at first inauguration: 62
Date of inaugurations: 20 January 1953; 21 January 1957
Vice-President: Richard M. Nixon
Sec. of State: John Foster Dulles, Christian A. Herter
Sec. of Treasury: George M. Humphrey, Robert B. Anderson

HIGHLIGHTS

1911–15 Attended U.S. Military Academy at West Point
1916, 1 July Married Mamie Geneva Doud
1917–18 Commander of Tank Corps Training Center, Camp Colt, Pennsylvania
1932–35 Aide to General Douglas MacArthur, chief of staff of the U.S. Army
1935–39 Senior military assistant to General Douglas MacArthur in the Philippine Islands
1942 Appointed commanding general of U.S. forces in Europe
1943–45 Supreme Commander of Allied Expeditionary forces in Europe
1948–50 President of Columbia University
1951–52 Appointed Supreme Commander of NATO
1953 Elected president of the United States
1953, July Korean War armistice signed
1954 Landmark Supreme Court desegregation decision, Brown v. Board of Education
1956 Reelected to a second term as president
1957 Dispatched federal troops to Little Rock,

> *The United States never lost a soldier or a foot of ground in my administration. We kept the peace. People ask how it happened – by God, it didn't just happen, I'll tell you that."*
>
> DWIGHT D. EISENHOWER

Arkansas high school to protect black students
1957 Succeeded in forming International Atomic Energy Agency, a plan for peaceful use of nuclear energy
1957, October Russia launched *Sputnik*, first man-made space satellite
1959 Russian Premier Krushchev visited U.S.
1959 Broke off diplomatic relations with China
1960 Russia shot down American U-2 plane

⪚35⪚
JOHN F. KENNEDY
(1917–1963)
President (1961–1963)

"An idealist without illusions" was how Kennedy described himself. The youngest man, and the first Roman Catholic, to be elected president, Kennedy captured the imagination of America's youth with his New Frontier program. He was assassinated after two years, ten months in office.

BIOGRAPHY

Date of birth: 29 May 1917
Place of birth: Brookline, Massachusetts
Father: Joseph Patrick Kennedy (1888–1969)
Mother: Rose Fitzgerald Kennedy (1890–1995)
Wife: Jacqueline Lee Bouvier (1929–1994)
Children: 3
Date of death: 22 November 1963
Place of death: Dallas, Texas
Burial: Arlington National Cemetery, Virginia
Length of term: 2 years, 10 months
Age at inauguration: 43
Date of inauguration: 20 January 1961
Vice-President: Lyndon B. Johnson
Sec. of State: Dean Rusk
Sec. of Treasury: C. Douglas Dillon

HIGHLIGHTS

1935 Attended Princeton University
1940 Graduated from Harvard University

> *In the long history of the world, only a few generations have been granted the role of defending freedom in this hour of maximum danger. I do not shrink from this responsibility – I welcome it. I do not believe that any of us would exchange places with any other people or any other generation. The energy, the faith, the devotion which we bring to this endeavor will light our country and all who serve it – and the glow from that fire can truly light the world. And so, my fellow Americans: ask not what your country can do for you – ask what you can do for your country."*
>
> JOHN F. KENNEDY, FROM HIS INAUGURAL ADDRESS, 20 JANUARY 1961

1940–41 Attended Stanford University Business School
1941–45 Served in the U.S. Navy, rising to lieutenant; skipper of PT-109 and earned Purple Heart
1945 Journalist for Chicago Herald-American and International News Service
1947–53 U.S. representative from Massachusetts
1953–61 U.S. senator from Massachusetts
1953, 12 September Married Jacqueline Lee Bouvier
1956 Won the Pulitzer Prize for book, *Profiles in Courage*
1961–63 President of the United States
1961–63 Continued sending advisers and military supplies, started under Eisenhower, to South Vietnam
1961 Unsuccessful Bay of Pigs invasion, a U.S.-led attempt to overthrow Fidel Castro
1961 Established the Peace Corps, a volunteer agency to support underdeveloped countries
1961 Space Program. Kennedy stated objective to put a man on the moon by end of decade
1961 23rd Amendment ratified, giving residents of District of Columbia the right to vote in presidential elections
1962, October Cuban Missile Crisis; Russia dismantled missile bases in Cuba
1962-63 Promoted legislative programs to end desegregation in education, housing, and employment.
1963 Nuclear Test Ban Treaty with Britain and Soviet Union, later signed by more than 100 countries
1963, 22 November Assassinated in Dallas, Texas

1955 ♦ ROSA PARKS REFUSED TO GIVE HER SEAT TO A WHITE MAN ON A BUS IN MONTGOMERY, ALABAMA.

1956 ♦ ELVIS PRESLEY'S APPEARANCE ON THE ED SULLIVAN TELEVISION SHOW SET A RECORD – 54 MILLION VIEWERS.

1958 ♦ FIRST DOMESTIC JET AIRLINE PASSENGER SERVICE IN U.S. BEGAN.

1959 ♦ BARBIE DOLL AND PANTY HOSE INTRODUCED.

1961 ♦ COSMONAUT YURI GAGARIN BECAME THE FIRST HUMAN IN SPACE. THREE WEEKS LATER ALAN SHEPARD, ABOARD *MERCURY CAPSULE FREEDOM 7*, WAS THE FIRST AMERICAN IN SPACE.

1961 ♦ CUBAN MISSILE CRISIS.

1962 ♦ MARILYN MONROE DIES.

1962 ♦ JOHN GLENN JR. BECAME FIRST AMERICAN IN ORBIT WHEN HE CIRCLED THE EARTH THREE TIMES.

John Glenn Jr.

1962 ♦ JAMES MEREDITH BECAME THE FIRST BLACK STUDENT AT THE UNIVERSITY OF MISSISSIPPI AFTER TROOPS PUT DOWN RIOTS.

1963 ♦ MARTIN LUTHER KING JR. DELIVERED HIS "I HAVE A DREAM" SPEECH AT THE MARCH ON WASHINGTON.

1963 ♦ TONKIN GULF RESOLUTION ESCALATES AMERICAN INVOLVEMENT IN VIETNAM.

> " *Mrs. Lincoln wanted what she wanted when she wanted it and no substitute! And as far as we know she always had it, including a President of the United States.*"
> JULIA TAFT, YOUNG FRIEND OF THE LINCOLN BOYS

BIOGRAPHY

Date of birth: 13 December 1818
Place of birth: Lexington, Kentucky
Father: Robert Smith Todd
Mother: Elizabeth Parker Todd
Husband: Abraham Lincoln
Marriage: 4 November 1842
Children: Robert Todd, William "Willie" Wallace, Thomas "Tad"
Date of death: 16 July 1882
Place of death: Springfield, Illinois
Burial: Springfield, Illinois

HIGHLIGHTS:

1839 Met Abraham Lincoln at a dance in Springfield, Illinois
1842, 4 November Married Lincoln at her sister's home
1847–48 Lived in Washington during Lincoln's term in Congress
1861 ca. Suspected of being a Confederate spy
1862 Death of son Willie in the White House
1864 Purchases in White House totaled over $27,000, more than her husband earned in a year
1865 Lincoln's assassination
1868–71 Lived in Frankfurt, Germany with son Tad

> " *I often think it would have been some solace to me and perhaps have lessened the grief, which is now breaking my heart – if my idolized had passed away, after an illness, and I had been permitted to watch over him and tend him to the last,*" [then she could have] "*...thanked him for his lifelong— almost – devotion to me and I could have asked forgiveness, for any inadvertent moment of pain, I may have caused him.*"
> MARY TODD LINCOLN, 1865

> " *She is no more insane than you or I are and if you come with me to talk with her, you would understand that.*"
> PHYSICIAN WHO TREATED MARY, 1881

1871 Death of son Tad
1875 Declared legally insane. Son Robert committed her to mental institution in Batavia, Illinois
1875, September Organized her own release from hospital
1875 Returned to Europe, living in Pau, France; then lived with sister in Springfield, Illinois, until her death in 1882

Eliza McCardle JOHNSON
(1810–1876)
First Lady (1865–1869)

> " *I knew he'd be acquitted; I knew it.*"
> ELIZA JOHNSON, AFTER SENATE VOTED TO ACQUIT HER HUSBAND IN IMPEACHMENT TRIAL, 1868

Married at 16, Eliza Johnson holds the record for marrying at the youngest age of any first lady. Better educated than her husband Andrew Johnson, she tutored him in writing and arithmetic. She became a semi-invalid in middle age; when Johnson became president she took to the White House second floor and appeared only twice in public. Eliza was fragile and had suffered from tuberculosis in the years before the Civil War. She had lost a son and a son-in-law. While her husband's political career prospered she concentrated on her domestic life. Her daughter, Martha Johnson Patterson, assumed Eliza's social duties.

BIOGRAPHY

Date of birth: 4 October 1810
Place of birth: Leesburg, Tennessee
Father: John McCardle
Mother: Sarah Phillips McCardle
Husband: Andrew Johnson
Marriage: 17 May 1827
Children: Martha, Charles, Mary, Robert, Andrew, Jr.
Date of death: 15 January 1876
Place of death: Greeneville, Tennessee
Burial: Greeneville, Tennessee

Mrs Lincoln was quite a spender and her lavish parties, held while men were dying on the battlefields of the Civil War, angered her critics.

Margaret Mackall Smith
TAYLOR
(1788–1852)
First Lady (1849–1850)

The daughter of a wealthy Maryland planter, educated at a New York City finishing school, Margaret Taylor married Lieutenant Zachary Taylor in 1810. Devoutly religious, she became reclusive because it is said she promised God she would renounce society if her husband returned safely from war. As first lady, she retired to the second floor, leaving her daughter, Betty Taylor Bliss, to substitute for her. No painting or photograph of Margaret survives.

BIOGRAPHY
Date of birth: 21 September 1788
Place of birth: Calvert County, Maryland
Father: Walter Smith
Mother: Ann Mackall Smith
Husband: Zachary Taylor
Marriage: 21 June 1810
Children: Ann Mackall, Sarah Knox, Mary Elizabeth "Betty", Richard
Date of death: 14 August 1852
Place of death: Pascagoula, Mississippi
Burial: Louisville, Kentucky

Abigail Powers
FILLMORE
(1798–1853)
First Lady (1850–1853)

In 1819, Abigail Powers, 21, taught school; her oldest pupil was 19-year-old Millard Fillmore. After a long courtship and marriage, Abigail continued a lifelong interest in education. She was the first wife of a future president to hold a job after marriage. As first lady, she started the first permanent White House library. Preferring the privacy of a "cheerful room" upstairs, she left the hostess duties to her daughter Mary. At Franklin Pierce's inauguration, Abigail developed pneumonia and died within a month.

BIOGRAPHY
Date of birth: 13 March 1798
Place of birth: Stillwater, New York
Father: Reverend Lemuel Powers
Mother: Abigail Newland Powers
Husband: Millard Fillmore
Marriage: 5 February 1826
Children: Millard Powers, Mary Abigail
Date of death: 30 March 1853
Place of death: Washington, D.C.
Burial: Buffalo, New York

> " *How lonesome this hotel room is in your absence....You have scarcely been out of my mind since you left. How I wish I could be with you!"*
> MILLARD FILLMORE, LETTER TO ABIGAIL, 1850

Jane Means Appleton
PIERCE
(1806–1863)
First Lady (1853–1857)

Frail and shy, a minister's daughter, Jane Pierce's life was marked by tragedy. After losing two young children, her surviving son Bennie, age 11, was killed in a train accident just two months before her husband became president. Bitterly opposed to political life, she fainted when she heard of Pierce's nomination for president and did not attend his inauguration.

BIOGRAPHY
Date of birth: 12 March 1806
Place of birth: Hampton, New Hampshire
Father: Reverend Jesse Appleton
Mother: Elizabeth Means Appleton
Husband: Franklin Pierce
Marriage: 19 November 1834
Children: Franklin, Frank Robert, Benjamin
Date of death: 2 December 1863
Place of death: Andover, Massachusetts
Burial: Concord, New Hampshire

> " *I hope he won't be elected for I should not like to be at Washington and I know you would not either."*
> BENNIE, IN A LETTER TO HIS MOTHER, 1852

Harriet
LANE
(1830–1903)
First Lady (1857–1861)

The only bachelor president, James Buchanan turned to his orphaned niece, Harriet Lane, 27, to serve as his hostess. As her guardian, Buchanan had provided for her education and political exposure during his years as congressman and foreign minister. Harriet was a popular and effective first lady, generous with appeals for access to the president. Her art collection became the basis of the National Collection of Fine Arts at the Smithsonian. After the White House, Harriet married a banker, had three sons, and devoted her life to charitable work.

Mary Todd
LINCOLN
(1818–1882)
First Lady (1861–1865)

A young lawyer summed her up in 1840: "the very creature of excitement." This quality marked Mary Todd Lincoln's life, bringing her both happiness and tragedy. She was witty, vivacious, moody, and mentally fragile. At the White House she indulged in spending sprees, and because her Confederate brothers were fighting the Union, she was rumored to be a spy. She suffered the death of her son Willie in 1862, Lincoln's assassination in 1865, and her son Tad's death in 1871. When she was 57, her son Robert had her committed to a mental institution. She organized her own release, then lived in France before illness brought her back to Illinois where she died.

> *We choose to go to the moon in this decade, and do the other things, not because they are easy but because they are hard....”*
>
> JOHN F. KENNEDY, 1961

≈36≈
LYNDON B. JOHNSON
(1908–1973)
President (1963–1969)

Johnson was a complex personality, a man who relished power and a master manipulator in Congress. He had major success in his extensive domestic program "The Great Society," and a major defeat for his policy of escalating the Vietnam War.

BIOGRAPHY
Date of birth: 27 August 1908
Place of birth: Gillespie County, Texas
Father: Sam Ealy Johnson, Jr. (1877–1937)
Mother: Rebekah Baines Johnson (1881–1958)
Wife: Claudia "Lady Bird" Taylor (1912–
Children: 2
Date of death: 22 January 1973
Place of death: ranch near Johnson City, Texas
Burial: Stonewall, Texas
Number of terms: 1 (after partial term)
Age at first inauguration: 55
Date of inaugurations: 22 November 1963; 20 January 1965
Vice-President: Hubert Humphrey
Sec. of State: Dean Rusk
Sec. of Treasury: C. Douglas Dillon, Henry H. Fowler, Joseph W. Barr

HIGHLIGHTS
1927–30 Attended Southwest Texas State Teachers College
1930–31 Taught public speaking and debate in Sam Houston High School, Houston, Texas
1932–35 Secretary to U.S. Representative Richard M. Kleberg
1934, 17 November Married Claudia "Lady Bird" Taylor

> *I will do my best. That is all I can do. I ask your help, and God's.”*
>
> LYNDON B. JOHNSON, 22 NOVEMBER 1963

> *As President, his brilliant leadership on the Civil Rights Act of 1964 and the Voting Rights Act of 1965 has earned him a place in the history of civil rights alongside Abraham Lincoln.”*
>
> SENATOR EDWARD M. KENNEDY, 1973

1935–37 Director of the National Youth Administration in Texas
1937–48 U.S. Representative from Texas
1941–42 Served in World War II as lieutenant commander in U.S. Navy; awarded the Silver Star
1949–60 U.S. Senator from Texas
1961–63 Vice President of the United States
1963–69 President of the United States
1964 Civil Rights Act passed, barring discrimination in employment
1964 24th Amendment ratified, outlawing poll tax
1965 Medicare and Medicaid programs established
1965–67 Four environmental protection acts passed to improve air and water quality
1964–68 Escalated U.S. role in Vietnam, building troop level to over half a million
1967 25th Amendment ratified, allowing presidents to fill a vacancy in vice-presidency

> *He can be as gentle and solicitous as a nurse, but as ruthless and deceptive as a riverboat gambler.”*
>
> ROWLAND EVANS AND ROBERT NOVAK

Lyndon Johnson's dynamism was reflected in his 'Great Society' legislation – the most ambitious in U.S. history.

≈37≈
RICHARD MILHOUS NIXON
(1913–1974)
President (1969–1974)

Lonely, hypersensitive, dishonest. Intelligent, decisive, courageous. Words describing Nixon are as conflicted as his record. In his first term he greatly improved relations with Russia and China, and ended the U.S. involvement in Vietnam. His second term was destroyed by the Watergate scandal that forced him to resign.

BIOGRAPHY
Date of birth: 9 January 1913
Place of birth: Yorba Linda, California
Father: Francis Anthony Nixon (1878–1956)
Mother: Hannah Milhous Nixon (1885–1967)
Wife: Thelma Catherine "Pat" Ryan (1912–1993)
Children: 2
Date of death: 22 April 1994
Place of death: New York City
Burial: Yorba Linda, California
Number of terms: 2 (partial second term)
Age at first inauguration: 56
Date of inaugurations: 20 January 1969; 20 January 1973
Vice-President: Spiro Agnew, Gerald R. Ford
Sec. of State: William P. Rogers, Henry A. Kissinger
Sec. of Treasury: David M. Kennedy, John B. Connally, Jr., George P. Shultz, William E. Simon

HIGHLIGHTS
1934 Graduated from Whittier (California) College
1937 Received degree from Duke University Law School, Durham, North Carolina
1937–41 Practiced law in Whittier, California
1940, 21 June Married Thelma Catherine "Pat" Ryan
1942 Attorney in the Office of Price Administration, Washington, D.C.

> *No words can describe the depths of my regret and pain at the anguish my mistakes over Watergate have caused the nation and the Presidency, a nation I so deeply love and an institution I so greatly respect.”*
>
> RICHARD M. NIXON, SEPTEMBER 1974

1964 ✦ CIVIL RIGHTS ACT PASSED.

1964 ✦ BEATLEMANIA SEIZES AMERICA WHEN THE FAB FOUR VISIT.

1965 ✦ MALCOLM X, ASSASSINATED AT THE AUDUBON BALLROOM IN HARLEM, NEW YORK.

1965 ✦ FOUR DAYS OF RACE RIOTING IN THE WATTS NEIGHBORHOOD OF LOS ANGELES.

1965 ✦ MEDICARE BILL SIGNED, PROVIDING HEALTH INSURANCE FOR AMERICANS OVER 65.

1965 ✦ SOFT CONTACT LENSES FIRST INTRODUCED.

1967 ✦ FIRST ISSUE OF *ROLLING STONE* MAGAZINE.

Martin Luther King Jr.

1968 ✦ JAMES EARL RAY ASSASSINATED MARTIN LUTHER KING JR. AT THE LORRAINE MOTEL IN MEMPHIS.

1968 ✦ ROBERT F. KENNEDY KILLED BY SIRHAN SIRHAN IN LOS ANGELES.

1968 ✦ *APOLLO 8* ORBITED THE MOON IN FIVE-DAY MISSION.

1969 ✦ *SESAME STREET* AIRS ON PUBLIC TV FOR FIRST TIME.

1969 ✦ WOODSTOCK FESTIVAL OPENED IN UPSTATE NEW YORK.

1970 ✦ KENT STATE KILLING OF FOUR STUDENT ANTI-WAR PROTESTORS BY NATIONAL GUARD.

1970 ✦ WORLD TRADE CENTER BUILT.

1942–46 Served in the U.S. Navy, rising to lieutenant commander
1947–50 U.S. Representative from California
1951–53 U.S. Senator from California
1953–61 Vice President of the United States
1960 Republican nominee for president, defeated by Kennedy
1962 Practiced law in New York City
1969–74 President of the United States
1969–74 Vietnam War. Despite 1973 peace agreement ending U.S. involvement, fighting continued between North and South Vietnam
1969, 20 July Astronaut Neil Armstrong, commander of Apollo 11, sets foot on the moon
1971 26th Amendment ratified, lowering voting age to 18
1971–72 Nixon was first president to visit China, opening relations with the communist government
1972 Strategic Arms Limitation Talks (SALT) Agreement signed with Soviet leader, Brezhnev
1972, 17 June Five agents from the Committee to Re-elect the President arrested after burglarizing Democratic National Committee offices at Watergate, touching off the worst political scandal in U.S. history
1974, 9 August Resigned to avoid impeachment

⬤38⬤
GERALD RUDOLPH FORD
(1913-
President (1974–1977)

Ford was the first man appointed to the vice-presidency under the new 25th Amendment, replacing Spiro Agnew. Just a year later, he took the oath as president at the climax of the Watergate scandal – Nixon's resignation.

BIOGRAPHY
Date of birth: 14 July 1913
Place of birth: Omaha, Nebraska
Father: Leslie Lynch King (1882–1941)
Mother: Dorothy Ayer Gardner Ford (1892–1967)
Wife: Elizabeth Bloomer Warren (1918–
Children: 4
Number of terms: 1 (partial)
Age at inauguration: 61
Date of inauguration: 9 August 1974
Vice-President: Nelson A. Rockefeller
Sec. of State: Henry A. Kissinger
Sec. of Treasury: William E. Simon

HIGHLIGHTS
1935 Graduated from the University of Michigan
1935–41 Assistant football coach at Yale University
1941 Received degree from Yale Law School
1941–42 Served in the U.S. Navy, rising to lieutenant commander
1948, 15 October Married Elizabeth Bloomer Warren
1949-73 U.S. representative from Michigan
1973 Appointed Vice President of the United States, at Spiro Agnew's resignation
1974–77 President of the United States at Nixon's resignation
1974, September Granted pardon to Nixon
1974 Offered conditional amnesty to Vietnam War draft evaders and deserters
1974 First American president to visit Japan
1975 Signed Helsinki Agreement, guaranteeing the European boundaries established after World War II

⬤39⬤
JIMMY CARTER
(1924–
President (1977–1981)

Born James Earl Carter, Jr. (he took the oath of office as "Jimmy"), Carter – a southern Democrat – vigorously supported the rights of blacks and women and all oppressed people throughout the world. His greatest triumph was the 1979 Middle East treaty, and his greatest defeat the Iran hostage crisis.

BIOGRAPHY
Date of birth: 1 October 1924
Place of birth: Plains, Georgia
Father: James Earl Carter, Sr. (1894–1953)
Mother: Lillian Gordy Carter (1898–1983)
Wife: Rosalynn Smith (1927–
Children: 4
Number of terms: 1
Age at inauguration: 52
Date of inauguration: 20 January 1977
Vice-President: Walter F. Mondale
Sec. of State: Cyrus R. Vance, Edmund S. Muskie
Sec. of Treasury: W. Michael Blumenthal, G. William Miller

HIGHLIGHTS
1946 Graduated from U.S. Military Academy at West Point

1946, 7 July Married Rosalynn Smith
1946–53 Served in U.S. Navy, rising to rank of lieutenant, senior grade
1963–67 Senator in Georgia legislature
1966 Unsuccessful candidate in primary election for governor of Georgia
1971–75 Governor of Georgia
1977–81 President of the United States
1977 Panama Canal Treaty, relinquishing Canal Zone to Panama
1978 Camp David accords, leading to Middle East peace treaty in 1979
1979 Established diplomatic relations with China
1979, 4 November American hostages held captive in Iran
1980 Defeated in bid for second term
1980-present Continues humanitarian work at Carter Center and Habitat for Humanity; author of memoirs, poetry, and fiction
2002 Awarded Nobel Peace Prize

⬤40⬤
RONALD REAGAN
(1911–2004)
President (1981–1989)

The oldest U.S. president on taking office, and the only president with "professional actor" on his resume, Reagan was called the Great Communicator. Cheerful, even-tempered, always optimistic, he achieved most of his domestic economic goals and signed an historic arms reduction treaty with the Soviet Union.

BIOGRAPHY
Date of birth: 6 February 1911
Place of birth: Tampico, Illinois
Father: John Edward Reagan (1883–1941)
Mother: Nelle Wilson Reagan (1885–1962)
Wife: (1) Jane Wyman (1914–); (2) Nancy Davis (1921–
Children: (1) 2; (2) 2
Date of death: 5 June 2004
Place of death: Bel Air, California
Burial: Simi Valley, California
Number of terms: 2

1975 → *SATURDAY NIGHT LIVE* PREMIERED ON TELEVISION.

1976 → 200TH ANNIVERSARY OF DECLARATION OF AMERICAN INDEPENDENCE.

1977 → APPLE COMPUTERS INTRODUCED THE FIRST COMMERCIAL PERSONAL COMPUTER.

1977 → ELVIS PRESLEY DIED AT AGE 42.

1977 → FIRST *STAR WARS* FILM PRODUCED.

1978 → FIRST "TEST TUBE BABY" BORN.

1979 → THREE MILE ISLAND NUCLEAR POWER PLANT OVERHEATED, CAUSING EVACUATION OVER A FIVE-MILE AREA.

1980 → JOHN LENNON SHOT AND KILLED BY MARK DAVID CHAPMAN IN NEW YORK CITY.

1983 → SALLY RIDE BECAME THE FIRST AMERICAN WOMAN TO TRAVEL IN SPACE.

1981 → SANDRA DAY O'CONNOR CONFIRMED AS FIRST WOMAN JUSTICE OF SUPREME COURT.

1983 → COMPACT DISCS INTRODUCED BY SONY AND PHILIPS.

1983 → INTERNET CREATED.

1986 → SPACE SHUTTLE *CHALLENGER* EXPLODED SECONDS AFTER TAKEOFF.

1987 → WALL STREET CRASH; STOCK MARKET DROPS 508 POINTS IN A SINGLE DAY (OCTOBER 19).

1987 → FIRST USE OF A DRUG, AZT, APPROVED TO FIGHT AIDS.

1988 → PAM AM FLIGHT 103 EXPLODED AND CRASHED IN LOCKERBIE, SCOTLAND.

Angelica Singleton
⚜ VAN BUREN ⚜
(1816–1877)
Acting First Lady (1838-1841)

Martin Van Buren had been a widower for almost twenty years when he became president. In 1838 when his son married, he called on his daughter-in-law Angelica to be his White House hostess. The parties became livelier, perhaps because Angelica called on Dolley Madison for advice. Angelica's lovely portrait by Henry Inman hangs in the White House.

> ❝ *Angelica Van Buren is a lady of rare accomplishments, very modest yet perfectly easy and graceful in her manners and free and vivacious in her conversation. She is universally admired.* ❞
> BOSTON POST, 1839

Anna Tuthill Symmes
⚜ HARRISON ⚜
(1775–1864)
First Lady (1841)

The wife of the 9th president and the grandmother of the 23rd president, Anna Harrison did not immediately accompany her husband to the White House. She sent her daughter-in-law, Jane Harrison, to attend the inauguration. While Anna remained in Ohio to prepare for her life as first lady, President Harrison suddenly died, just a month after taking office. The marriage was apparently a happy one, despite the fact that Anna outlived eight of their nine children.

BIOGRAPHY

Date of birth: 25 July 1775
Place of birth: Flatbrook, New Jersey
Father: John Cleves Symmes
Mother: Anna Tuthill Symmes
Husband: William Henry Harrison
Marriage: 25 November 1795
Children: Elizabeth Bassett, John Cleves Symmes, Lucy Singleton, William Henry, Jr., John Scott, Benjamin, Mary Symmes, Carter Bassett, Anna Tuthill
Date of death: 25 February 1864
Place of death: Morristown, New Jersey
Burial: North Bend, Ohio

> ❝ *I wish that my husband's friends had left him where he is, happy and contented in retirement.* ❞
> ANNA HARRISON, AT HARRISON'S ELECTION, 1840

Letitia Christian
⚜ TYLER ⚜
(1790–1842)
First Lady (1841–1842)

Julia Gardiner
⚜ TYLER ⚜
(1820–1889)
First Lady (1844–1845)

Married at age 22 to John Tyler, and mother of seven children, Letitia Christian Tyler at 51 was in failing health when her husband became president. She asked her daughter-in-law Priscilla Cooper Tyler to fill in, a role she relished. Letitia remained upstairs at the White House, coming down only once to her daughter's wedding in 1842. Later that year, Letitia died, the first first lady to die in the White House. Two years later, Tyler married Julia Gardiner, 24, having proposed at the 1843 George Washington's Ball. Lively and exuberant, Julia thoroughly enjoyed the duties of first lady and hosted a White House ball for 3,000 guests. She started the tradition of musicians greeting the president with "Hail to the Chief."

> ❝ *Nothing appears to delight the President more than...to hear people sing my praises.* ❞
> JULIA GARDINER TYLER

Sarah Childress
⚜ POLK ⚜
(1803–1891)
First Lady (1845–1849)

Well educated for a woman of her time, Sarah Polk, like Abigail Adams, was a full partner in her husband's career. She cultivated a strong network of achieving women, even those who opposed her husband politically. She also enjoyed her social role, though she banned dancing and liquor at White House receptions. She survived her husband by 42 years and never remarried.

> ❝ *If I get to the White House, I expect to live on $25,000 a year and I will neither keep house nor make butter.* ❞
> SARAH POLK, RESPONDING TO REMARK THAT OPPONENT HENRY CLAY'S WIFE MADE GOOD BUTTER AND KEPT A GOOD HOUSE.

BIOGRAPHY

Date of birth: 4 September 1803
Place of birth: Murfreesboro, Tennessee
Father: Joel Childress
Mother: Elizabeth Whitsitt Childress
Husband: James Knox Polk
Marriage: 1 January 1824
Children: none
Date of death: 14 August 1891
Place of death: Nashville, Tennessee
Burial: Nashville, Tennessee

HIGHLIGHTS:

1816 Attended Moravian Female Academy, Salem, North Carolina, the best girls' school in the South
1824 1 January Married James K. Polk at her family's plantation home in Tennessee
1825–41 Congressman's wife during three presidents' administrations
1829–31 Supported social ostracism of Peggy Eaton during Jackson's first term
1845 ca. Hosted first annual Thanksgiving dinner at White House
1849 Retired with former president to Nashville, Tennessee

Dolley Payne Todd MADISON

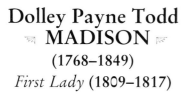

(1768–1849)

First Lady (1809–1817)

A vivacious beauty, Dolley Madison charmed the capital as official hostess in both Jefferson's and her husband's administrations. She oversaw the remodeling of the White House, and during the War of 1812 she saved its treasures, notably a Gilbert Stuart portrait of George Washington.

> ❝ *I am still here within sound of the cannon! Mr. Madison comes not; may God protect him! Two messengers covered with dust come to bid me fly; but I wait for him.*❞
> DOLLEY MADISON, LETTER FROM THE WHITE HOUSE TO HER SISTER, 1814

BIOGRAPHY

Date of birth: 29 May 1768
Place of birth: New Garden Quaker Settlement, North Carolina
Father: John Payne
Mother: Mary Coles Payne
Husband: (1) John Todd; (2) James Madison
Marriage: (1) 1790; (2) 15 September 1794
Children: (1) John Payne
Date of death: 12 July 1849
Place of death: Washington, D.C.
Burial: Washington, D.C; later Montpelier, Virginia

HIGHLIGHTS

1790 Married John Todd; he died of yellow fever in 1793
1794, May Introduced to Congressman James Madison by friend Aaron Burr
1794, 15 September Married Madison, a non-Quaker; Dolley expelled from Society of Friends
1797 Moved to Montpelier, Madison's Virginia plantation
1801–1809 Served as official hostess during terms of Thomas Jefferson, a widower
1809 Oversaw remodeling of the White House
1814 White House burned; Madisons move to

Octagon House during three-year restoration
1817 Retired with President to Montpelier, Virginia
1836 Moved back to Washington at Madison's death
1849 Attended her last White House party given by President Polk, just months before her death

Elizabeth Kortwright MONROE

(1768–1830)

First Lady (1817–1825)

Unlike her predecessor Dolley Madison, Elizabeth Monroe insisted on privacy and refused the hostess role in the White House. A statuesque beauty, called "la belle Americaine" when she lived in Paris, she helped secure the release of Lafayette's wife from prison during the Reign of Terror.

BIOGRAPHY

Date of birth: 30 June 1768
Place of birth: New York City
Father: Laurence Kortwright
Mother: Hannah Aspinwall Kortright
Husband: James Monroe
Marriage: 16 February 1786
Children: Eliza, Maria Hester
Date of death: 23 September 1830
Place of death: Oak Hill, Loudoun County, Virginia
Burial: Oak Hill; later Richmond, Virginia

> ❝ *Her dress was superb black velvet; neck and arms bare and beautifully formed; her hair in puffs and dressed high on the head and ornamented with white ostrich plumes; around her neck an elegant pearl necklace. Though no longer young, she is still a very handsome woman.*❞
> GUEST'S DESCRIPTION OF ELIZABETH MONROE AT NEW YEAR'S DAY RECEPTION, 1825

Louisa Catherine Johnson ADAMS

(1775–1852)

First Lady (1825–1829)

The only foreign-born first lady, Louisa Johnson grew up in London and in Nantes, France where her family took refuge during the American Revolution. She first met her future husband in France on a trip with his father, John Adams. As first lady she planted a variety of trees and shrubs on the White House grounds, experimenting to find a suitable climate for silkworms.

BIOGRAPHY

Date of birth: 12 February 1775
Place of birth: London, England
Father: Joshua Johnson
Mother: Catherine Nuth Johnson
Husband: John Quincy Adams
Marriage: 26 July 1797
Children: George Washington, John II, Charles Francis
Date of death: 15 May 1852
Place of death: Washington, D.C.
Burial: Quincy, Massachusetts

HIGHLIGHTS

1797 Married John Quincy Adams, a foreign minister during his father's presidency, in London
1801 Moved to America when Adams elected Massachusetts state senator
1809-25 Lived periodically in Berlin, St. Petersburg, and Paris with husband on diplomatic business
1813 Infant daughter died in Russia
1814 Traveled 40 days through war-ravaged Europe with eight-year-old son from St. Petersburg to join husband in Paris
1824, 8 January Hosted Ball to General Jackson at White House
1825 Hosted Lafayette during his U.S. visit.

Note: Rachel Donelson Robards Jackson died in 1828, the year before Andrew Jackson acceded to the presidency. Emily Donelson, his wife's niece, acted as first lady.

My view is that President Gorbachev is different from previous Soviet leaders....I want the new closeness to continue...as long as they continue to act in a helpful manner. If and when they don't, then first pull your punches. If they persist, pull the plug. It's still trust but verify; it's still play but cut the cards."

RONALD REAGAN, FAREWELL ADDRESS, 1989

Age at first inauguration: 69
Date of inaugurations: 20 January 1981; 21 January 1985
Vice-President: George H.W. Bush
Sec. of State: Alexander M. Haig, Jr., George P. Shultz
Sec. of Treasury: Donald T. Regan, James A. Baker III, Nicholas Brady

HIGHLIGHTS

1932 Graduated from Eureka College, Illinois
1934 Radio sports announcer in Des Moines, Iowa
1937 Hollywood screen test and first movie offer, Love Is on the Air
1937–65 Actor and president of Screen Actors Guild
1940, 25 January Married actress Jane Wyman; divorced in 1948
1942–45 Captain in U.S. Army Air Force
1952, 4 March Married Nancy Davis
1967–75 Governor of California
1981–89 President of the United States
1981, 30 March Wounded in assassination attempt
1982–87 "Reaganomics" program – the longest economic expansion in peacetime since World War II
1983–88 Terrorist attacks against U.S. and western nations
1985 Iran-Contra scandal
1983 Grenada invasion
1985–88 Series of summit meetings with Soviet leader Gorbachev on nuclear arms reduction

What I'd really like to do is go down in history as the President who made Americans believe in themselves again."

RONALD REAGAN, 1981

↜41↝
GEORGE HERBERT WALKER BUSH
(1924-
President (1989–1993)

Despite a sluggish economy and unfilled promises on the domestic front, Bush earned respect even from critics for his leadership in foreign policy. He signed major nuclear disarmament treaties and presided over the end of the Cold War and the collapse of Communism and the Soviet Union.

BIOGRAPHY

Date of birth: 12 June 1924
Place of birth: Milton, Massachusetts
Father: Prescott S. Bush (1895–1972)
Mother: Dorothy Walker Bush (1901–92)
Wife: Barbara Pierce (1925–
Children: 6
Number of terms: 1
Age at inauguration: 64
Date of inauguration: 20 January 1989
Vice-President: J. Danforth "Dan" Quayle
Sec. of State: James A. Baker III, Lawrence Eagleburger
Sec. of Treasury: Nicolas F. Brady

HIGHLIGHTS

1942–45 Served in U.S. Navy in World War II, receiving Distinguished Flying Cross
1945, 6 January Married Barbara Pierce
1948 Graduated from Yale College
1948–66 Oil businessman in Texas, forming own company in 1951
1966 Elected U.S. representative from Texas
1971–72 U.S. Ambassador to United Nations
1974–75 Chief, U.S. Liaison Office in Beijing, China
1976–77 Director, Central Intelligence Agency
1981–89 Vice President of the United States
1989–83 President of the United States
1989 Tiananmen Square demonstration, Beijing, China
1989–90 Invasion of Panama and capture of Noriega
1989–92 End of the Cold War and collapse of Communism in eastern Europe and Soviet Union
1990–91 Persian Gulf War
1992 Sent U.S. troops to aid Somalia
1992–93 Signed two nuclear missile agreements with Boris Yeltsin of the new Republic of Russia

...a brilliant diversity spread like stars, like a thousand points of light in a broad and peaceful sky."
GEORGE H.W. BUSH, REFERRING TO THE NATION IN ACCEPTANCE SPEECH AT REPUBLICAN CONVENTION, 1988

↜42↝
WILLIAM JEFFERSON CLINTON
(1946–)
President (1993–2001)

One of the brightest and most empathetic politicians, Clinton presided over the longest peacetime economic expansion in U.S. history. His unprecedented popular approval ratings survived his personal indiscretions and an impeachment trial.

BIOGRAPHY

Date of birth: 19 August 1946
Place of birth: Hope, Arkansas
Father: William Jefferson Blythe, III (1917–46)
Mother: Virginia Cassidy Blythe Clinton (1923–94)
Wife: Hillary Rodham (1947–
Children: 1
Number of terms: 2
Age at first inauguration: 46

1989 → TANKER *EXXON VALDEZ* RAN AGROUND OFF COAST OF ALASKA, CAUSING WORST OIL SPILL IN U.S. HISTORY.

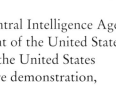

Exxon Valdez

1989 → BERLIN WALL COMES DOWN.

1989 → TEENAGE MUTANT NINJA TURTLES.

1992 → FIRST EARTH SUMMIT IN RIO DE JANEIRO WITH DELEGATES FROM 153 COUNTRIES.

1993 → A BOMB EXPLODED BENEATH THE WORLD TRADE CENTER, KILLING SIX PEOPLE (26 FEBRUARY).

1993 → FBI OFFICERS STORM BRANCH DAVIDIAN COMPOUND AT WACO TEXAS. 76 DEAD.

1993 → GUN-CONTROL LEGISLATION ("BRADY BILL") SIGNED INTO LAW.

1995 → OKLAHOMA CITY BOMBING. 168 DEAD.

1995 → "MILLION MAN MARCH" AND RALLY IN WASHINGTON DC.

1998 → TERRORIST BOMBS KILL AT LEAST 257 IN U.S. EMBASSIES IN KENYA AND TANZANIA.

1997 → PRINCESS DIANA KILLED IN CAR CRASH IN PARIS (31 AUGUST).

1999 → COLUMBINE HIGH SCHOOL MASSACRE.

1999 → JOHN F. KENNEDY, JR. DIED IN A PLANE CRASH WITH HIS WIFE AND SISTER-IN-LAW.

> *We're now at the end of a century when generation after generation of Americans answered the call to greatness, overcoming Depression, lifting up the dispossessed, bringing down barriers to racial prejudice, building the largest middle class in history, winning two world wars and the 'long twilight struggle' of the Cold War."*
>
> BILL CLINTON, STATE OF THE UNION ADDRESS, 19 DECEMBER 1999

Date of inaugurations: 20 January 1993; 20 January 1997
Vice-President: Albert Gore, Jr.
Sec. of State: Warren M. Christopher, Madeleine K. Albright
Sec. of Treasury: Lloyd M. Bentsen, Robert E. Rubin, Lawrence H. Summers

HIGHLIGHTS

1968 Graduated from Georgetown University
1968–70 Attended Oxford University, England, as Rhodes Scholar
1973 Graduated from Yale Law School
1973–76 Taught at University of Arkansas at Fayetteville
1975, 11 October Married Hillary Rodham
1976 Elected Attorney General of Arkansas
1979–81; 1983–92 Governor of Arkansas for five terms
1993–2001 President of the United States
1993 Whitewater affair investigations began
1993 Health care reform bill defeated
1993–94 North American Free Trade Agreement (NAFTA) and General Agreement on Tariffs and Trade (GATT) passed
1995 Oklahoma City federal building bombed
1995–96 Intervened in Bosnia conflict
1997 Balanced budget plan signed
1998 Monica Lewinsky scandal; Clinton testified before federal grand jury
1998 Middle East agreement signed between Palestine and Israel
1998, 19 December Congress voted to impeach Clinton
1999, 12 February Senate voted to acquit Clinton
1999 Kosovo bombed; peace treaty signed
1999 Financial Reform bill signed
2000 Breakdown of talks between Palestine and Israel at Camp David

⁘43⁘
GEORGE WALKER BUSH
(1946–
President (2001–2009)

After a tumultuous first term, George Bush won re-election in 2004, defeating John Kerry in one of the largest voter turnouts in American history. On 9/11/01, just eight months into his first term – which he had won largely on a domestic platform – George Bush became a war president. Dedicating himself to defeating global terrorism, he attacked the Taliban in Afghanistan and invaded Iraq. The decision to invade Iraq became an important issue in the 2004 election.

> *All of this was brought upon us in a single day, and night fell on a different world."*
>
> GEORGE W. BUSH, 20 SEPTEMBER 2001

Nine-eleven was the defining moment for President Bush.

BIOGRAPHY

Date of birth: 6 July 1946
Place of birth: New Haven, Connecticut
Father: George Herbert Walker Bush (1924-
Mother: Barbara Pierce Bush (1925-
Wife: Laura Welch (1946-
Children: 2
Number of terms: 2
Age at first inauguration: 54
Date of inaugurations: 20 January 2001; 20 January 2005
Vice-President: Richard Cheney
Sec. of State: Colin L. Powell, Dr Condoleezza Rice
Sec. of Treasury: Paul H. O'Neill; John W. Snow

> *Great harm has been done to us. We have suffered great loss. And in our grief and anger we have found our mission and our moment."*
>
> GEORGE W. BUSH, SEPTEMBER 2001

HIGHLIGHTS

1968 Graduated from Yale College
1968-73 Served in the Texas Air National Guard
1975 Graduated from Harvard Business School
1977, 5 November Married Laura Welch
1978 Defeated in election to U. S. House of Representatives
1989-93 Managing Partner, Texas Rangers baseball team
1995-2000 Governor of Texas
2001, 7 November Election Day; no clear winner in presidential contest with Al Gore
2001, 13 December Formally accepted the presidency after Supreme Court ruling against a manual recount of votes
2001, 20 January Inaugurated President
2001, 11 September World Trade Center attack
2002, 25 November Created new cabinet-level Department of Homeland Security
2003, 28 January Presented Case for War in Iraq in second State of the Union speech
2003 19 March Declared war with Iraq
2003, 28 May Signed $350 billion tax cut, the third-largest in U.S. history
2003, September Called for revision of Patriot Act
2003, 8 December Medicare bill signed covering prescription drugs
2003, 13 December Saddam Hussein captured
2004, 28 June Bush administration handed over power to Iraqis
2004, July Publication of 9/11 Commission Report
2004, 2 November Re-elected to a second term

2001 ⁘ 11 SEPTEMBER TWO HIJACKED AIRPLANES STRUCK AND DESTROYED BOTH TOWERS OF THE WORLD TRADE CENTER, THE WORST ATTACK EVER ON AMERICAN SOIL. A THIRD PLANE STRUCK THE PENTAGON, AND A FOURTH CRASHED IN PENNSYLVANIA.

2001 ⁘ ENRON FILED FOR BANKRUPTCY.

2001 ⁘ EXPOSURE TO ANTHRAX IN U.S. MAIL KILLED FIVE PEOPLE.

2001 ⁘ ARTIFICIAL LIVER INVENTED.

2002 ⁘ WILDFIRES CONSUMED LARGE AREAS IN WESTERN STATES.

2001 ⁘ SELF-CLEANING WINDOWS (PPG INDUSTRIES).

2002 ⁘ RANDOM SNIPER SHOOTINGS IN WASHINGTON, D.C. AREA. JOHN ALLEN MUHAMMAD AND JOHN LEE MALVO CONVICTED IN 2003.

2002 ⁘ WORLDCOM FILED FOR BANKRUPTCY.

2003 ⁘ SPACE SHUTTLE *COLUMBIA* DISINTEGRATED, KILLING 7 ASTRONAUTS (3 FEBRUARY).

2003 ⁘ THE IRAQ WAR STARTS (19 MARCH).

2003 ⁘ BIGGEST BLACKOUT EVER TO HIT NORTH AMERICA (14 AUGUST).

Martha Dandridge Custis
☞ WASHINGTON ☜
(1731–1802)
First Lady (1789–1797)

When she married George Washington, Martha Custis was a widow and a wealthy Virginia landowner with two children. During the Revolution she joined her husband each winter at field headquarters. Hailed as "Lady Washington," she hosted formal receptions in both New York and Philadelphia during Washington's presidency.

BIOGRAPHY
Date of birth: 21 June 1731
Place of birth: New Kent County, Virginia
Father: John Dandridge
Mother: Frances Jones Dandridge
Husband: (1) Daniel Parke Custis; (2) George Washington
Marriage: (1) 1749; (2) 6 January 1759
Children: (1) John Parke Custis, Martha Parke Custis
Date of death: 22 May 1802
Place of death: Mount Vernon, Virginia
Burial: Mount Vernon, Virginia

HIGHLIGHTS
1749 Married Daniel Parke Custis; he died in 1757

> ❝ *I cannot blame him [Washington] for having acted according to his ideas of duty in obeying the voice of his country.... I am still determined to be cheerful and happy, in whatever situation I may be; for I have also learned from experience that the greater part of our happiness or misery depends upon our dispositions, and not upon our circumstances.*❞
> MARTHA WASHINGTON, IN A LETTER TO A FRIEND

> ❝ *I suppose, Mr. Washington, you think people are going to take every grist from you as pure grain; but what would you have been if you hadn't married the rich widow Custis!*❞
> DAVID BURNS, PROPERTY OWNER, TO PRESIDENT GEORGE WASHINGTON

1759, 6 January Married George Washington, a member of the Virginia House of Burgesses
1759–1789 Lived at Mount Vernon, Virginia
1789, 30 April George Washington inaugurated first president of the United States
1789, May Arrived by presidential barge in New York City, the nation's temporary capital, to settle in rented house on Cherry Street
1789–1797 As president's wife, hosted formal events, and a weekly "drawing room" party, in New York and Philadelphia
1790, 1 January Held first New Year's reception, beginning a tradition that continued until Hoover's term in 1933
1790 Moved to Market Street in Philadelphia, the nation's new capital
1797 Washingtons retired from public life and returned to Mount Vernon
1799 At Washington's death, Congress granted Martha the franking privilege which she used until her death in 1802

Abigail Smith
☞ ADAMS ☜
(1744–1818)
First Lady (1797–1801)

Wife of one president and mother of another, Abigail Adams became one of the most learned first ladies. Her writings – in their volume and literary quality—are unsurpassed by those of any other American woman of her time. Her husband John Adams, her "dearest Friend," respected her opinions and in frequent letters they remained in touch through long separations. When Washington became the nation's capital in 1800, Abigail – called "Mrs. President"– became the first president's wife to live in the White House.

> ❝ *I never wanted your advice and assistance more in my life. The times are critical and I must have you here to assist me...I can do nothing without you.*❞
> JOHN ADAMS IN A LETTER TO HIS WIFE, ABIGAIL

BIOGRAPHY
Date of birth: 23 November 1744
Place of birth: Weymouth, Massachusetts
Father: Reverend William Smith
Mother: Elizabeth Quincy Smith
Husband: John Adams (1735-1826)
Marriage: 25 October 1764
Children: Abigail, John Quincy, Charles, Thomas Boylston
Date of death: 28 October 1818
Place of death: Quincy, Massachusetts
Burial: United First Parish Church, Quincy, Massachusetts

HIGHLIGHTS
1764, 25 October Married John Adams at her parent's home, Weymouth, Massachusetts
1764 The couple moved to John's home in Braintree (now Quincy), Massachusetts
1784–85 Lived in Auteuil, France, when Adams was diplomat in Paris
1785–88 Lived in London when Adams was Ambassador to Court of St. James
1797 Moved to capital in Philadelphia on Adams' inauguration as president
1800 Became first president's wife to live in White House (then called the President's House) when the capital moved to Washington D.C.
1801 Returned home to Massachusetts until her death in 1818

> ❝ *Remember the ladies and be more generous and favorable to them than your ancestors!*❞
> ABIGAIL ADAMS IN A LETTER TO HER HUSBAND, JOHN, 1776

Note: Thomas Jefferson became president (1801) after his wife, Martha Wayles Skelton Jefferson, died giving birth to their sixth child, Lucy Elizabeth, in 1782. He was devastated, and wrote two months later that he was "...emerging from the stupor of mind which had rendered me as dead to the world as [she] was whose...loss occasioned it."

The
TIMECHART
of
PRESIDENTS
& FIRST LADIES

HISTORY OF THE PRESIDENTS • THE WHITE HOUSE • ASSASSINATIONS & NEAR MISSES •

MILITARY PRESIDENTS • PETS • SPORTS & PASTIMES • CHILDHOOD • FIRSTS & LASTS

Thomas Jefferson leaving for his inauguration, 1801.

James Madison in his twenties when he was contributing to Virginia's constitution.

Admiral Perry's victory of the British on Lake Erie, 10 September 1813.

James Monroe in the 1820s, still dressed in the old-fashioned clothes of an earlier era.

wilderness, the President's House far from completion.

The Adams retired to Quincy in 1801, and for 17 years enjoyed the companionship that public life had long denied them. Abigail died in 1818. On July 4, 1826, John Adams whispered his last words: "Thomas Jefferson survives." But Jefferson had died at Monticello a few hours earlier.

Thomas Jefferson

Thomas Jefferson was born in 1743 in Albemarle County, Virginia, inheriting land from his father and social standing from his mother. He attended the College of William and Mary, and later studied law.

In 1772 he married a widow, Martha Wayles Skelton, and they lived in his partly constructed mountaintop home, Monticello. Throughout their ten years of marriage, they appear to have been totally devoted. Seven pregnancies weakened Martha and she died giving birth to her last child. Two daughters lived to maturity. Jefferson never remarried.

As a powerful prose stylist and an influential Virginia representative, Jefferson, at 33, was chosen to draft the Declaration of Independence – a document that is a brilliant assertion of fundamental human rights and America's most succinct statement of its philosophy of government.

He served as minister to France in 1785, and Secretary of State in President Washington's cabinet, resigning in 1793.

When Jefferson became president (1801), the crisis in France was over. He slashed military expenditures, cut the budget, eliminated a whiskey tax, and reduced the national debt. He sent a naval force to Tripoli in North Africa to fight the Barbary pirates who were harassing American ships in the Mediterranean.

In 1803, Jefferson acquired the Louisiana Territory from Napoleon – land comprising 15 present-day states from Louisiana to Montana. Even before the Louisiana Purchase, Jefferson had wanted to explore the vast expanse between the Missouri River and the Pacific Ocean. Now with that territory in U.S. hands, he commissioned his private secretary Meriwether Lewis and William Clark to lead the expedition. It was a two-year, 8,000 mile trek, ascending the Missouri, crossing the Continental Divide, along the Columbia River to the Pacific.

In 1809, Jefferson retired to Monticello to design and direct the construction of the University of Virginia. After a long and fascinating correspondence with John Adams while both men were in the twilight of their lives, Jefferson died on July 4, 1826. Adams died on the same day, exactly fifty years after the signing of the Declaration of Independence.

James Madison

A native Virginian, well-educated in history and law, James Madison helped frame the Virginia

Constitution in 1776, and at age 29, served in the Continental Congress. An emphatic debater at the Constitutional Convention and co-author of the Federalist Papers, Madison earned the title "Father of the Constitution."

In 1794 he married Dolley Payne Todd, a widow with a young son. The marriage, though childless, was happy – "our hearts understand each other," Dolley said. For half a century, she was the most important woman in the social circles of America.

At the start of Madison's administration (1809), the U.S. had a trade embargo with both Britain and France. The next year, Madison urged Congress to pass a law stating that if either country would accept America's neutral rights, he would forbid trade with the other. Napoleon complied, and Madison suspended trade with Britain.

The British seizure of American seamen and cargoes impelled Madison to give in to the war hawks in Congress. On June 1, 1812 he asked for a declaration of war. It began disastrously for America; its forces were unprepared. The British entered Washington and set fire to the White House and the Capitol. But a few notable military victories, climaxed by General Andrew Jackson's triumph at New Orleans, fueled the idea that the War of 1812 had been gloriously successful. With both Britain and America war weary, the Treaty of Ghent ended the conflict in 1814, with neither side the victor.

However, the War of 1812, often called the Second War of Independence, marked the end of American economic dependence on Britain. Domestic industry prospered and America took its first steps from a largely farming to an industrial nation.

In retirement at Montpelier, his Virginia estate, Madison spoke out against the issue of states rights that threatened to shatter the Union. He wrote, "The advice nearest to my heart and deepest in my convictions is that the Union of the States be cherished and perpetuated."

James Monroe

Born in Westmoreland County, Virginia, in 1758, James Monroe attended the College of William and Mary, fought with distinction in the Continental Army, and later studied law under Thomas Jefferson.

As a young politician, he was a member of the Virginia Assembly, the Continental Congress, and in 1790, a United States Senator. As Minister to France in 1794–96, he displayed strong sympathies for the French cause; later, he helped negotiate the Louisiana Purchase.

Monroe's wife Elizabeth accompanied her husband to France, arriving in Paris in the midst of the French Revolution, and she played a dramatic role in saving Lafayette's wife from the guillotine.

Early in his administration (1817), Monroe undertook a good will tour, beginning what was called the "Era of Good Feelings."

Unfortunately, these feelings did not last. Beneath the façade of nationalism, there was sectional unrest. The people of the Missouri Territory applied and failed for admission to the Union as a slave state. The Missouri Compromise bill resolved the struggle, naming Missouri a slave state and Maine a free state, and prohibited slavery north and west of Missouri forever.

In foreign affairs Monroe responded to the threat that Europe might try to aid Spain in regaining her former Latin American colonies. Not only must Latin America be left alone, Monroe said, but "the American continents…are henceforth not to be considered as subjects for future colonization by any European Power." Some 20 years after Monroe died (4 July 1831) this became known as the Monroe Doctrine, and it remained the cornerstone of American foreign policy for the rest of the 19th century.

John Quincy Adams

John Quincy Adams, the son of John Adams, was born in Braintree (now Quincy), Massachusetts in 1767, graduated from Harvard College and became a lawyer. At age 26 he was appointed minister to the Netherlands. While abroad, he met his future wife, Louisa Johnson, born in London to an English mother—our only first lady born outside the United States.

Adams served as Senator, Minister to Russia, and later, under President Monroe, a gifted Secretary of State. He fixed the present US-Canadian border from Minnesota to the Rockies, obtained the territory of Florida from Spain, and helped formulate the Monroe Doctrine.

Elected president in 1824, Adams announced an ambitious national program. He proposed a network of roads and canals to link the country. He also urged Congress to lead in developing the arts and sciences through a national university, to finance scientific expeditions, and to erect an observatory. With little support from Congress or the people, Adams did not achieve his program.

Badly defeated by Andrew Jackson for a second term, Adams returned to Massachusetts. Unexpectedly, in 1830, he was elected to the House of Representatives, and there for the rest of his life he served as a powerful leader.

Andrew Jackson

Born in a frontier log cabin in the Carolinas in 1767, Andrew Jackson received a meager education. In his late teens he studied law; in his spare time he gambled, drank, chased women, and took dancing lessons. Fiercely jealous of his honor, he killed a man in a duel over an

The ailing 78-year-old Andrew Jackson on 15 April 1845.

unjustified slur about his wife Rachel (Rachel died in 1828, just as she and the President-elect were preparing for his inauguration.)

Jackson was the first man elected from Tennessee to the House of Representatives; then he served briefly in the Senate. A major general in the War of 1812, Jackson became a national hero when he defeated the British at New Orleans.

Jackson defeated Adams for the presidency in 1828, and was re-elected to a second term in 1832. Like George Washington, Jackson combined the art of a seasoned politician with the decision-making ability of a successful general. Unlike his predecessors, Jackson did not defer to Congress in policy-making but used the power of his veto and his party to command.

The greatest party battle concerned what Jackson called "the Monster"—the Bank of the United States, virtually a government-sponsored monopoly. Jackson opposed it and the American voters backed him.

A firm believer in preserving the Union, there was no serious talk of secession under Jackson's rule. He pledged to reduce the national debt, and in 1835 he did so, the first time in the nation's history.

At age 78, "Old Hickory" died at the Hermitage, his home in Nashville. His last words to the members of his household: "I hope to see you all in Heaven, both white and black, both white and black."

Martin Van Buren

Of Dutch descent, Martin Van Buren was born in 1782, the son of a tavern keeper and farmer, in Kinderhook, New York. His formal education ended at age 14 when he became a legal apprentice.

A contemporary caricature of Martin Van Buren as an opossum.

In 1807 he married his childhood sweetheart, Hannah Hoes. She died of tuberculosis just ten years later.

In a span of twelve years, Van Buren served as senator, governor of New York, secretary of state, vice president, and president. Just two months after his inauguration, in 1837, hundreds of banks and businesses failed. Thousands lost their lands – the worst depression in the country's history to that date. Van Buren's support was ruined, though he was not responsible for the crisis.

When Texas applied for statehood, Van Buren opposed it, believing it would expand slavery and lead to war with Mexico.

Van Buren was defeated for a second term and again as a candidate for president in 1848. He died at age 79 at Lindenwald, his New York home.

The stubbornly independent John Quincy Adams: "I am a man of reserved, cold, austere, and forbidding manners…."

After his inaugural Andrew Jackson threw open the White House to the public – it quickly degenerated into a rout.

William Harrison died only a month into his presidency, the shortest in American history.

> *His manner was remarkably unaffected. I thought that in his whole carriage he became his station well."*
> CHARLES DICKENS, AT THE WHITE HOUSE, 1842 (OF TYLER)

President John Tyler was aboard the frigate Princeton *when an experimental gun exploded. By a stroke of luck he was below decks at the time.*

> *The Mississippi, so lately the frontier of our country, is now only its center...."*
> JAMES K. POLK, STATE OF THE UNION MESSAGE, 1848

General Zachary Taylor at the battle of Buena Vista, 23 February 1847.

William Henry Harrison

Born into the Virginia planter aristocracy, William Henry Harrison studied classics and history at Hampden-Sydney College, then studied medicine under Dr. Benjamin Rush in Philadelphia.

In 1791, Harrison embarked on a military/political career highlighted by the Indian wars in the Northwest Territory, delegate to Congress, governor of Indiana Territory, general in the War of 1812, and U.S. senator.

Harrison was elected president in 1840. But before he had been in office a month, he caught a cold that developed into pneumonia. On April 4, 1841 he died—the first president to die in office, ending the shortest term in American history. Because of her husband's sudden death, his wife Anna never occupied the White House. She outlived him by 23 years.

John Tyler

Called "His Accidency" by his opponents, John Tyler was the first vice president to attain the White House by the death of his predecessor. His first presidential decision was his most important. He had himself sworn in immediately, thus paving the way for future orderly transfers of power after the deaths of presidents while in office.

Born into a prosperous Virginia family in 1790, Tyler graduated from the College of William and Mary, studied law, and served Virginia as representative, governor, and senator.

On domestic issues he relied heavily on his veto power, resulting in 1843 in the first impeachment resolution against a president. The resolution failed.

Tyler, a states'-righter, strengthened the presidency, but he also increased sectional differences that led toward civil war. When the first southern states seceded, Tyler led a compromise movement; failing, he worked to create the Southern Confederacy. He died in 1862, a member of the Confederate House of Representatives.

Tyler's first marriage, to Letitia Christian, lasted almost 30 years. She died just a year after Tyler became president. His second wife, Julia Gardiner, captivated Washington with glittering White House receptions. Tyler had 14 children to live to maturity.

James K. Polk

James K. Polk was born on a farm in Mecklenburg County, North Carolina, in 1795. Studious and industrious, Polk graduated with honors from the University of North Carolina. As a young lawyer he entered politics, served in the Tennessee legislature, and became a protégé of Andrew Jackson.

In 1824 he married Sarah Childress, a politically astute partner to her husband and a charming though strait-laced first lady. She appeared at the inaugural ball, but did not dance.

In the House of Representatives, Polk was a chief supporter of Jackson in his attack on the

A popular lithograph of James K. Polk, who said of the presidency: "I am heartily rejoiced that my term is so near its close. I will soon cease to be a servant and will become a sovereign."

Bank of the U.S. He served as speaker until 1839, leaving to become governor of Tennessee.

In 1844 Jackson, correctly sensing that America favored expansion, urged the choice of a presidential candidate committed to "Manifest Destiny"—the desire to own the continent from coast to coast. Polk, though the dark-horse candidate, won the election.

Even before he could take office, Congress passed a resolution offering annexation to Texas, raising the possibility of war with Mexico. And Polk himself seemed to be risking war with Britain in his stand on the Oregon Territory. He at first would settle for nothing less than the entire region but agreed to a compromise, granting to the U.S. the present states of Washington and Oregon.

Acquisition of the southwest territory from Mexico proved far more difficult. To bring pressure, Polk sent General Zachary Taylor to the disputed area on the Rio Grande River. To Mexico, this was aggression, and they attacked. Congress declared war and although outnumbered, American forces won repeated victories and occupied Mexico City. Finally, in 1848, Mexico ceded all or part of modern California, Nevada, Utah, Wyoming, Colorado, Texas, New Mexico, and Arizona.

Polk added more than 500,000 square miles to the nation, but its acquisition began a bitter quarrel between the North and the South over the expansion of slavery.

Leaving office in poor health in March 1849, Polk died three months later.

Zachary Taylor

Born in Virginia in 1784, Zachary Taylor grew up in Kentucky, a southern slave-owner at the edge of the western frontier. But Taylor did not defend slavery or southern sectionalism; 40 years in the army made him a strong nationalist.

In 1810, Taylor married Margaret Smith, daughter of a prosperous Maryland planter. For 40 years, Margaret accompanied her husband to frontier posts across the country, often tending the sick and wounded. She gave birth to six children, three of whom survived. As first lady, Margaret Taylor took no part in formal social functions, relying on her daughter Betty to act as hostess.

During Taylor's short term as president (1849–50) northerners and southerners argued whether the new Mexican territories should be opened to slavery. Some southerners even threatened secession. Standing firm, Taylor was prepared to hold the Union together by armed force rather than by compromise.

Taylor laid the cornerstone of the Washington Monument on a blistering July 4, 1850. He fell ill; within five days he was dead. After his death, the forces of compromise triumphed, but the war Taylor had been willing to face came 11 years later.

Millard Fillmore

Millard Fillmore, 13th president. "In the North I was charged with being a pro-slavery man...and in the South I was accused of being an abolitionist. But I am neither."

Born in the Finger Lakes region of New York in 1800, Millard Fillmore worked on his father's farm, attended one-room schools and, at 19, fell in love with his redheaded teacher, Abigail Powers, who later became his wife.

A lawyer, a state and federal Congressman, then vice president, Fillmore became president at Zachary Taylor's death in 1850.

The Compromise of 1850 dominated Fillmore's three years in office. A supporter despite his anti-slavery views, Fillmore signed the bill into law. It provided for:

- Admission of California as a free state.
- Settlement of the Texas borders.
- Territorial status to New Mexico and Utah.
- The Fugitive Slave Act, requiring the government to aid in recovering runaway slaves.
- Abolishment of the slave trade in the District of Columbia.

The Compromise favored southern slave interests and fatally divided Fillmore's supporters. Denied re-nomination for a second term, Fillmore lost both his wife and daughter the next year, and later remarried. He died in 1874.

Franklin Pierce

Born in Hillsboro, New Hampshire, in 1804, Franklin Pierce attended private schools and graduated from Bowdoin College, where he made a lifelong friend, the writer Nathaniel Hawthorne. Pierce studied law, served in the New Hampshire legislature, then went to Washington as a representative and a senator. In 1834 he married Jane Means Appleton.

After serving in the Mexican War, Pierce won the Democratic nomination and the presidency. Two months before he took office, the Pierces saw their 11-year-old son Bennie killed—the only fatality of a train accident. The Pierces had already lost two sons in infancy. Pierce was devastated; his wife did not attend his inauguration or any White House affair for two years.

Pierce became president at a time of apparent tranquility, but he misjudged his times. Although a New Englander, he ignored the abolitionists. And when he signed the Kansas-Nebraska Act and the repeal of the Missouri Compromise, he let loose a storm that made slavery a greater national issue than ever before, and hastened the disruption of the Union.

Internationally, Pierce encouraged the expansion of trade. The ports of Japan were opened in 1854 in a treaty negotiated by Commodore Matthew Perry.

Refused the re-nomination, Pierce returned to New Hampshire, leaving his successor to face the rising storm. He died in 1869.

James Buchanan

Born in a log cabin near Mercersburg, Pennsylvania, in 1791, Buchanan graduated from Dickinson College. He was elected five times to the House of Representatives, was minister to Russia, a senator, Polk's secretary of state, and Pierce's minister to Britain.

Taking office as president in 1857, Buchanan presided over a rapidly dividing nation. Like Pierce, a northern Democrat, he favored southern interests. He supported Kansas' admission as a slave state, infuriating the North and splitting his party. In 1859, antislavery zealot John Brown was hanged for treason after capturing the federal arsenal at Harpers Ferry, Virginia. In the last months of his term, seven southern states seceded from the Union, forming the Confederate States of America under Jefferson Davis.

Buchanan, our only president who never married, retired to Pennsylvania in 1861 and died seven years later, leaving his successor to resolve the cataclysm facing the nation.

Abraham Lincoln

Before becoming president, Abraham Lincoln wrote a brief sketch of his life:

"I was born February 12, 1809 in Hardin County, Kentucky. My parents were both born in Virginia of undistinguished families....My mother...died in my tenth year....My father...removed from Kentucky to...Indiana in my eighth year....It was a wild region, with many bears and other wild animals. There I grew up....Of course when I came of age I did not know much. Still somehow, I could read, write, and cipher...but that was all." Lincoln said that he had about one year of formal education.

Lincoln worked hard to gain knowledge while farming, splitting rails for fences, and clerking at a store at New Salem, Illinois. He was a captain in the Black Hawk War, studied law, was postmaster, and spent eight years in the Illinois legislature. His law partner said, "His ambition was a little engine that knew no rest."

In 1842, Lincoln married Mary Todd. They had four boys, but only one lived to maturity. Witty and vivacious as a girl, Mary's adult life was tragic, with episodes of paranoia, phobias, spending sprees, and uncontrollable temper. In 1875 she was committed to a mental institution by her surviving son Robert.

In 1858, Lincoln ran for the Senate against

A cartoon pillorying Franklin Pierce for his accident-prone performance as a brigadier-general during the Mexican War.

Buchanan (seated on right) in this 1859 photograph with his cabinet. He wrote to his successor, Lincoln: "If you are as happy, my dear sir, on entering [the White House] as I am in leaving it, you are the happiest man in the country!"

Abraham Lincoln makes a surprise visit to troops in 1865.

Lincoln's opponent during the Civil War: Jefferson Davis (1808–1889), President of the Confederate States of America.

> *Fondly do we hope, fervently do we pray, that this mighty scourge of war may speedily pass away....With malice toward none, with charity for all, with firmness in the right as God gives us to see the right, let us strive on to finish the work we are in, to bind up the nation's wounds, to care for him who shall have borne the battle and for his widow and orphan, to do all which may achieve and cherish a just and lasting peace among ourselves and with all nations."*
> ABRAHAM LINCOLN, 2ND INAUGURAL ADDRESS, 1865

Stephen A. Douglas. Lincoln lost the election, but in debating Douglas he gained a national reputation that brought him the Republican nomination—and election—as president in 1860.

In 1861, eleven southern states seceded from the Union to form the Confederate States of America. Lincoln thought secession illegal, and was willing to use force to defend the Union. When Confederate troops fired on Fort Sumter, SC, and forced its surrender, he called on the states for 75,000 volunteers. The Civil War had begun.

In 1862, Lincoln issued the Emancipation Proclamation, freeing slaves within Confederate states still at war. The proclamation had little effect in the South, but in the North it turned the war into a moral crusade. Lincoln won re-election in 1864, as Union victories heralded an end to the war. On April 9, 1865, Grant accepted Lee's surrender at Appomattox, VA.

The Civil War ended slavery forever. The South remained under northern rule for more than ten years. Union casualties were 365,000; the number of Confederate casualties is unknown.

On April 14, 1865, Lincoln was assassinated at Ford's Theater in Washington by John Wilkes Booth.

Andrew Johnson

With the assassination of Lincoln, the presidency fell upon Andrew Johnson, a southern Democrat. Although an honorable man, Johnson was one of the most unfortunate of presidents. Opposing him were the Republicans in Congress who favored a "radical" reconstruction of the South.

Born in Raleigh, NC, in 1808, Johnson grew up in poverty and never attended school. He was apprenticed to a tailor as a boy, opened a tailor shop, and, at age 18, married Eliza McCardle.

Entering politics, he championed the common man, advocating the Homestead Act to provide a free farm for poor settlers. In 1864 he was nominated for vice president under Lincoln.

President Johnson treated the South more as a wayward friend than as a conquered enemy. For that he was vigorously opposed by the Radical Republicans in Congress. Overriding Johnson, Congress passed the Civil Rights Act of 1866 and the 14th Amendment, requiring states to grant civil rights and citizenship to blacks as a condition for readmission to the Union.

In 1867, Johnson was impeached for dismissing his Secretary of War, who had opposed him. He was tried by the Senate and acquitted by one vote.

In 1875, Tennessee returned Johnson to the Senate. He died a few months later.

Ulysses S. Grant

Born in 1822, Ulysses Grant was the son of an Ohio tanner. At 17, he won an appointment to West Point and graduated in the middle of his class. He fought in the Mexican War under Zachary Taylor.

At the outbreak of the Civil War, Grant organized volunteers, commanded a regiment, and, by 1862, rose to the rank of major general. After his victories at Shiloh and Vicksburg, Grant was appointed Commander of the Union Army by President Lincoln.

Elected president in 1868 as a war hero, Grant and his wife Julia began what she called "the happiest period" of her life. She entertained lavishly, true to the spirit of the Gilded Age.

As president, however, Grant provided neither vigor nor reform. Although a man of scrupulous honesty, he was welcomed to Washington by unscrupulous politicians. He accepted lavish gifts from admirers, and allowed himself to be bribed by speculators. Grant's administration was the first to be marked by major scandals.

At retirement the Grants made a trip around the world. But in 1884 Grant went bankrupt in a banking swindle, then learned he had cancer. He started writing his memoirs to pay off his debts and provide for his family. Soon after completing the last page, in 1885, he died.

Rutherford B. Hayes

Winner of the most fiercely disputed election until Bush-Gore in 2000, Rutherford Hayes brought dignity, honesty, and moderate reform to the presidency.

Born in Ohio in 1822, Hayes was educated at Kenyon College and Harvard Law School. He fought in the Civil War with the rank of brevet major general. He was a congressman and governor of Ohio before running for president.

Hayes' election over his Democratic opponent Samuel J. Tilden, who won the popular vote, depended upon contested electoral votes in three states (Florida was one). An Electoral Commission decided the contest. The final vote: 185 to 184 – just two days before inauguration date.

President Hayes insisted that his appointments be made on merit, not political loyalty. In 1877 he launched a major civil service reform, barring government workers from political activity. Hayes pledged protection of the rights of blacks in the South, but also advocated local self-government and the withdrawal of troops.

First Lady Lucy Hayes, a temperance advocate nicknamed "Lemonade Lucy", was a popular hostess and one of the best-loved women to preside over the White House.

Andrew Johnson's impeachment trial in the Senate, 1867.

President Grant (standing on the right) with wife Julia on a visit to a Virginia mine, 1879. He bet a dollar she wouldn't go down the mine. He lost.

President Hayes (who had been a Union major-general in the Civil War) at a servicemen's reunion clambake at Rhode Island.

Hayes had announced in advance that we would serve only one term. He died at his Ohio home in 1893.

James A. Garfield

Born in Orange, Ohio, in 1831, James Garfield graduated from Williams College in Massachusetts, taught classics, fought as a major general in the Civil War, and served 17 years in Congress. A Republican, he was elected president in 1880 but was assassinated after just 200 days in office.

Garfield restored prestige to the presidency by attacking political corruption in the New York Customhouse and the mail route contracts in the West.

In foreign affairs, Garfield's secretary of state invited all republics to a conference in Washington in 1882. The conference never took place. On July 2, 1881, in a railroad station, Charles Guiteau shot the president. Mortally wounded, Garfield lingered near death for weeks. For a few days he seemed to rally but on September 19, 1881, he died from an infection and internal hemorrhage.

First Lady Lucretia Garfield, her husband's inseparable companion, was herself recovering from illness. During the months the president fought for his life, her grief and devotion won the respect and sympathy of the nation.

Chester A. Arthur

The son of a Baptist preacher, Chester Arthur was born in Fairfield, Vermont, in 1829. He graduated from Union College, taught school, was admitted to the bar, and practiced law in New York City.

As Collector of the Port of New York, Arthur was a firm believer in the spoils system. As president, however, he transformed himself into a champion of civil service reform, notably signing the Pendleton Act of 1883.

Chester Arthur, although robust-looking, suffered from Bright's Disease.

During Arthur's administration, the first general Federal immigration law was enacted. Over his veto, Congress suspended Chinese immigration for ten years.

Suffering from Bright's disease, Arthur ran unsuccessfully for re-nomination in 1884, and died in 1886. One of his last public acts was the dedication of the Washington Monument.

Grover Cleveland

Grover Cleveland was the only president to leave the White House and return for a second term four years later.

He was born in Caldwell, New Jersey, in 1837, and raised in upstate New York. At 44, he began a political career that carried him to the White House in three years. Running as a reformer and a Democrat, he was elected mayor of Buffalo and later governor of New York.

In 1886 he married Frances Folsom on her twenty-first birthday, the first bride of a president to marry in the White House.

As president, Cleveland was no innovator, but he exemplified honesty. He fought corruption and vetoed favors to special interest groups. He signed the Interstate Commerce Act, the first law establishing Federal regulation of the railroads.

His first administration spanned four prosperous years which continued during Harrison's term. However, on re-election in 1892, Cleveland faced a severe economic depression—the Panic of 1893. He lost nearly all his public support, and lost the re-nomination. He died in 1908.

Benjamin Harrison

Benjamin Harrison was born in 1833 on a farm in North Bend, Ohio. He attended Miami University in Ohio and studied law in Cincinnati. After the Civil War—he was a brigadier general by 1865 – Harrison served in the Senate before winning the presidency from Cleveland in 1888.

The most important development of Harrison's term was the continuing growth of the United States. Six new states were admitted, bringing the total to 44. In 1890 the western frontier no longer existed—the country was settled from coast to coast.

First Lady Caroline Harrison renovated the White House, started the famous collection of White House china, and raised funds for Johns Hopkins University, while giving elegant receptions and dinners.

Harrison was defeated for a second term by Cleveland, and he died in 1901.

William McKinley

Born in Niles, Ohio, in 1843, William McKinley attended Allegheny College, and was teaching school when the Civil War began. He enlisted in the Union army, and by the end of the war was brevet major of volunteers. He studied law, and won a seat in Congress and the governorship of Ohio as a Republican. In 1871, he married Ida Saxton. His marriage was a devoted, though tragic one; both daughters died young, and his wife became a lifelong invalid.

The Spanish-American War dominated McKinley's administration. Cuban revolt against Spanish rule had escalated, and the American public, siding with the Revolutionaries, was pressuring McKinley for a U.S. invasion. In April 1898, he asked Congress for a declaration of war. The U.S. destroyed the Spanish fleet, seized Manila, and occupied Puerto Rico. Later, the U.S. annexed the Philippines, Guam, and Puerto Rico.

McKinley's second term came to a tragic end in September, 1901. A deranged anarchist shot him in Buffalo, New York. He died eight days later.

James Garfield with his daughter Molly before he became president. He would become the second of four American presidents to be assassinated.

Grover Cleveland is the only president to have had two non-contiguous administrations.

An 1892 cartoon depicting Benjamin Harrison being swamped by his grand-father's (President William Harrison) hat.

President McKinley just a short time prior to his assassination at Buffalo, New York, 6 September 1901.

Teddy Roosevelt, always an intrepid outdoorsman, with John Muir on Glacier Point, Yosemite Valley, California, c. 1906.

William Howard Taft was affable and likeable but lazy: "My sin is indisposition to labor...a disposition to enjoy the fellowship of others more than I ought."

Woodrow Wilson on a month-long tour of America to sell the people the peace treaty ending World War I, of which he had been a principal architect.

Theodore Roosevelt

With McKinley's assassination, Vice President Theodore Roosevelt became the youngest president in the nation's history. He brought new excitement to the office, and vigorously led the country toward progressive reforms and strong foreign policy.

Roosevelt was born in New York City in 1858 into a wealthy family, but he struggled against ill health in his youth and became an advocate of the strenuous life. In 1884 his first wife Alice and his mother died on the same day. Two years later, he married Edith Carow with whom he had five children—a fun-loving, rambunctious family.

During the Spanish-American War, Roosevelt, a colonel of the Rough Rider Regiment, led a charge at the battle of San Juan which made his political career. In 1898, Roosevelt won election as governor of New York, and in 1900 was nominated as McKinley's running mate on the Republican ticket.

As president, "TR" steered the United States more actively into world politics. Aware of the need for a strategic shortcut between the Atlantic and Pacific, he proposed the construction of the Panama Canal and encouraged Panama's independence from Colombia. He expanded the Monroe Doctrine, preventing foreign bases in the Caribbean.

In 1906 Roosevelt won the Nobel Peace Prize for mediating the Russo-Japanese War and easing immigration quotas with Japan.

Some of Roosevelt's most important achievements were in conservation. He preserved 125 million acres of public land in national forests, established the first wildlife refuge, and fostered large irrigation projects.

Leaving the presidency in 1909, Roosevelt went on an African safari, then re-entered politics. In 1912 he ran unsuccessfully for a third term as president.

He died in 1919. He had said "No man has had a happier life than I have led; a happier life in every way."

William Howard Taft

Born in 1857, the son of a distinguished judge, William Taft graduated from Yale, studied law, and made his way to the White House via administrative posts. He was the first governor of the Philippines under McKinley. Roosevelt made him secretary of war, and decided Taft should be his successor.

Taft's administration had many positive accomplishments. Arizona and New Mexico were admitted as states, making a total of 48. Taft prosecuted more than twice the number of anti-trust suits than Roosevelt had—notably against Rockefeller's Standard Oil Company and the American Tobacco Company. Two Constitutional amendments were proposed, providing for an income tax and direct election of senators.

First Lady Helen Herron Taft, widely traveled

and politically astute, was an enthusiastic hostess. The Tafts celebrated their silver wedding anniversary at the White House with a glittering evening garden party. She planted the capital's famous Japanese cherry trees around the Tidal Basin.

After leaving office, Taft was named Chief Justice of the United States, a position he held until just before his death in 1930. To Taft, the appointment was his greatest honor.

Woodrow Wilson

Woodrow Wilson was born in Virginia in 1856 and grew up during the Civil War in Georgia, and during Reconstruction in the devastated city of Columbia, South Carolina. After graduation from Princeton and the University of Virginia Law School, Wilson earned his doctorate at Johns Hopkins and started an academic career. He married Ellen Louise Axson in 1885. (She died in 1914.) He was president of Princeton for eight years and then elected governor of New Jersey.

Wilson won the presidency in 1912 on the Democratic ticket, campaigning against both Roosevelt and Taft on a program called the "New Freedom" which stressed individualism and states' rights. In his first term, he maneuvered through Congress the most far-reaching social justice legislation of any president to that time: the Underwood Act; the Federal Reserve Act; the Federal Trade Commission; a law prohibiting child labor; another limiting railroad workers to an eight-hour-day. With these successes, and the perception that "he kept us out of war," Wilson won re-election.

In 1917 when German submarines resumed sinking U.S. ships, Wilson concluded that America could not remain neutral in the World War. On April 2, 1917, he asked Congress for a declaration of war.

Wilson enunciated America's war aims—the Fourteen Points, the last of which would establish "A general association of nations...affording mutual guarantees...to great and small states alike." American troops and supplies poured into Europe, turning the tide of war against Germany.

After the Germans signed the Armistice in November 1918, Wilson went to Paris to try to build an enduring peace. He presented to Congress the Versailles Treaty, containing the League of Nations Covenant.

But the election of 1918 had favored the Republicans who opposed the Treaty. The president made a national tour to rally support. Exhausted, he suffered a stroke and nearly died. The Versailles Treaty failed in the Senate. Nursed by his second wife Edith, who had assumed many routine presidential duties during her husband's illness, he lived until 1924. Edith lived to ride in President Kennedy's inaugural parade in 1961.

Warren G. Harding

Warren Harding was born near Marion, Ohio, attended Ohio Central College, and became the publisher of a successful newspaper, the Marion Star. He served Ohio as a Republican in the state senate and as lieutenant governor, and ran unsuccessfully for governor. In 1914, he was elected to the U.S. Senate. He won the White House by an unprecedented 60 percent of the popular vote, the first man to move directly from the Senate to the presidency.

By 1923 the postwar depression seemed to be giving way to a new surge of prosperity, and Harding enjoyed strong support for his domestic programs. He was the first post-Civil War president to speak in the South for the rights of blacks. First Lady Florence Harding, a popular hostess, restored gaiety and openness to the White House.

Behind the scenes, however, rumors of scandal began circulating. Like Grant, Harding trusted his political cronies who betrayed him for their own gain. And after he died in office, in 1923, the Teapot Dome oil-leasing scandal was exposed, along with reports of extra-marital affairs.

Calvin Coolidge

In Vermont early in the morning of August 3, 1923, Calvin Coolidge heard that he was president. His father, a notary public, read him the oath of office. Coolidge signed it and then went back to sleep.

Born in Plymouth, Vermont, in 1872, Coolidge graduated with honors from Amherst College in Massachusetts and entered law and politics. A Republican, he rose from local councilman to governor of Massachusetts to vice president.

At his inauguration as president, he said that the nation had achieved "a state of contentment seldom seen before," and pledged to maintain the status quo. He rapidly became popular. In 1924, he was the beneficiary of what was called "Coolidge prosperity." He believed that the government that governs least, governs best.

Coolidge was both the most witty and taciturn of presidents. Shortly before leaving office in 1929, he gave President-elect Hoover advice on getting rid of talkative visitors: "If you keep dead still, they will run down in three or four minutes." About her husband, Grace said that when a woman bet she could get at least three words of conversation from him, Coolidge quietly said to her, "You lose."

The Coolidges suffered their younger son's sudden death at 16, but Grace Coolidge never let her grief interfere with the wit and exuberance she brought to the White House.

By 1929 when the Depression hit the country, Coolidge was in retirement. He died in 1933, confiding to a friend, "...I feel I no longer fit in with these times."

Herbert Hoover

Herbert Hoover was born in an Iowa village in 1874, grew up in Oregon, and graduated from Stanford University as a mining engineer. In 1899, he married his college sweetheart, Lou

President Hoover recording a speech into a new-fangled "talkie" machine.

Henry. The newlyweds went to China, the first of dozens of homes around the globe until war broke out in 1914.

During and after World War I, Hoover won an international reputation as a great humanitarian, feeding and clothing Belgians and, later, directing war relief in Europe under President Wilson. Lou Hoover, who spoke five languages, helped establish canteens, ambulances, and hospitals in London.

Hoover, a Republican, was elected president in 1928. On October 29, 1929 – seven months into his term—Wall Street collapsed, thousands of businesses failed, 9 million Americans lost their savings, and 12 million lost their jobs. Despite Hoover's efforts, the crisis worsened. He became the scapegoat for the Depression and was badly defeated in 1932.

After World War II, Presidents Truman and Eisenhower appointed Hoover to several humanitarian and government commissions. He died at age 90 in New York City.

Franklin Delano Roosevelt

Franklin D. Roosevelt was born in 1882 on his father's estate in Hyde Park, New York—now a national historic site. He graduated from Harvard College and Columbia Law School. In 1905, he married Anna Eleanor Roosevelt, his fifth cousin.

Roosevelt entered public service through politics, as a Democrat. He won election to the New York senate in 1910, and served as assistant secretary of the Navy under President Wilson.

In the summer of 1921, when he was 39, Roosevelt was stricken with poliomyelitis. During three years of painstaking convalescence, he strengthened his upper body but never regained the use of his legs. In 1924 he began one of the most remarkable comebacks in American history when he appeared on crutches to nominate Alfred E. Smith. In 1928 Roosevelt was elected governor of New York.

In 1932, in the midst of the Great Depression, "FDR" was elected president, to the first of four terms. By inauguration day, there were 13,000,000 Americans unemployed, and almost every bank was closed. In his first months in office, Roosevelt launched the New Deal, a vigorous program of social justice, bringing recovery to business and relief to the unemployed. The Tennessee Valley Authority (TVA), the Works Progress Administration (WPA), and the Social Security Act were among dozens of

Warren Harding prided himself on his showmanship: "I am a man of limited talents, from a small town. I do not seem to grasp that I am President."

Calvin Coolidge was said to have a face that looked as if it had been "weaned on a pickle." He also had a predilection for dressing up.

Faces of grief at FDR's funeral procession.

Truman with Churchill and Stalin. He liked both men.

"Hail the conquering hero." Ike in New York City after victory in Europe, 1945.

new reforms. To reassure the nation, Roosevelt began his famous radio speeches called "fireside chats." In 1935 he was re-elected in a landslide.

Eleanor Roosevelt transformed the role of first lady. Sensitive to the needs of the underprivileged of all creeds, races, and nations, she worked tirelessly to improve their lot. She held weekly press conferences, traveled across the country, lectured, gave radio broadcasts, and wrote a daily newspaper column. During World War II she visited troops around the world, and, after her husband's death, she was America's representative to the UN, earning the title "First Lady of the World."

Roosevelt had pledged the country to the "good neighbor" policy, laying the groundwork for the Western Hemisphere's strong stand against the Axis powers—Germany, Japan, and Italy—during World War II. After France fell and England was attacked in 1940, he began aid to England but stopped short of military involvement.

The Japanese attacked Pearl Harbor on December 7, 1941. The next day Roosevelt asked Congress for a declaration of war. The vote was unanimous. Roosevelt organized the nation's manpower and resources for global war. Under his leadership home-front Americans went all out for victory.

In 1942, at Roosevelt's suggestion, the 26 Allied countries agreed to call themselves the "United Nations," the basis for the UN organization formed at the end of the war.

In 1945, Roosevelt met with Winston Churchill and Joseph Stalin at Yalta to discuss plans for peace but by this time Roosevelt's health had deteriorated, and on April 12, 1945, at Warm Springs, Georgia, he died of a cerebral hemorrhage.

Harry S. Truman

Harry S Truman had just finished presiding over a Senate session on April 12, 1945, when he heard that Roosevelt was dead. During his few weeks as vice president Truman had scarcely seen the president and had received no briefing on the development of the atomic bomb or the growing tensions with Soviet Russia. Overnight, these and other wartime problems became Truman's to solve.

Truman was born in Lamar, Missouri, in 1884, and grew up in Independence, Missouri. He went to France during World War I as a captain in the Field Artillery. Returning, he married Elizabeth "Bess" Wallace, his childhood sweetheart; it was a devoted marriage that lasted 53 years.

Active in the Democratic party, Truman was elected a county court judge in 1922, and a U.S. senator in 1934.

As president, Truman made some of the most crucial and controversial decisions in history. Soon after V-E Day—less than a month after Truman took the oath—the war against Japan had reached its final stage. A plea to Japan to surrender unconditionally was rejected. Truman, after consulting his advisers, ordered atomic

bombs dropped on the cities of Hiroshima and Nagasaki. Five days later Japan surrendered.

Truman led the nation in helping create the United Nations, and in June 1945 the charter was signed.

Truman's domestic policy, known as the Fair Deal, included the expansion of Social Security, a full-employment program, a permanent Fair Employment Practices Act, and public housing and slum clearance.

Dangers and crises marked the foreign scene when Truman campaigned successfully in 1948. The Soviet Union had begun installing Communist regimes in neighboring countries. Truman enunciated the program that bears his name—the Truman Doctrine—pledging to aid all countries threatened by Communist revolution. The Marshall Plan (1948–52), named for his secretary of state, stimulated spectacular economic recovery in war-ravaged Western Europe. Truman ordered the Berlin airlift; in 1949 he negotiated the North Atlantic Treaty Organization (NATO) – a military alliance to protect Western nations.

Fear of Communist activity in the U.S. was whipped to a hysterical pitch when Senator Joseph McCarthy listed names of "card-carrying Communists," later culminating in the Army-McCarthy hearings during Eisenhower's administration.

In June 1950, when the Communist government of North Korea attacked South Korea, Truman was faced with what he said was his most difficult decision as president. He ordered U.S. forces into action, joining the UN Army. The fighting lasted more than three years. Truman kept the war a limited one, rather than risk a wider conflict with China and perhaps Russia.

Deciding not to run again, Truman retired to Independence with Bess, who, unlike Eleanor Roosevelt, had preferred to remain in the background as first lady. Truman died at age 88, on December 26, 1972.

Dwight D. Eisenhower

Born in Denison, Texas, in 1890, brought up in Abilene, Kansas, Dwight Eisenhower excelled in sports, and won an appointment to the U.S. Military Academy at West Point. Stationed in Texas as a second lieutenant, he met Mamie Geneva Doud, whom he married in 1916.

In his early army career, Eisenhower served under Generals John J. Pershing and Douglas MacArthur. After Pearl Harbor, he was called to Washington for a war plans assignment. He commanded the invasions of North Africa in 1942, and as Supreme Commander of Allied Forces in Europe, directed the cross-channel assault on Normandy on June 6, 1944 – the greatest amphibious invasion in history.

After the war, he became president of Columbia University, and later was appointed Supreme Commander of NATO.

An adoring public all but forced the presidency

upon Eisenhower. He was an authentic American hero; "I Like Ike" was an irresistible slogan, and he won a sweeping victory for the Republicans in 1952. In the White House, the Eisenhowers entertained an unprecedented number of heads of state and leaders of foreign governments, and Mamie's evident enjoyment of her role endeared her to her guests and to the public.

Eisenhower went to Korea to revive the stalled peace talks, and, in 1953, a truce brought an armed peace along the border of South Korea. The death of Stalin the same year caused shifts in relations with Russia.

Meanwhile, both Russia and the U.S. had developed hydrogen bombs. With the threat of destruction hanging over the world, Eisenhower met with the leaders of Britain, France, and Russia in Geneva in 1955, but he was unable to reach agreement on ways to reduce Cold War tensions.

In September 1955, Eisenhower suffered a heart attack and was hospitalized for seven weeks. He recovered, and was elected for a second term.

A year after the election, Russia startled the world by launching Sputnik, the first man-made space satellite. U.S. prestige suffered, and a debate began about the merits of American education.

In domestic policy, Eisenhower continued the New and Fair Deal programs. Brown v. Board of Education, the landmark 1954 Supreme Court decision, had outlawed segregation in public schools. As desegregation began, Eisenhower sent troops into Little Rock, Arkansas, to assure compliance. He also ordered the complete desegregation of the Armed Forces.

Eisenhower concentrated on maintaining world peace. He developed the "atoms for peace" program and the formation of the International Atomic Energy Agency.

Before he left office in 1961, he gave a prayer for peace "in the goodness of time." The Eisenhowers returned to their home in Gettysburg, Pennsylvania. He died after a long illness on March 28, 1969.

John Fitzgerald Kennedy

John F. Kennedy was born in Brookline, Massachusetts, in 1917, and grew up in Bronxville, New York and the Kennedy summer home in Hyannis Port, Massachusetts. In addition to the usual childhood ailments, he contracted Addison's disease and suffered back pain—conditions that lasted his lifetime. Graduating from Harvard in 1940, he entered the Navy. In 1943, when his PT boat was rammed and sunk by a Japanese destroyer, Kennedy, though injured, led the survivors to safety.

After the war, he was elected to Congress as a Democrat, advancing in 1953 to the Senate. He married Jacqueline Bouvier in 1953. In 1955, while recovering from a back operation, he wrote *Profiles in Courage,* which won the Pulitzer Prize in history.

In 1960, Kennedy was a first-ballot nominee for president, running on a program called the "New Frontier." Millions watched the televised debates with the Republican, Richard Nixon. Winning by a narrow margin of popular vote, Kennedy became the youngest, and the first Roman Catholic, president.

A beautiful young wife and two small children entered the White House and the hearts of a nation. Jacqueline Kennedy brought beauty, intelligence, and taste to the role of First Lady. She made the White House a museum of American history as well as an elegant family home.

In his inaugural address, Kennedy said: "Ask not what your country can do for you—ask what you can do for your country." He hoped America would resume its mission as the first nation dedicated to the revolution of human rights. The Alliance for Progress provided billions of dollars in aid to Latin America. In 1961, the Peace Corps—the signature success of the New Frontier—brought American idealism to the aid of developing nations. But the hard reality of the Communist challenge remained, and the focus of Kennedy's presidency was on foreign affairs.

In 1961, Kennedy permitted a band of Cuban exiles, armed and trained by the C.I.A., to invade their homeland at the Bay of Pigs. The attempt to overthrow the regime of Fidel Castro was a failure. The Soviet Union then renewed pressure against West Berlin, erecting a wall between West and East Berlin. Kennedy responded by increasing the U.S. military strength, including new efforts in outer space.

In 1962, the Russians installed nuclear missiles in Cuba, bringing the Cold War to a climax. In October, Kennedy ordered a blockade on all offensive weapons bound for Cuba. After six days, while the world waited on the brink of nuclear war, the Russians backed down and agreed to dismantle the missiles.

Believing that both America and Russia had a vital stake in stopping the spread of nuclear weapons, Kennedy led negotiations for the Nuclear Test Ban Treaty in 1963. It was ratified by more than 100 nations.

On November 22, 1963, Kennedy was assassinated in Dallas, Texas. His charisma, the glitter of Camelot, and his assassination have made JFK as much a phenomenon as a president. Historians disagree on his greatness, and an assessment of both the man and his administration continues today.

Lyndon B. Johnson

On November 22, 1963, not two hours after Kennedy died, Lyndon B. Johnson was sworn in as president aboard Air Force One at Dallas's Love Field.

Johnson was born in 1908 in central Texas, near Johnson City, which his family had helped settle. He worked his way through Southwest Texas State Teachers College; he taught poor students of Mexican descent.

In 1937 he won election to the House of

JFK, Jackie, Caroline, and John Jr at Hyannis Port, Massachusetts, 4 August 1962 in a photograph by Cecil Stoughton. Just over a year later Kennedy would be dead.

President Johnson liked to get up close and personal. The recipient of his attention is Supreme Court appointee, Abe Fortas.

An ebullient Betty Ford dancing on the Cabinet Room table, 19 January 1977.

Representatives on a New Deal platform, helped by his wife, Claudia "Lady Bird" Taylor Johnson, whom he had married in 1934.

During World War II, Johnson served as a lieutenant commander in the Navy, winning a Silver Star. After six terms in the House, he was elected to the Senate in 1948, serving as both minority and majority leader.

As president, Johnson urged the nation to "build a great society, a place where the meaning of man's life matches the marvels of man's labor." Nominated by acclamation in 1964, Johnson won the presidency in his own right with a record popular margin—more than 15 million votes.

In his first years in office, Johnson won passage of one of the most extensive legislative platforms in American history—the Great Society program. It provided aid to education, urban renewal, beautification and conservation; established Medicare; attacked poverty, disease, crime, and delinquency. The Civil Rights Act of 1964 barred discrimination in employment. The Voting Rights Act of 1965, Johnson's proudest achievement, outlawed poll taxes, literacy tests, and promoted voter registration.

Lady Bird Johnson was a prime force behind the beautification of the capital and the nation. And she was active in the war on poverty, especially the Head Start program for pre-schoolers.

Johnson had less success in foreign affairs. His greatest disaster was the Vietnam War. He escalated U.S. involvement, but succeeded only in making it one of America's costliest wars and severely dividing public opinion. In 1967 demonstrators marched on the Pentagon, men burned their draft cards and fled to Canada or Sweden to avoid arrest. Meanwhile racial riots broke out. In 1968, the Reverend Martin Luther King, Jr. was assassinated; two months later, Senator Robert F. Kennedy was assassinated, changing the Democrats' political prospects.

Deciding not to run for a second term, Johnson retired to the LBJ Ranch in Texas. He died on January 22, 1973, just one day before an agreement to end the fighting in Vietnam.

Richard Milhous Nixon

Born in Yorba Linda, California, in 1913, Richard Nixon had a brilliant record at Whittier College and Duke University Law School before practicing law. In 1940, he married Thelma Catherine "Pat" Ryan. During World War II, he served as a Navy lieutenant commander in the Pacific.

After the war he was elected to Congress as a Republican, and in 1950 he won a Senate seat. Two years later, Eisenhower chose him for his vice-presidential running mate.

Nominated for president by acclamation in 1960, Nixon lost the election to Kennedy by a narrow margin. In 1962, he ran, again unsuccessfully, for governor of California. In 1968, he again won his party's presidential nomination, and in a stunning political comeback, defeated Vice President Hubert Humphrey.

Richard Nixon, flanked by his daughter Tricia, announces his resignation on 9 August 1974.

Nixon's domestic accomplishments as president included consumer product safety, the end of the draft, new anticrime laws, and a broad environmental program. One of the most dramatic events was the first moon landing in 1969 by astronauts Neil Armstrong and Edwin Aldrin on Apollo 11.

Nixon's most important achievements were in his quest for world peace. In a dramatic departure in U.S. foreign policy, Nixon visited China, the first American president to do so. He called it a "journey for peace", easing tensions with China by an agreement to broaden scientific, cultural, and trade contacts. Four months later, he met with Russian leader Leonid Brezhnev and signed the SALT agreement, limiting nuclear weapons.

In his 1972 bid for a second term, Nixon defeated Democrat George McGovern in a landslide election. Three days after his inaugural address, Nixon announced that an agreement with North Vietnam had been reached: American troops would be withdrawn and American prisoners of war released. The Vietnam War cost the U.S. 58,000 dead, 304,000 wounded, and $110 billion.

Within a few months, Nixon's administration was besieged by the Watergate scandal—one of the most severe constitutional crises in U.S. history. In 1972, a break-in at the offices of the Democratic National Committee was traced to officials of Nixon's reelection committee. Several administration officials resigned; and some were later convicted of covering up the affair. Nixon denied any personal involvement, but tape recordings indicated he had tried to divert the investigation.

Faced with almost certain impeachment, Nixon resigned the presidency on August 9, 1974. As he spoke, his wife Pat, perhaps the most dutiful and underrated First Lady, stood tearfully beside him. The Nixons retired, settling on the East coast. In his last years Nixon regained a measure of public acclaim, especially abroad. He died on April 22, 1994.

Gerald Rudolph Ford

On August 9, 1974, minutes after Nixon resigned, Gerald Ford took the oath of office. He said, "Our long national nightmare is over. Our Constitution works; our great Republic is a government of laws and not of men."

Born in Omaha, Nebraska, in 1913, Ford grew up in Grand Rapids, Michigan. He starred on the University of Michigan football team, was offered a professional contract, but instead went to Yale, where he coached football while earning his law degree. In World War II, he served in the Navy in the South Pacific, earning the rank of lieutenant commander. After the war he served 25 years in Congress, eight as minority leader. In 1948, he married Elizabeth "Betty" Bloomer, a popular, outspoken first lady whose candor about her breast cancer and alcoholism won wide respect.

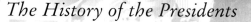

As president, Ford immediately tried to calm controversy by granting Nixon a full pardon. Instead the pardon aroused scathing criticism which crippled his presidency.

Throughout Ford's administration, the country suffered a severe economic recession. Consumer prices hit record highs; unemployment rose to the highest level since the 1930s and Ford was unable to push his programs through a Democratic-controlled Congress.

He turned to foreign affairs to buttress U.S. prestige and revive his leadership. On a trip to the Far East in 1974, he visited Japan—a first for an American president—and South Korea, reaffirming U.S. support and friendship. A summit meeting with Soviet leader Brezhnev set new limitations on nuclear weapons. But American prestige sank to a low ebb in 1975 when South Vietnam, Cambodia, and Laos fell to communist North Vietnam.

Ford won the Republican nomination in 1976 but lost the election to his Democratic opponent, Jimmy Carter.

The Fords live in Rancho Mirage, California. Nearby is the main campus of the Betty Ford Center where thousands of people have been helped with alcohol and drug addiction.

Jimmy Carter

Jimmy Carter was born in 1924 in Plains, Georgia—the first president born in a hospital. He preferred his nickname, Jimmy, to his full name, James Earl Carter, Jr. Peanut farming, politics, and devotion to the Baptist faith were mainstays of his upbringing. In 1946 he graduated from the U.S. Naval Academy and married Rosalynn Smith.

After seven years as a naval officer, Carter returned to Plains to take over the peanut farm left by his late father. In 1962 he was elected to the Georgia senate; and in 1970 became governor of Georgia. As a southern governor, Carter stood out by supporting ecology, efficiency in government, and the removal of racial barriers. At the 1976 Democratic convention, he was nominated for president and defeated Ford. Carter was the first man from the Deep South elected president since Zachary Taylor in 1848.

Despite opposition in Congress, Carter had successes in domestic affairs. He dealt with the energy shortage with a new energy bill and a new cabinet-level Department of Energy. He worked to improve the environment with a ban on dumping raw sewage in the ocean. He doubled the size of the national parks and wildlife refuges, adding 104 million acres of Alaskan lands. He created the Department of Education, bolstered Social Security, and appointed a record number of women, blacks, and Hispanics to government.

Carter's most lasting achievement as president was the Middle East peace treaty that he helped to negotiate between Egypt and Israel at Camp David in 1978. He concluded the Panama Canal Treaty, ceding the Canal Zone to Panama.

Building upon the work of his predecessors, he established full diplomatic relations with China and completed negotiation of the SALT II nuclear limitation treaty with the Soviet Union. In person and in speeches, he called for human rights around the world.

There were serious setbacks, however. In November, 1979, Iranian militants seized the U.S. embassy in Tehran and took more than 60 American hostages. This incident, together with continuing inflation at home, contributed to Carter's defeat for a second term in 1980. Iran finally released the hostages, the same day Carter left office.

Jimmy Carter's life after leaving the White House has been one of the most extraordinary in history, eclipsing John Quincy Adams, Teddy Roosevelt, and Taft. Today, through the Carter Center, he and Rosalynn, who proved a skillful speaker and hardworking first lady, pursue the same goals—peace, health care, and human rights—by writing, traveling around the globe, building for Habitat for Humanity, and promoting mental health rights.

Ronald Reagan

Ronald Reagan was born in 1911 in Tampico, Illinois. During high school he earned money as a lifeguard, and then worked his way through Eureka College. After graduation, he became a radio sports announcer. A screen test in 1937 won him a contract with Warner Brothers, and during the next two decades he appeared in over 50 films. In World War II, Reagan served in the U.S. Army Air Forces as a captain, but his nearsightedness disqualified him for combat duty.

In 1940 Reagan married actress Jane Wyman; they divorced in 1948. In 1952 he married Nancy Davis.

After serving as president of the Screen Actors Guild, Reagan toured the country as television host of "General Electric Theater," becoming a spokesman for conservatism. In 1966 he was elected governor of California by a wide margin; he was re-elected in 1970.

Reagan won the Republican presidential nomination in 1980. Voters, troubled by inflation and the year-long confinement of the American hostages in Iran, swept the Republicans into office.

At age 69, Reagan was the oldest man ever elected president,

Jimmy and Rosalynn Carter in Mike Peter's 1977 cartoon in the Dayton Daily News.

Ronald Reagan on the presidency: "Since I came to the White House I got two hearing aids, a colon operation, skin cancer, and a prostate operation and I was shot. The damn thing is, I've never felt better in my life."

The Bush dynasty during the elder Bush's presidency. Neil Bush on the far left (as we view it), George W. is next, and Jeb is on the far right.

Bill Clinton on the presidency: "I don't know whether it's the finest public housing in America or the crown jewel of prison life."

All of you know I'm having to become quite an expert in this business of asking for forgiveness. And I ----. It gets a little easier the more you do it. And if you have a family, an Administration, a Congress and a whole country to ask, you're going to get a lot of practice.

BILL CLINTON, 28 AUGUST, 1998

but his youthful, vigorous appearance belied his age. Shortly after ending his inaugural address, he announced that the 444-day captivity of the Iran hostages had ended. Two months later, he was shot by John W. Hinckley, Jr., but quickly recovered. His grace and wit after the near-fatal incident caused his popularity to soar.

Called the "Great Communicator" with the public and Congress, Reagan signed legislation— called "Reaganomics"—to cut taxes and government spending, curb inflation, increase employment, and strengthen national defense. But late in 1981, the country slid into recession; unemployment rose to its highest level since the 1930s, and defense spending brought a large budget deficit.

By 1984 an economic recovery helped Reagan win a second term with a record number of electoral votes. In 1986 Reagan reformed the income tax, lowering tax rates and simplifying the tax code. By the end of his administration, despite the stock panic of 1987, the nation was enjoying its longest recorded period of peacetime prosperity.

In foreign policy, Reagan worked to achieve "peace through strength", leading to a decisive end to the Cold War. In dramatic meetings with Soviet leader Gorbachev, he negotiated a treaty that would eliminate intermediate-range missiles. In 1985, the West suffered several attacks of international terrorism—the hijacking of a TWA airliner, the Achille Lauro hijacking at sea, and bombings in Vienna, Rome, and Berlin.

The scandal of the Reagan years was the 1986 Iran-Contra affair. It was revealed that the administration had secretly sold arms to Iran and diverted the proceeds to the Contra forces in Nicaragua.

In January 1989, the Reagans retired to Bel-Air, California. President Reagan told the American people in 1994 that he had been diagnosed with the memory-robbing Alzheimer's disease. His "long goodbye" with Nancy at his side, ended with his death on 5 June 2004.

George Herbert Walker Bush

Born in Milton, Massachusetts, in 1924, George Bush attended Phillips Academy in Andover. On his eighteenth birthday he enlisted in the Navy. The youngest pilot when he received his wings, he flew 58 combat missions during World War II. On one mission he was shot down over the Pacific and rescued from his life raft. He was awarded the Distinguished Flying Cross. In 1945 he married Barbara Pierce.

Bush completed his education at Yale University; he was captain of the baseball team and a member of Phi Beta Kappa. After graduating, he embarked on a career in the oil industry in Texas and became active in the Republican Party, serving two terms as a representative to Congress from Houston. After unsuccessful runs for the Senate, he was appointed to a series of positions: Ambassador to the UN, Chairman of the Republican National Committee, Chief U.S. liaison in China, and Director of the Central Intelligence Agency.

In 1980 Bush lost the nomination for president, but was chosen as running mate by Reagan. In 1988 he won the nomination for president and defeated Michael Dukakis in the election.

Immediately Bush faced a sluggish economy and the scandal of the failure of the government's Savings and Loans banks. He broke his campaign pledge not to raise taxes, which he later called a "mistake."

In foreign affairs there was dramatic change. Presidents from Truman to Reagan had tried to contain Communism. The payoff came during Bush's term. The Communist empire broke up, and the Berlin Wall fell, ending the Cold War.

Bush's greatest crisis came in 1990 when Iraqi President Saddam Hussein invaded Kuwait. Bush rallied the UN, the American people, and Congress, and sent 500,000 U.S. troops to join the allied coalition. After weeks of air and missile strikes, the 100-hour ground war—called Operation Desert Storm—overwhelmed the Iraqi army and liberated Kuwait.

Despite Bush's high marks for this military and diplomatic success, voters focused on the weak economy, rising violence in inner cities, and the continued high deficit. In 1992 he lost his bid for a second term to Democrat Bill Clinton.

First Lady Barbara Bush, endearingly unpretentious, captivated the American people. She chose adult literacy as her special cause and today heads the Barbara Bush Foundation for Family Literacy. The Bushes live in Houston, Texas, and in the family summer home in Kennebunkport, Maine.

William Jefferson Clinton

Bill Clinton was born William Jefferson Blythe IV in 1946, in Hope, Arkansas, three months after his father died in an accident. When he was four, his mother married Roger Clinton, whose name he took when he was fifteen. As a high school delegate to Boys Nation, he met President

Kennedy in the White House Rose Garden, an encounter that inspired Clinton to enter public service.

Clinton graduated from Georgetown University and in 1968 won a Rhodes scholarship to Oxford University in England. He received a law degree from Yale in 1973 and entered politics in Arkansas. In 1975 he married Hillary Rodham, a graduate of Wellesley College and Yale Law School.

Clinton, a Democrat, was elected Arkansas attorney general in 1976; two years later he won the governorship. After losing a second term, he regained the office and served until he defeated incumbent George Bush in the 1992 presidential election.

Clinton outlined an ambitious domestic program to balance the federal budget and lower national debt. He set health care reform as a major priority. But the new administration met conflict and controversy at every turn—the Whitewater affair; the suicide of White House aide Vince Foster; the botched raid on the Branch Davidians in Waco, Texas; the bombing in Oklahoma City; and the defeat of health care reform.

The chairman of the unsuccessful National Health Care Reform was Hillary Rodham Clinton. Undeterred by critics, as First Lady she won many admirers for her support for women and children around the world. She is currently one of the U.S. senators for New York.

In foreign affairs, President Clinton favored allied coalitions over military missions. He replaced U.S. troops with UN peacekeepers in Somalia and Haiti. And he supported NATO air raids in war-torn Bosnia. He bombed Iraq when Saddam Hussein stopped UN weapons inspections. In 1998, Clinton joined U.S. with NATO forces to oust Yugoslavia's President Milosevic for his offenses against ethnic Albanians in Kosovo. Clinton became a global supporter for an expanded NATO, more open international trade (NAFTA agreement), and a campaign against drug trafficking. Peace in the Middle East, however—his major goal—eluded him.

In 1998, as a result of issues surrounding indiscretions with a White House intern, Clinton was impeached by the House of Representatives. He was tried in the Senate and found not guilty of the charges. He apologized to the nation and continued to have unprecedented popular approval ratings for his job as president.

On leaving the White House, the Clintons moved to Chappaqua, New York, Senator Hillary Clinton's home base. Bill Clinton keeps an office in New York City. Both have written mega-selling memoirs: *My Life* (his) and *Living History* (hers).

George Walker Bush

The son of former president George H.W. Bush, George W. Bush was born in 1946 in New Haven, Connecticut and grew up in Midland, Texas. After graduating from Yale, he served in the Texas Air National Guard, received an MBA degree from Harvard, ran unsuccessfully for Congress, and began a career in the oil industry. In 1989 he purchased the Texas Rangers baseball franchise. In 1994 he was elected governor of Texas and served for eight years.

Bush's run for president against Vice President Al Gore in 2000 ended in the closest and most disputed election in modern U.S. history. The election was decided by the Supreme Court, making Bush the first man in over a century to become president without winning the popular vote.

The terrorist attacks of 9/11/01 changed George Bush's priorities from those of the "compassionate conservative" on which he had run, to an aggressive war president embracing preemptive strikes and regime change in his war on worldwide terrorism.

Bush demanded that Afghanistan's Taliban regime turn over Osama Bin Laden, head of Al Qaeda, but without success. In October 2001 U.S. and coalition forces ousted the Taliban and three years later, in 2004, Afghanistan held its first free presidential election.

In 2002, in his first State of the Union address, the President labeled Iran, Iraq, and North Korea as "an axis of evil." Focusing on Iraq, the administration took a forceful stand over weapons of mass destruction it believed Iraq held. Despite strong opposition from many European allies, the president demanded Saddam Hussein step down or face invasion. On March 19, 2002 the U.S. and Britain invaded Iraq. Saddam was captured and jailed, but coalition troops became involved in violent confrontations with Iraqi insurgents in what became a chaotic occupation.

On the domestic front, Bush signed the No Child Left Behind Act (2002), which the president described as "the cornerstone of my administration" and overhauled Medicare (2003), providing a prescription drug benefit for the first time.

President Bush authorized deep tax cuts which, combined with the cost of the Iraq war and domestic anti-terrorisism efforts (under the umbrella of the Patriot Act, passed in October 2001), produced record levels of budget deficit.

The run-up to the 2004 presidential election was extremely close, but Bush eventually won both the popular and electoral college votes against Democratic challenger, John Kerry.

"All of this was brought upon us in a single day, and night fell on a different world."
George W. Bush, September 2001.
The catastrophe that visited America on 11 September 2001 not only traumatized the nation but galvanized George W. Bush, casting him in the role of war president.

President Bush and Laura Bush leaving Camp David, 2 March 2001.

> *This house, for example—I was thinking of it as we walked down this hall, and I was comparing it to some of the great houses of the world that I have been in. This isn't the biggest house. Many, and most, in even smaller countries, are much bigger. This isn't the finest house. Many in Europe, particularly, and in China, Asia, have paintings of great, great value, things that we just don't have here and, probably, will never have until we are 1,000 years old or older.*
> *But this is the best house. It is the best house, because it has something far more important than numbers of people who serve, far more important than numbers of rooms or how big it is, far more important than numbers of magnificent pieces of art.*
> *This house has a great heart, and that heart comes from those who serve.*
> FROM NIXON'S FAREWELL TO WHITE HOUSE STAFF, AUGUST, 1974

Home, office, museum, and historic gathering place – the White House is one of the most renowned and symbolic buildings in the world. It is certainly the most famous house in America. For over 200 years it has been the home of 41 presidents and first families. Once officially known as the "President's House," later as the "Executive Mansion," Americans began calling it the "white house" as early as its first coat of whitewash in 1798. Finally, in 1901, President Theodore Roosevelt made that name official.

1790–91 A site for the new national capital is selected along the Potomac River. President Washington chooses Pierre L'Enfant as city planner.

Pierre L'Enfant updating President George Washington on his plans for the new capital.

1792 James Hoban selected as architect for the President's House; cornerstone is laid.
1800 John and Abigail Adams move into the White House; government relocates from Philadelphia to Washington, DC.
1801 President Jefferson plans a garden and a stone wall around the house; a cooking stove replaces the kitchen's open-hearth fireplace.

British troops burning Washington D.C., 24 August 1814.

1814, 24 August Burning of the White House and Capitol by the British in the War of 1812.
1817 President Monroe moves into the reconstructed White House.
1822 Pennsylvania Avenue was cut on the north side of the President's Park.
1824 South Portico constructed; the park north of the White House is named to honor General Lafayette.
1825 John Quincy Adams develops the first flower garden on the White House grounds and plants ornamental trees.
1830 North Portico completed.
1833 Running water is piped into the White House for the first time.
1835 First central heating system installed; Andrew Jackson creates the White House orangery and plants the famous Jackson magnolia on the south side of the house.
1848 Gas lamps installed for James K. Polk replace candles and oil lamps; installation of a second and improved central heating system completed.
1850 First lady Abigail Fillmore obtains Congressional funds to establish an official library in the White House.
1853 An efficient hot-water heating system installed for President Pierce; running hot water is first piped into the second floor bathroom; the White House orangery is expanded into a greenhouse.
1857 Orangery is demolished and a replacement greenhouse is constructed on the west, adjoining the State Floor of the White House.
1866 The first telegraph office is installed in the White House.
1871 President Grant extends the grounds south and a great round pool is built on the south lawn.
1877 First telephone installed for President Hayes, using the phone number "1."
1878 Hundreds of trees are planted; the tradition of planting commemorative trees to represent each president and state is begun.
1870s–80s The conservatory is expanded, rambling beside and over the West Wing and providing a spring garden all year long.
1880 White House staff starts using typewriters; the Ellipse south of the White House is completed.
1881 The White House has its first hydraulic elevator, and crude air conditioning, installed.
1891 Electric wiring installed
1898 First electric elevator installed

The White House after the fire of 24 August 1814.

1901 The official name of the Executive Mansion is changed to the "White House."

Jerry Smith, one of Mrs Harrison's staff, engaged in the most thorough cleaning the White House had seen for many decades.

The White House, far right, during the John Adams administration.

The White House kitchen, 1890.

1902 Theodore Roosevelt Renovation by McKim, Mead & White; conservatory is removed and a new "temporary" Executive Office Building, later called the West Wing, is erected. Edith Roosevelt plants a colonial garden to the west.

1909 West Wing office building is doubled in size by a southern expansion and includes the first presidential Oval Office; President Taft purchases official automobiles for the White House and converts the stable into a garage.

The floral splendor of the East Room in anticipation of a formal dinner during the Theodore Roosevelt administration.

1913 President Wilson holds the first presidential press conference at the Executive Offices of the White House. Ellen Wilson replaces the colonial garden with a formal rose garden and a new East Garden.

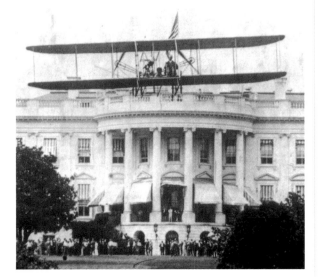

An airplane takes off from the White House lawn in 1911 during the Taft administration.

1922 Electric vacuum cleaners are used in the White House for the first time; President Harding has a radio set installed in a bookcase in his study on the second floor.

1925 President Coolidge makes the first national radio broadcast from the White House.

1926 The White House acquires its first electric refrigerator; iceboxes had been in use since the Polk administration.

1933 President Franklin D. Roosevelt begins radio broadcasts to the nation from the White House, known as "fireside chats." A heated indoor swimming pool is built in the west terrace for President Roosevelt's therapy. (The pool was covered in 1974 and the space was converted into a room for press briefings.)

1934 West Wing is rebuilt and expanded and a new Oval Office and Cabinet Room is built in an eastern extension.

1942 An East Wing office building erected, including a bomb shelter; movie theater is added to the east terrace.

1947, 5 October The first presidential address telecast from the White House is delivered by President Truman.

1948 The Truman Renovation begins; four years later the project completely reconstructs the interior of the White House and adds two new underground levels and the Truman Balcony.

1961 President Kennedy has the Rose Garden redesigned to serve presidential functions. Jacqueline Kennedy begins restoration of furniture and works of art.

1964 Lady Bird Johnson has the East Garden completed in honor of Jacqueline Kennedy.

1993 President Clinton gets e-mail.

1994 First White House Web site – *Welcome to the White House* – launched.

During World War I President Wilson allowed sheep to graze on the White House lawn.

Fireworks at a congressional barbecue at the White House on 23 September 1987 during Ronald Reagan's administration.

Assassinations and Near Misses

The Zero Years and Tecumseh's Curse

Some people believe that the curse of Indian chief Tecumseh has killed U.S. presidents before the end of their term in office, if they were elected in a year that ended with 0. The first victim of the curse was William Henry Harrison, whose troops killed the Indian chief in 1813.

HARRISON, *elected in 1840, died of pneumonia after serving 31 days in office.*

LINCOLN, *elected in 1860, assassinated in 1865*

GARFIELD, *elected in 1880, assassinated in 1881*

McKINLEY, *elected to a second term in 1900, assassinated in 1901*

HARDING, *elected in 1920, died of a stroke in office in 1923.*

ROOSEVELT, *elected to a third term in 1940, died of a cerebral hemorrhage in office in 1945.*

KENNEDY, *elected in 1960, assassinated in 1963*

REAGAN, *elected in 1980, survived an attempted assassination. He seems to have broken the curse.*

Abraham Lincoln

On the morning of April 14, 1865, John Wilkes Booth stopped at Ford's Theater in Washington, D.C. and heard that President Lincoln was planning to attend the evening performance of Our American Cousin. Wilkes, 27, an actor, and a racist and Confederate sympathizer, hated Lincoln and wanted revenge for the South's defeat. His attempt the previous month to kidnap Lincoln had failed. Now, with his co-conspirators, Booth saw his chance. He would kill Lincoln at the theater. Two other men would target Vice-President Andrew Johnson and Secretary of State William Seward.

Lincoln and his wife Mary arrived at Ford's Theater at 8:30 pm. Booth arrived about 10 pm, left his horse in a back alley, and made his way to the presidential box where the Lincolns were sitting. The president's bodyguard had left his post. Booth opened the door to the box and shot Lincoln in the back of the head at close range.

Booth jumped to the stage, hit the floor and broke his left leg. Flashing his knife, Booth crossed the stage to the back door, mounted his horse and fled.

Lincoln was taken across the street to a bedroom in the Petersen boarding house. The wound was fatal, the bullet having split in two on impact, one piece stopping mid-brain, the other lodging near the right eye. Gideon Welles, Secretary of the Navy, was a witness. "The giant sufferer lay extended diagonally across the bed, which was not long enough for him," he wrote. "He had been stripped of his clothes. His large arms…were of a size which one would scarce have expected from his spare appearance. His slow, full respiration lifted the clothes with each breath that he took. His features were calm and striking…. The respiration of the President became suspended at intervals, and at last entirely ceased at twenty-two minutes past seven." [morning of April 15]

Welles watched Mary Lincoln and her oldest son Robert struggle with their sorrow. As Lincoln's life ebbed away, Mary wailed, "Where is my husband?" She begged him to take her with him. Lincoln's body lay in state in 14 different cities before burial in Springfield, Illinois.

Booth and his accomplices were captured by federal troops on April 26 at Garrett's farm near Port Royal, Virginia. Hiding in a barn, Booth refused to surrender. The barn was set on fire and still he resisted. One of the soldiers claimed that he shot Booth; other reports say Booth killed himself. Booth's co-conspirators (the plots against Seward and Johnson had failed) were tried by a military tribunal and found guilty. Some were hanged; some were imprisoned.

James Garfield

On July 2, 1881, President Garfield went to the Baltimore and Potomac railroad station in Washington, D.C. to begin a trip to his 25th college reunion in Williamstown, Massachusetts. There Charles J. Guiteau, 39, a mentally disturbed man who had been rebuffed for a diplomatic post, shot him. Guiteau had been stalking the president for weeks. One of the bullets grazed Garfield's arm; the other lodged in his back and could not be located. In an attempt

The execution of Lincoln's assassins, including Mary Surratt on the far left.

to find the bullet, Alexander Graham Bell devised a metal detector, but the metal frame of Garfield's bed confused Bell's device.

Garfield lived for 11 weeks in increasing pain, suffering the infamous July heat typical of Washington. The first lady, Lucretia Garfield, ordered blocks of ice delivered to the president's bedside; then she, her children, staff, and volunteers took turns waving fans to circulate the air cooled by melting ice. 500,000 pounds of ice were contributed by the public that July. Several inventors offered their electrical devices, and on July 12, it is said that the world's first "air conditioning machine" went into action.

Garfield weakened, however, and died in Elberon, New Jersey on September 19, 1881.

Charles Guiteau pleaded not guilty by reason of insanity, was convicted and publicly hanged on June 30, 1882.

Garfield's assassination by a disappointed office seeker led to the passage in 1883 of the Pendleton Civil Service Act which rewards merit rather than patronage.

William McKinley

On September 5, 1901, President McKinley addressed the Pan-American Exposition in Buffalo, New York. The next day, as he stood shaking hands with a long line of well-wishers, Leon Czolgosz, 28, a Detroit native, approached with his right hand wrapped in a bandage. As McKinley extended his hand, two shots were fired from a concealed pistol. One bullet was apparently stopped by a button; the second penetrated the president's stomach and lodged in his pancreas.

Gripping his chest, McKinley fell back into the arms of a security guard. "My wife – be careful how you tell her – oh, be careful," he said.

Removed to a hospital for two operations, McKinley seemed to improve, then relapsed, and died on September 14. The official cause of death was listed as gangrene of the stomach and pancreas. McKinley was 58 years old.

Czolgosz, an admitted anarchist, was convicted and sentenced to death in the electric chair.

The assassination of McKinley confirmed Americans' fears, already stirred by recent assassinations in Europe linked to anarchists. Congress passed laws to target suspected immigrants, prohibiting their entry into the United States.

> *Fellow citizens, God reigns, and the Government at Washington still lives."*
> JAMES A. GARFIELD, OHIO REPRESENTATIVE, ON THE MORNING LINCOLN DIED. GARFIELD WAS HIMSELF ASSASSINATED 16 YEARS LATER.

Charles Guiteau ambushed President Garfield in the Baltimore & Potomac railroad station in Washington DC, July 2, 1881.

The Kennedy family, in deep mourning, leaving the Capitol on November 24, 1963, two days after the assassination.

To John Kennedy, a fatalist with serious chronic illnesses, thoughts of death were not new. On October 28, 1962, at the successful conclusion of the Cuban Missile Crisis, Kennedy joked to his brother Robert, *"This is the night I should go to the theater,"* referring to Lincoln's visit to Ford's Theater after the Civil War was won.

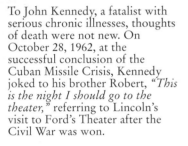

We in this country, in this generation, are – by destiny rather than choice – the watchmen on the walls of world freedom. We ask therefore that we may be worthy of our power and responsibility – that we may exercise our strength with wisdom and restraint – and that we may achieve in our time and for all time the ancient vision of 'peace on earth, good will toward men.' That must be our goal – and the righteousness of our cause must always underlie our strength. Or, as was written long ago: "Except the Lord keep the city, the watchman waketh but in vain."

FROM THE SPEECH KENNEDY WAS SCHEDULED TO GIVE AT THE DALLAS TRADE MART, NOVEMBER 22, 1963

John F. Kennedy

In November 1963, President and Mrs. Kennedy traveled to Texas to mend differences between factions in the Democratic Party. On November 22, the Kennedys, with Texas Governor John Connally and his wife, proceeded in an open limousine to the Dallas Trade Mart where Kennedy was scheduled to speak. The greeting from the crowds lining the streets was warm and enthusiastic. Mrs. Connally said to Kennedy, "You can't say that Dallas doesn't love you."

Moments later, at about 12:30 P.M. as the limousine reached Dealey Plaza, shots rang out. Kennedy clutched his throat with both hands. Jacqueline Kennedy, seated to his left, turned to her husband. Connally also appeared to have been shot. Seconds later, the fatal bullet hit the right side of the president's head. Blood gushed from the President's head. "Jack!" Jackie cried, "Oh, no! No!"

A photographer looked up at a building on the corner – the Texas School Book Depository – and caught a glimpse of a rifle barrel being withdrawn from a window on the sixth floor.

Jackie bent low, cradling her husband's head in her lap as the limousine sped to Parkland Hospital. A Secret Service man, who had jumped onto the rear bumper of the car, flung himself across the trunk, and in his anger and frustration pounded it repeatedly with his fist.

Kennedy never regained consciousness. At 1 P.M. he was pronounced dead. His body was flown to Washington that night, and millions watched his funeral on television three days later. Kennedy was buried in Arlington National Cemetery; an eternal flame marks his grave.

The Dallas police arrested Lee Harvey Oswald, 24, a former marine and communist sympathizer who worked in the book depository from which the shots apparently were fired. Oswald never made it to trial; two days after the assassination, as Americans watched on television, he was gunned down by Jack Ruby, a nightclub owner.

There is no other murder in history that has produced as much speculation as Kennedy's assassination. There are many reasons. Assassination itself, then unknown in 20th-century America, conveyed a kind of instant martyrdom. Americans, from the beginning, refused to accept the idea that a lone gunman had murdered the president with no apparent motive. One poll, taken right after the assassination, found that only 29 percent of Americans believed that Oswald had acted alone.

A week after the assassination, President Lyndon Johnson appointed the Warren Commission to investigate. In 1964 the Commission concluded that Oswald, acting alone, shot Kennedy; that there was no conspiracy; that Oswald fired three shots, one of which missed the limousine entirely.

In 1979, the House of Representatives issued a report that Kennedy was probably killed as a result of a conspiracy and that four shots, not three, were fired.

Conspiracy theories continue to circulate. Polls taken in 2003, on the 40th anniversary of Kennedy's death, indicate that most Americans still believe there was a conspiracy to kill him.

Near Misses

GEORGE WASHINGTON

In 1776 during the Revolutionary War, a conspiracy was uncovered to kidnap and murder General Washington. The plot involved the mayor and governor of New York and a bodyguard, Thomas Hickey, who was publicly hanged on June 28.

On January 30, 1835 Andrew Jackson defended himself successfully against would-be assassin Richard Lawrence.

ANDREW JACKSON

In 1835, Richard Lawrence, 32, approached Jackson on a Washington street and aimed a derringer at close range. The gun misfired. Lawrence drew another gun; it also misfired. Lawrence was found insane and died in an institution.

ABRAHAM LINCOLN

In 1861 Lincoln traveled by train to Washington for his inauguration. His guard, Charles Pinkerton, uncovered a plot to kill Lincoln when the train arrived in Baltimore. He convinced Lincoln to continue to Washington on horseback.

Pinkerton later formed the Pinkerton Detective Agency.

MARY TODD LINCOLN

Once when returning to the White House after a visit to a friend, Mrs. Lincoln suffered minor head injuries when a wheel dislodged on her buggy, causing it to overturn. It is thought that the wheel was tampered with.

THEODORE ROOSEVELT

In 1902 as President Roosevelt was receiving guests in the White House, a suspicious stranger approached. Security guards noticed a bulge in the man's back pocket, later revealed as a pistol. The man was arrested and taken to jail.

FRANKLIN ROOSEVELT

In 1933 President-elect Roosevelt was preparing to speak at a rally in Miami, Florida when shots rang out. Chicago's Mayor Cermak, on stage with Roosevelt, was killed and five bystanders were wounded. Roosevelt was uninjured. Joseph Zangara, 32, was convicted of murder. He attempted suicide and was electrocuted.

HARRY TRUMAN

Oscar Collazo lies wounded after his attempt on President Truman's life. Collazo survived.

During a renovation of the White House, the Trumans lived at Blair House across the street.

On November 1, 1950, two Puerto Rican Nationalists tried to shoot their way into the home and killed a White House policeman. One of the assassins was killed; the other was sentenced to death. Truman reduced the death sentence to life imprisonment, and in 1979 Jimmy Carter granted a full pardon.

James Brady and police officer Thomas Delahanty lie wounded after the attempt on Ronald Reagan's life outside the Washington Hilton Hotel, March 30, 1981.

GERALD FORD

In September 1975, Gerald Ford survived two assassination attempts in California. Lynette Fromme, 27, a cult follower of Charles Manson, attempted to shoot the president in Sacramento. Secret servicemen disarmed her before she could fire. In San Francisco, Sara Jane Moore, 45, a civil rights activist, fired a revolver at Ford, but a bystander deflected the shot. Both women are currently in prison serving life sentences.

RONALD REAGAN

John W. Hinckley, Jr., 25, shot Reagan outside a Washington, D.C. hotel on March 30, 1981. The bullet entered his chest, narrowly missing his heart. Reagan survived. Hinckley was found not guilty by reason of insanity and committed to St. Elizabeth's, a mental institution in Washington.

In December 2003, Hinckley was granted limited home visits under his parents' supervision.

BILL CLINTON

On October 29, 1994, Francisco Durran fired shots at the White House from Pennsylvania Avenue. He was found guilty of attempted assassination and sentenced to life in prison.

Military Presidents

I do not think there was ever a more wicked war than that waged by the United States against Mexico. I thought so at the time, when I was a youngster, only I had not moral courage enough to resign."

ULYSSES S. GRANT

"To see men without clothes to cover their nakedness, without blankets to lie on, without shoes…marching through frost and snow…and submitting to it without a murmur, is a mark of patience and obedience which in my opinion can scarce be paralleled."

George Washington at Valley Forge, December 1777

Before there were sports legends or movie stars, there were war heroes. Americans have been enchanted by them since the birth of the nation. Historians agree that the importance to political success of having been a soldier changes over time, rising in wartime and declining in peacetime.

Military experience has helped many presidents launch their national political careers. Elections after the Civil War virtually required military service. Hayes and Garfield entered politics from the springboard of their high rank in the Union army. Teddy Roosevelt made a spectacular rise to high office, helped by his heroics at San Juan Hill in the Spanish-American War. Kennedy, Nixon, Ford, and George H.W. Bush pointed with pride to their Navy service during World War II. In 2004, the contrast between the military service of John Kerry and George Bush exploded into a campaign issue.

Conversely, our history is littered with the unsuccessful presidential bids of military men. General Winfield Scott (1852), Admiral George Dewey (1900), General Douglas MacArthur (1951), and more recently George McGovern, Alexander Haig, Robert Dole, John McCain, and Wesley Clark – all sought the office and failed.

Six of America's professional soldiers (as against presidents who have had some military experience, like Garfield, Teddy Roosevelt, Truman, Kennedy etc) – all generals—did win the White House, all swept into office on a wave of popular enthusiasm:

George Washington at the battle of Princeton, January 2, 1777. Painting by John Trumbull (1756–1843).

George Washington

The young George Washington was consumed with military passion, partly instilled by his beloved half-brother, Lawrence, who had served as an officer in the Royal Navy. At age 20 George was appointed a major in the Virginia militia during the French and Indian War but his experiences were not altogether encouraging. On July 4, 1754 he was forced to surrender Fort Necessity to French attackers, and on July 9, 1755 he was with British Major-General Edward Braddock at his disastrous defeat at the Monongahela River, although the young colonel Washington acquitted himself with bravery.

On June 15, 1775 he was unanimously elected commander-in-chief of the American Revolutionary army. During the eight hard years of fighting he suffered several defeats (for example, New York, Brandywine, Germantown) and experienced only minor victories (at Trenton and Princeton) and one major success as field commander – the last battle of the war, at Yorktown, which capitulated October 19, 1781. But he achieved something no other American general could have – he kept his army together and against all odds prevented its dissolution.

On the day the British fleet sailed out of New York harbor, Washington met with his officers at Fraunces' Tavern, embraced them, resigned his commission, and left for the comforts of his home in Mount Vernon.

Though Washington did not flaunt his war credentials, his victory for independence led to his unanimous choice in 1789 as America's first president. The founding fathers attached the title "commander-in-chief of armed forces" to the presidency.

General Andrew Jackson at the battle of Tallushatchee, November 3, 1813 fought against the Creek Indian allies of the British during the War of 1812.

Andrew Jackson

At age 13, Andrew Jackson and his brother Robert joined the Continental army and fought at the battle of Hanging Rock, South Carolina, on August 6, 1780. Jackson's entire family perished in the Revolutionary War.

In 1802 he was elected major-general of Tennessee militia and after victory against the Creeks in March 1814 was made a major-general of the U.S. Army. During the War of 1812 he marched to New Orleans where, on January 8, 1815, he achieved a stunning victory over the British invaders. News spread across the country and Jackson emerged a national hero, leading the crusade for democratic reform. One of his soldiers called him "tough as hickory" and the nickname "Old Hickory" remained with Jackson through his political campaigns.

A mounted William Harrison, then the governor of Indiana Territory, at the battle of Tippecanoe, November 8, 1811 in which the Shawnee were defeated and their chief, Tecumseh, was killed.

William Henry Harrison

In 1791, William Henry Harrison gave up his medical studies and joined the Continental army as an ensign. He fought in the Indian wars in the Northwest Territory, and won his first national fame in defeating the Shawnees in the battle of Tippecanoe (November 7, 1811).

In the War of 1812, Major-General Harrison defeated a British-Indian force in the battle of the Thames River (October 5, 1813), in which the Shawnee chief Tecumseh was killed.

Harrison resigned his commission in 1814 and served in congress and as foreign minister. In the presidential election of 1840, with John Tyler as running mate, he ran successfully against incumbent Martin Van Buren. Harrison's slogan – "Tippecanoe and Tyler Too!"

Zachary Taylor

Zachary Taylor (center) at the battle of Palo Alto, May 8, 1846, an American victory in the Mexican-American War of 1846-48.

Zachary Taylor – "Old Rough and Ready" – spent 40 years in the army, fighting in the War of 1812, the Black Hawk War, and the Second Seminole War. His greatest victories were in the Mexican War, first at Palo Alta and Resaca de la Palma and then at Monterrey, before defeating General Santa Anna at Buena Vista in 1847.

Leaving the army as major general and a war hero, Taylor – who had never held office – ran for the White House on a platform that extolled his military record. He won the election of 1848.

Ulysses S. Grant

Ulysses S. Grant, an 1843 graduate of West Point, fought in the Mexican War (under Zachary Taylor and Winfield Scott) and in the Civil War, retiring as general of the army, the first commander since Washington to hold that rank.

In 1862 he led the first major Union victory at Forts Henry and Donelson, Tennessee, followed by successes at Shiloh, Vicksburg, Chattanooga, and Richmond. Promoted to commander of all Union armies, Grant defeated the Confederate forces under Robert E. Lee. Lee surrendered to Grant at Appomattox, Virginia, on April 9, 1865.

Grant was the unanimous choice at the 1868 Republican Convention. His acceptance message was, "Let us have peace."

Dwight D. Eisenhower with, in his description, one of the "coffins on wheels", of the Tank Corps at Fort Meade, 1919.

Dwight D. Eisenhower

Dwight D. Eisenhower, also a West Point graduate (1915), rose to five-star general during World War II before becoming president. Like Grant, he had no political experience or had ever held public office.

During World War I, Eisenhower was posted in the United States as an instructor at various military camps. After the war he was assigned to the Panama Canal Zone, later to the Philippines, where he was assistant to General Douglas MacArthur.

Five days after Pearl Harbor, Eisenhower was ordered to report for duty with the War Department. He developed a strategy for opening a "second front", with the invasion of German-occupied France. Gaining a reputation as an organizer, planner, and a man who could reconcile conflicting views, he commanded the successful Allied invasions of French North Africa (1942) and of Sicily and Italy (1943). Named Supreme Commander of all Allied forces in Europe, he directed the D-Day assault on Normandy in June, 1944 – the greatest amphibian invasion in history.

> *I hate war as only a soldier who has lived it can, only as one who has seen its brutality, its futility, its stupidity."*
> DWIGHT D. EISENHOWER

General Grant (far left) leans over the shoulder of a fellow officer on May 21, 1864 during a rest stop on the way to Richmond.

James Garfield was the youngest major general in the Union army during the Civil War.

Theodore Roosevelt with his Rough Riders after the battle of San Juan, July 1, 1898.

Presidential Pets

Did you know?

A museum dedicated to the nation's first pets, the Presidential Pet Museum, is located near Washington DC in Lothian, MD. A collection of prints and memorabilia is on display. Call (410) 741-0899 for more information.

> *"Do not be disturbed by Curious. I needed something to love, and when I found a little mockingbird, I tamed it and became its friend."*
>
> President Thomas Jefferson, greeting a White House visitor with Curious on his shoulder

Nearly 400 pets have called 1600 Pennsylvania Avenue home. Whoever makes it to the White House can appreciate the loyal companionship of pets. Running the country can be a hard and lonely job.

George and Martha Washington never lived in the White House, but they had the very first first pets. George was devoted to Nelson, the horse he was riding when he accepted Cornwallis' surrender at Yorktown. But the Washingtons' most famous, or infamous, pet was Martha's parrot. Apparently George and the parrot did not get along, and each kept a close eye on the other.

Birds were popular presidential pets early in our history. Thomas Jefferson had a favorite mockingbird named Curious, which he taught to take food from his lips and to ride on his shoulder.

Dolley Madison owned a green parrot who would announce to guests: "Constitution…Constitution" which, of course, her husband had helped draft. Dolley was so fond of her parrot that she rescued it – along with a painting and a few pieces of silver – from the burning White House during the War of 1812.

John Quincy Adams owned an alligator given to him by General Lafayette. Adams' wife, Louisa, raised silkworms. Andrew Jackson owned a number of pets, most of which accompanied him to the White House, including his wartime mount, Sam Patches.

Martin Van Buren had two tiger cubs given to him, but they didn't stay very long. William

Warren Harding's Airedales, c.1924

Henry Harrison came with a Billy goat and a Durham cow, but they didn't stay long, either, because Harrison himself didn't stay very long. (He died after 30 days in office.)

John Tyler had his favorite horse named The General. When The General died, Tyler had a grave dug on his estate. He placed a headstone with the following inscription: *"Here lies the body of my good horse 'The General.' For twenty years he bore me around the circuit of my practice, and in all that time he never made a blunder. Would that his master could say the same! John Tyler."*

Zachary Taylor provided a home on the White House grounds for his favorite horse, Old Whitey. Whitey had a problem, however. Many of the visitors to the White House pulled a hair or two from Whitey's tail for a souvenir.

The Lincoln White House was a menagerie of rabbits, turkeys, horses and goats. The family also had a dog named Fido, and Tad and Willie Lincoln had a pony. Tad had a white rabbit and goats named Nanny and Nanko, and a turkey named Jack. Jack originally was on the Lincoln's dinner menu, but Tad became fond of the bird and begged his father to spare Jack's life. Lincoln's favorite dog was Jip. Lincoln is also credited with having the first pet cat at the White House.

William Taft's pet cow, Pauline, in front of the State, War and Navy building, Washington DC, c.1911.

ABOVE *The very glum Calvin Coolidge with his equally subdued-looking hound.*

Herbert Hoover's crazed-looking pet possum apprehended by Officer Snodgrass of the White House Police Force, 6 May 1929.

A rare photograph of a wheelchair-bound FDR with his Scottie Fala in his lap, Hyde Park, 1941. On the campaign trail in the Fall of 1944 FDR complained: "These Republican leaders have not been content with attacks on me, or my wife, or on my sons. No, not content with that, they now include my little dog, Fala. Well, of course, I don't resent attacks…but Fala does resent them…his Scotch soul was furious."

Ulysses Grant had a variety of animals. Most were horses. He kept Jeff Davis, a wartime mount and Cincinnatus, his saddle horse. He also had mares, carriage horses, Shetland ponies, and a racer named Julia. His son Jesse had a parrot, gamecocks, and a Newfoundland dog named Faithful.

Rutherford Hayes kept pedigreed Jersey cows and carriage horses, and a Siamese cat. Scott Hayes, his son, kept dogs and goats.

James Garfield's daughter Molly had a mare named Kit.

Grover Cleveland's wife Frances kept a number of canaries and mockingbirds, as well as a Japanese poodle.

Benjamin Harrison's son Russell had a pet goat named His Whiskers. This goat was so ornery that one day the president was forced to chase him down Pennsylvania Avenue when he decided to run away with the Harrison grandchildren.

William McKinley had an Angora cat and a Mexican double-yellow-headed parrot.

But Theodore Roosevelt wins the prize for pet variety. Roosevelt and his six children shared dogs, cats, squirrels, raccoons, bears, lizards, guinea pigs, a hyena, a badger, a blue macaw, chickens, a barn owl, rabbits, a pony, two parrots, a garter snake, a zebra, and a pig named Maude.

William Howard Taft kept a cow named Pauline Wayne. This was the last cow kept at the White House. After that, the White House purchased its milk.

During World War I, Woodrow Wilson kept a flock of sheep at the White House. They kept the grass short, and their wool was sold with the proceeds going to the American Red Cross.

Warren Harding had one of the more famous first pets. His Airedale, named Laddie Boy, was well known across the nation. When Harding died, a song was written, "He's Gone, Laddie Boy," in honor of his dog.

Calvin Coolidge wins as the president who owned the most unusual pets. Besides dogs, cats,

and birds, he had an antelope, a bear, a tiger, lion cubs, and a wallaby.

The most famous presidential dog was Fala, a Scottish terrier beloved of Franklin Roosevelt. The President loved Fala so much that he rarely went anywhere without him. Fala was present when Roosevelt and Winston Churchill signed the Atlantic Charter in 1941 aboard the USS *Augusta*. Fala was also the subject of the first presidential pet biography, a tradition continued by first ladies Barbara Bush and Hillary Clinton.

The Kennedy household included Macaroni the pony, a gift to Caroline from Vice President Lyndon Johnson. Macaroni shared the spotlight with a host of dogs, rabbits, and guinea pigs. Macaroni roamed freely around the White House grounds and received thousands of fan letters from the American public. Caroline also had a dog named Pushinka, who was given to her by the then head of the Soviet Union, Nikita Khrushchev.

Lyndon Johnson created a stir when he picked up his beagles Him and Her by the ears.

Checkers, Richard Nixon's cocker spaniel, has a secure place in the history books. In his 1952 "Checkers Speech", Nixon defended his use of a private slush fund by admitting the one gift he intended to keep – the little cocker spaniel that had been given to his daughters.

Barbara Bush provided a birthing room in the White House for the family dog Millie. In 1990 *Millie's Book* was published, the first "autobiography" by a presidential pet.

The Clinton family dog Buddy was a chocolate Labrador retriever who was careful to keep his distance from the Clintons' cat, Socks. Buddy was killed by a car outside his home in New York in 1992.

George W. Bush has a family dog, Barney, a Scottish terrier who was a gift to Laura Bush. The Bushes also have a cat named India. Their English Springer spaniel, Spot, who was born in the White House and daughter of Barbara Bush's Millie, died in early 2004.

Ten Most Unusual Presidential Pets

Pygmy hippo: *Calvin Coolidge*

Alligator: *John Quincy Adams*

Elephant: *James Buchanan*

Zebra: *Theodore Roosevelt*

Antelope: *Calvin Coolidge*

Bears: *Thomas Jefferson; Theodore Roosevelt; Calvin Coolidge*

Coyote: *Theodore Roosevelt*

Hyena: *Theodore Roosevelt*

Tigers/lions: *Martin Van Buren; Theodore Roosevelt, Calvin Coolidge*

Wallaby: *Calvin Coolidge*

If you want a friend in Washington, get a dog."
PRESIDENT HARRY S TRUMAN

Barbara Bush's dog, Millie, gazing at a painting of Grace Coolidge and her dog, Rob Roy.

Nancy Reagan with Victory at Rancho del Cielo, 13 August 1981.

LEFT *Gerald Ford with his lab Liberty in the Oval Office, 7 November 1974.*

Ronald Reagan on presidential helicopter Marine 1 with Lucky, 1 November 1985.

Presidential Pastimes

George Washington was an accomplished flautist, as befitted a gentleman of the period.

An 1882 cartoon pokes fun at Chester Arthur's many fishing trips.

"*When you play, play hard; when you work, don't play at all.*"

Theodore Roosevelt

How a president filled his rare leisure hours gives us fascinating glimpses into his character. John Quincy Adams liked skinny-dipping in the Potomac River, Teddy Roosevelt was a wrestler, Eisenhower a skilled chef, and Coolidge rode a mechanical horse to keep in shape! And for many people, Jefferson's polymath interests – architecture, botany, meteorology, inventing – are more memorable than the events of his administration.

What presidents did for recreation also reflects the changing customs through our nation's history. For most early presidents – from George Washington to Theodore Roosevelt – the favorite sports were hunting, fishing, and horseback riding. President Taft was the first to take up golf (1909) – and golf has since been the favorite of eleven presidents. Swimming, jogging, skiing, and tennis have also been popular with recent presidents.

Walking, however, wins as the most enduring form of exercise from the early 1800s to today.

Recreational walking began with George Washington, and its devotees included John Adams and his son John Q., Madison, both Harrisons, Coolidge, and Truman who regularly walked two miles at a fast pace.

Washington was a hunter (foxes) and so was Monroe, Tyler, Hayes, Garfield, Cleveland, and Benjamin Harrison (ducks). Teddy Roosevelt hunted big game in Africa. Lincoln, however, detested hunting.

Lincoln was an avid reader, especially of Shakespeare and the Bible, and could recite whole passages by heart. But perhaps his favorite pastime was swapping jokes with friends.

Presidential fishermen were legion – Van Buren, Pierce, Hayes, Garfield, Arthur, Coolidge, Hoover, Teddy Roosevelt, Eisenhower, Carter, and both the Bushes were all devotees.

"*Fishing is the chance to wash one's soul with pure air. It brings meekness and inspiration, reduces our egotism, soothes our troubles, and shames our wickedness. It is discipline in the equality of men; for all men are equal before fish.*"

Herbert Hoover

Eisenhower was probably the most serious presidential golfer; it was a bad day if his score reached 85. The U.S. Golf Association built a putting green for him adjacent to the White House. The best golfer was Kennedy who typically shot in the upper 70s. Nixon's score was about 15 strokes higher.

Taft, Wilson, Harding, and Coolidge didn't like to talk about their scores.

Before their presidencies many presidents were adept sportsmen. For example, Eisenhower played minor league baseball (center field), and football (halfback) at West Point. George Bush Sr. was an All-American in baseball (first base) at Yale. Gerald Ford, a star center at Michigan, was the only president to be drafted by the National

Herbert Hoover once wrote "The Declaration of Independence is firm that all men (and boys) are endowed with certain inalienable rights...which obviously includes the pursuit of fish."

RIGHT *William Taft was a dedicated horseman, although a contemporary once wondered if the horse got as much pleasure carrying the president's formidable 300-plus pounds.*

Taft tried to control his monumental bulk with daily exercise, including golf.

FAR RIGHT *Warren Harding was one in a long line of presidential golfers – although his real love was poker.*

Grover Cleveland was a dedicated hunter, seen here in his well-provisioned camp.

Poker-faced Calvin Coolidge (right) working out with less than unrestrained enthusiasm in the Capitol gym.

"You know all those Secret Service men you've seen around me? When I play golf, they get combat pay."
Gerald Ford

Football League.

Ford was the first president to take to the ski slopes. He had no rival there until Carter succeeded him.

Painting was a hobby of Grant and Eisenhower.

Jefferson was the first president to perform publicly on a musical instrument – the violin. Tyler also played the violin; Truman and Nixon played the piano.

Teddy Roosevelt was our first tennis playing president, followed by Taft, Ford, and Carter. Roosevelt tried practically every strenuous sport known in his day – hiking, polo, wrestling, boxing, jujitsu, horseback riding, and swimming in the icy Potomac River.

Some presidents chose less strenuous activities. John Q. Adams was skillful at billiards. He installed a billiard table covered with green felt in the White House. Poker was Harding's game – as well as Truman's and Nixon's. McKinley played euchre and cribbage. Wilson was an avid bridge player. Chess was a diversion for Madison, Lincoln, Garfield, and Hayes, while Bill Clinton did crosswords in ink at championship-rate speed.

Ronald Reagan riding on his 688-acre Rancho del Cielo in California's Santa Ynez Mountains.

27

Presidents in the Making

William Taft was always on the chunky side. His mother Louise, wrote, "He is very large of his age and grows fat every day...." He would grow up to top 350 pounds.

A child of the American Revolution, John Quincy Adams witnessed the Battle of Bunker Hill at eight years of age.

Teddy Roosevelt, who became a strapping outdoorsman, sportsman, and soldier, was a sickly child. It was his father who encouraged him to develop both his physical and intellectual sides.

The six-year-old Warren Harding with his sisters. His family nickname was "Winnie".

Calvin Coolidge aged three (the only president to be born on the 4th of July). The sweet-faced baby would grow up to be the famously stern-faced president.

The infant FDR on the shoulders of his father, James, in 1883.

Andrew Johnson did not attend a single day of school. At 14 he became an indentured servant as apprentice to a tailor.

The 13-year-old Harry Truman wearing his signature thick-lens eyeglasses: "Without my glasses I was as blind as a bat...."

Ike in 1907 aged 17 on a camping trip in his native Kansas. Born into a poor family he had to pitch in on family chores: "...scrubbing the floors on Saturday morning... washing the dishes or it could be taking care of the horses or the cows or the chickens...."

JFK aged about eight-years-old, in a photograph taken around 1925.

> *The manner by which women are treated is good criterion to judge of the true state of society. If we knew but this one feature in a character of a nation, we may easily judge the rest.*
>
> BENJAMIN HARRISON AT AGE 16

The baby Richard Nixon.

> *The largest Babe I ever had, he looked like a red Irishman.*
>
> JAMES GARFIELD'S MOTHER

Gerald Ford would not learn that he had been adopted until he was in his teens.

The Log Cabin Myth

An endearing American legend is that anyone can grow up and become president. And of course, for political reasons, many presidents have poor-mouthed their own origins. So the log cabin myth endures. Several presidents born in the 1800's were born in log cabins, yet based on the standards of their day, most of their families ranked as middle class. Even Abraham Lincoln, of log cabin fame, was decidedly middle class at birth – his father was a skilled carpenter as well as a farmer.

The majority have come from wealth and high social standing. The early presidents nearly all attended college. Most were lawyers or generals or both. Born when there were perhaps a dozen colleges in the entire nation, and one percent of Americans attended, these facts alone place them in the highest economic tier.

Lyndon Johnson in 1915 aged seven.

> *I haven't liked it since I was a little kid and my mother made me eat it. And I'm President of the United States, and I'm not going to eat any more broccoli!"*
>
> GEORGE H. W. BUSH, 1990

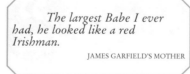

Presidential Birth States

Presidents born before the United States became independent:
- George Washington
- John Adams
- Thomas Jefferson
- James Madison
- James Monroe
- John Quincy Adams
- Andrew Jackson
- William Henry Harrison

Presidents born in Arkansas
- Bill Clinton

Presidents born in California
- Richard Nixon

Presidents born in the Carolinas
- Andrew Jackson (*historians are not sure whether he was born in North or South Carolina*)
- James Polk (North Carolina)
- Andrew Johnson (North Carolina)

Presidents born in Connecticut
- George W. Bush

Presidents born in Georgia
- Jimmy Carter

Presidents born in Illinois
- Ronald Reagan

Presidents born in Iowa
- Herbert Hoover

Presidents born in Kentucky
- Abraham Lincoln

Presidents born in Massachusetts
- John Adams
- John Quincy Adams
- John Kennedy
- George H.W. Bush

Presidents born in Missouri
- Harry Truman

Presidents born in Nebraska
- Gerald Ford

Presidents born in New Hampshire
- Franklin Pierce

Presidents born in New Jersey
- Grover Cleveland

Presidents born in New York
- Martin Van Buren
- Millard Fillmore
- Theodore Roosevelt
- Franklin Roosevelt

Presidents born in Ohio
- Ulysses Grant
- Rutherford Hayes
- James Garfield
- Benjamin Harrison
- William McKinley
- William Taft
- Warren Harding

Presidents born in Pennsylvania
- James Buchanan

Presidents born in Texas
- Dwight Eisenhower
- Lyndon Johnson

Presidents born in Vermont
- Chester Arthur
- Calvin Coolidge

Presidents born in Virginia
- George Washington
- Thomas Jefferson
- James Madison
- James Monroe
- William Henry Harrison
- John Tyler
- Zachary Taylor
- Woodrow Wilson

Jimmy Carter in his young teens. Like the young George Washington he would copy out his personal "rules of life."

At age 5, Jimmy Carter sold boiled peanuts on the streets of Plains, Georgia. He was free to play with black children but attended segregated schools.

The Reagan family Christmas card, c. 1916. Ronald, aged five, the smaller of the two children, with his brother Neil and parents Jack and Nelle.

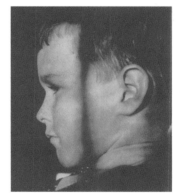

George Bush the elder aged six.

William Jefferson Blythe III (later William Jefferson Clinton) in 1950 aged four.

Firsts and Lasts

George Washington
- Only president elected unanimously
- Only president inaugurated in New York City
- Shortest inaugural address (2nd, in Philadelphia) – 135 words
- First redhead
- Only president who never lived in Washington, DC
- Only founding father to free his slaves

John Adams
- First Vice President
- First to move into the White House, 1800
- First father of a future president
- Second to die on the 4th of July
- Longest sentence in an inaugural address – 727 words, twice the number of Washington's entire 2nd inaugural address.

Thomas Jefferson
- First grandfather (daughter Mary gave birth to first child born in the White House)
- First to be inaugurated in Washington DC
- First to double the size of the nation
- First to shake hands in greeting – Washington and Adams met people with a slight bow
- First to die on 4th of July
- Last redhead

James Madison
- First to wear trousers – rather than knee britches
- Shortest – 5 feet 4 inches
- Lightest; he weighed about 100 pounds
- His widow, Dolley, sent the first personal message by Morse telegraph, 1844

James Monroe
- First Purple Heart – for wound suffered in Revolutionary War
- Only President to have a foreign capital named after him – Monrovia, Liberia
- Third to die on the 4th of July
- First father of the bride – daughter Maria's wedding was the first of a president's child in the White House.

John Quincy Adams
- First son of a former president
- Only foreign-born First Lady (Louisa Johnson was born in England)
- First whose son – John Adams II – was married in the White House
- First published poet

Andrew Jackson
- First use of opinion polls in a presidential campaign
- First target of an assassination attempt
- First to be born in a log cabin
- First bathtub installed in the White House – 1834
- First to marry a divorcee
- First to ride on a train
- Greatest step-father – to 11 children

Martin Van Buren
- First president born a US citizen (not born a British subject)

- Most nicknames
  Old Kinderhook – after Kinderhook, New York, his birthplace. From this nickname comes the term "OK."
- First to marry a distant cousin
- Only pet tiger in the White House

William Henry Harrison
- First grandfather of a president
- First to die in office
- Longest inaugural address, 8445 words – 1 hour and 45 minutes
- Shortest term (32 days)
- Most grandchildren (48) and great-grandchildren (106) including one president
- Only president that studied medicine
- First president to be photographed in office

John Tyler
- First to become president at predecessor's death
- First whose wife died while in office
- First to marry while in office
- Only president to join the Confederacy
- Fathered the most children – 15

James K. Polk
- First to be photographed while in office, by Matthew Brady, 1849
- First to provoke a foreign war
- Greatest territorial expansion –about one third of what the United States is now
- Only to keep all of his campaign promises

Zachary Taylor
- First career Army officer
- First Mexican War veteran
- Last veteran of War of 1812
- Last to own slaves

Millard Fillmore
- First kitchen stove in White House
- First born in 19th century
- First library in the White House

Franklin Pierce
- First to have central heating in the White House
- First to be arrested for murder – ran down an elderly woman with his carriage. The charges against him could not be proven and were dropped
- First to put up a Christmas tree in the White House
- Only to recite his inauguration speech from memory
- Only to retain his entire cabinet during his term

James Buchanan
- First presidential inauguration to be photographed
- First to send a transatlantic telegram – to Queen Victoria, 1858
- Only bachelor
- Only pet eagle
- Last War of 1812 veteran

Abraham Lincoln
- First born outside of the original thirteen

colonies – Kentucky
- First orphan
- First beard
- First seance in the White House
- Only to receive a patent – for adjustable buoyant chambers for steamboats
- First to have his portrait on both a coin and paper money
- Tallest – 6 feet 4 inches
- Most future presidents to attend an inauguration – Rutherford B. Hayes, James A. Garfield, Chester Arthur, and Benjamin Harrison attended Lincoln's first inaugural.
- First to receive a transcontinental telegram, 1861

Andrew Johnson
- First never to have attended school
- First to be impeached

Ulysses S. Grant
- First Civil War veteran
- Black men were first granted the vote during his administration
- First speeding ticket
- Last former slave owner
- Last Mexican War veteran

Rutherford B. Hayes
- His wife Lucy was first to be called "First Lady"
- First Easter egg roll on the White House lawn
- First telephone in White House (1879)
- First Presidential Library
- First to have electricity in White House

James A. Garfield
- First College Professor – Hiram College
- First left-handed
- First American citizen for whom a day of mourning was proclaimed in the royal courts of Europe
- Last born in a log cabin

Chester A. Arthur
- First elevator in the White House
- First dandy; nicknamed "Elegant Arthur", he at one time owned 80 pairs of trousers and changed clothes several times a day.
- First somnambulist; he enjoyed walking at night and seldom went to bed before 2:00am
- Only to destroy all of his personal papers before his death.

Grover Cleveland
- Only to marry in the White House
- Youngest first lady – Frances Folsom (21)
- First and only first father – daughter Esther, only incumbent's child born in the White House
- Only to have a candy bar named after another daughter – Baby Ruth
- Only former hangman, as sheriff of Buffalo, New York

Benjamin Harrison
- First grandson of a former President
- First pet possum
- First electric lights installed in the White House, 1891
- Only Hoosier

- Last bearded president
- First to have a Christmas tree in the White House

William McKinley

- First inauguration recorded by movie camera
- Thought to hold the record for presidential handshaking – 2,500 per hour
- Last Civil War veteran
- First to ride in an automobile – after being shot, he was taken to the hospital in a 1901 Columbia electric ambulance.

Theodore Roosevelt

- Youngest at inauguration – 42 years, 10 months
- Youngest to leave the presidency
- Only Spanish-American War veteran
- First to win Nobel Prize – 1906
- First to travel outside the US during term of office – 1906 Panama
- First to fly in an airplane, 1910, in a Wright Brothers plane
- First to publish a book while in office; he wrote 14 books before he took office
- First to call "President's House" the White House
- First to invite a black man to the White House – Booker T. Washington

William Howard Taft

- First to throw out the first pitch on opening day of major league baseball
- First presidential car – a model M touring car
- First to play golf
- First presidential funeral broadcast on radio
- First to be buried at Arlington National Cemetery
- Heaviest, at over 300 pounds

Woodrow Wilson

- First Ph.D. – Johns Hopkins University, 1886
- First university president – Princeton
- First to hold a presidential news conference
- Second president to be a Nobel Prize winner, 1919
- Only president buried in Washington DC (National Cathedral)
- Last to ride to his inauguration in a horse-drawn carriage
- First to cross the Atlantic

Warren G. Harding

- First to address the nation by radio, 1922
- First elected with women's votes
- Only newspaper publisher

Calvin Coolidge

- Only born on 4th of July
- First to be sworn in at his family home – Plymouth Notch, Vermont
- First to take naps
- First national Christmas Tree lighting ceremony on the White House lawn
- Most press conferences (520)
- First to broadcast by radio, 1925
- Largest menagerie – a goose, a wallaby, a donkey, a thrush, a lion cub, lots of cats, many dogs, several birds and a raccoon named Rebecca.

Herbert Hoover

- Only Quaker
- First born west of the Mississippi River –West Branch, Iowa
- First high school drop-out
- First engineer
- First self-made millionaire
- Only president to speak Chinese
- Youngest student in Stanford University's first class

Franklin D. Roosevelt

- Longest time in office
- First to appoint a woman to the cabinet – Secretary of Labor Frances Perkins
- First to appear on television as president – at the opening of the 1939 World's Fair
- First president named *Time Magazine's* Man of the Year
- Related by blood or marriage to more former presidents – a total of 11

Harry S Truman

- First to speak from the White House on television
- First World War I veteran
- First to pardon the Thanksgiving turkey
- Last not to graduate from college
- Only president to fire a 5 star general (MacArthur)

Dwight D. Eisenhower

- First president of all 50 states
- First college football letterman
- First putting green on the White House lawn(1953)
- First licensed pilot
- First to appear on color television
- Last born in 19th century
- Only president to serve in both World Wars
- Last cigarette smoker

John F. Kennedy

- First to give a live, televised news conference, 1961
- First Navy veteran
- First born in 20th century
- First Roman Catholic
- Youngest at election
- Youngest at death
- Only president to win Pulitzer Prize – 1957 for biography – Profiles in Courage
- Only to be survived by both parents

Lyndon B. Johnson

- First Texan
- First to be sworn in on an airplane
- First to appoint a black cabinet member
- First to appoint a black Supreme Court Justice

Richard M. Nixon

- First former vice president to become president who did not succeed the president under whom he served
- First presidential election in which 18-year-olds could vote
- First to resign from office
- First to visit all 50 states while in office
- First to visit China
- First to call the moon

Gerald R. Ford

- Only to hold the office of vice-president and president without ever having been elected to either
- Only All American football player
- First professional male model (*Look* magazine)
- First to pardon a former president
- First to visit Japan
- Only president whose two assassination attempts against him were made by women

Jimmy Carter

- First sworn in using his nickname, Jimmy
- First Annapolis graduate
- First nuclear engineer
- First born in a hospital
- Third president to win Nobel Prize, 2002

Ronald Reagan

- Only president to have been a lifeguard
- First movie actor
- First to appoint a woman to the Supreme Court
- Only divorced president
- Oldest at election
- Oldest former president
- First to survive Tecumseh's Curse ("Assassinations & Near Misses", pages 18–21)

George H. W. Bush

- First bomber pilot to be shot down
- First first baseman
- First to host *Saturday Night Live* October 15, 1994
- Second to be a father of a future president
- First to jump out of an airplane, three times in retirement

Bill Clinton

- First Arkansan
- First Rhodes Scholar
- First woman White House press secretary – Dee Dee Myers
- First woman Secretary of State – Madeleine Albright
- First elected president impeached
- First White House Website

George W. Bush

- First wartime president to seek a tax cut
- First Asian-American woman appointed to Cabinet – Elaine Chao
- First to light a Hanukkah menorah at the White House
- First State of the Union Webcast
- Second president to be son of a president
- Fourth to assume the presidency without winning the popular vote
- Most money raised (and spent) in a presidential campaign

Published by

CHARTWELL BOOKS, INC.

A Division of BOOK SALES, INC.

114 Northfield Avenue
Edison, New Jersey 08837

ISBN 0-7858-1914-2

CIP catalog records for this book are available from the Library of Congress.

Printed in China

Designed by Casebourne Rose Design Associates

CHARTWELL BOOKS, INC.

PICTURE CREDITS

fc = front concertina
bc = back concertina
Library of Congress: *fc:* 2 Washington inauguration; 9 Puck cartoon; 10 Teapot dome.
bc: 17 Martha Washington; 17 Abigail Adams; 18 Dolly Madison; 19 Angelica Van Buren; 19 Julia Tyler; 20 all; 21 both; 23 all; 24 all; 25 all; 26 both; 27 Bess Truman, Mamie Eisenhower; 28 both; 29 both. Book pages: 1-19 all; 13 top; 14 bottom; 16 bottom left, middle left and right, bottom right; 17 all left column, top right; 19 both; 22 both; 23 left-hand column, all right-hand column; 24 all; 26 all; 27 top four; 28 Taft, Teddy Roosevelt, Harding, Coolidge; 29 bottom right.
Architect of the Capitol: p.16 top.
Harry S. Truman Library: *fc* 11 'Dewey Defeats...'; p.10 top; p.28 second column, third from top.
Ash Lawn Highland: *bc* 18 Elizabeth Monroe.
US Department of the Interior, National Park Service, Adams Historical Site: *bc* 18 Louisa Adams.
President Benjamin Harrison Home: *bc* 19 Anna Harrison.
James K. Polk Memorial Association: *bc* 19 Sarah Polk.
John F. Kennedy Library: *bc* 27 Jacqueline Kennedy; p.11 top; p.20; p.28 third column top.
Bush Presidential Materials Project: *bc*30; p.14 top; p.25 top right; p.29 top right.
Lyndon Baines Johnson Library: *fc* 13 bottom center; p.11 bottom; p.28 far right.
Gerald R. Ford Library: p.12 top; p.25 bottom left; p.27 far left; p.28 third column.
US National Archives: *fc* 3 Declaration of Independence; p.12 bottom; p.28 third column middle.
Ronald Reagan Library: *bc* 30 Nancy Reagan; p.13 bottom; p.17 bottom right; p.21 top right; p.25 center bottom, bottom right; p.27 bottom right; p.29 center.
Carter Library: p.29 left.
Dwight D. Eisenhower Library: p.10 bottom; p.28 bottom second column; p.23 center.
Clinton Library: *bc* 31 Hillary Clinton.
Many thanks to **David Gibbons** for presidents' portraits, front concertina, Washington through Reagan.

REFERENCES

BOOKS
Caroli, Betty Boyd. *Inside the White House.* Garden City, New York: GuildAmerica Books, 1992
Caroli, Betty Boyd. *The First Ladies, 3rd edition.* Garden City, New York: GuildAmerica Books, 2001
DeGregorio, William A. *The Complete Book of U.S. Presidents.* New York: Random House Value Publishing, 2001
Garrison, Webb. *A Treasury of White House Tales.* Nashville, Tennessee: Rutledge Hill Press, 2002
Humes, James. *Which President Killed a Man?* New York: McGraw Hill, 2003
Rubel, David. *Mr. President.* Alexandria, Virginia: Time-Life Books, 1998
Whitney, David C. and Robin Vaughn Whitney. *The American Presidents,* 9th edition. Garden City, New York: GuildAmerica Books, 2001
World Almanac and Book of Facts 2004. New York: World Almanac Books, 2004

WEB SITES
www.americanpresident.org
http://ap.grolier.com
www.infoplease.com
www.whitehouse.gov

THE AUTHOR

Barbara Greenman has published several books of American history as Director of Book Development for the Literary Guild and Doubleday Book Clubs (now Bookspan). She edited regular revised editions of *The American Presidents* by David and Robin Whitney; and *The First Ladies, America's First Ladies,* and *Inside the White House* by Betty Boyd Caroli. Recently she compiled *A Treasury of American Quotations.*